Murder in Spite

A Doyle and Acton Mystery

Anne Cleeland

ARTEMIS
—PRESS—

The series in order:

Murder in Thrall

Murder in Retribution

Murder in Hindsight

Murder in Containment

Murder in All Honour

Murder in Shadow

Murder in Misdirection

Murder in Spite

For David Putman, a happy copper; and for all others like him.

Chapter 1

It was a shame, about the little baby. Not that she'd ever cared much for babies, of course.

Doyle considered the elegant menu-card laid before her and could not help but compare this train-trip with the last one she'd taken, the day she'd traveled from Dublin to London, two-thirds terrified and one-third hopeful. Her mother had packed her a lunch because they weren't certain whether there would be any food available. Doyle, of course, had been too self-conscious to eat it, sitting cheek-by-jowl between two strangers in third-class.

"Perhaps you could finally make your peace with the fish," Acton teased as he glanced at her over the top of his own menu. Doyle didn't care for fish, having worked a stint in a Dublin fish-market; an occupation that played no small part in her decision to strike out for London.

"There is not the smallest chance," she declared. "Fish are the work o' the devil, and those starin' eyes still give me the willies."

She was traveling with her husband in the train's first-class dining room, going to Holyhead before taking the ferry over to Dublin for a holiday. Doyle had recently given birth to their first child, and Acton thought it would be a good time to take a trip to see Doyle's hometown. He'd wanted to hire a private train, but Doyle had found that idea a bridge too far, and so they'd compromised on public first-class.

"Somethin' quick," Doyle cautioned. She'd discovered that when one had a baby, one lived the other parts of one's life in forty-five-minute intervals. "The soup sounds good."

Acton signaled to the waiter who'd been hovering at a discreet distance, and as he placed the order Doyle decided that she'd shown enough restraint, and it was past time to reach for the bread basket.

"Ah," she sighed after a blissful bite. "There's nothin' better than Irish butter, but I'd best watch myself; have to get back to fightin' trim or you'll leave me for the next fishmonger who wanders by your window."

"Nonsense; you are perfectly delightful."

As she slathered more butter along the remaining end, she gave him a look. "Meanin' that I actually have a bosom for the first time, and you are findin' it fascinatin'."

"I will miss it, when it is gone," he admitted.

"As will baby Edward—faith, you'd think he'd blow up like a balloon, what with all the eatin' he's doin'. He must be naturally scrawny, like me—or like I used to be, anyways."

Acton reviewed the selections in the bread basket, and decided to take a slice, himself. "What you lack in stature, you make up for in resilience."

"I'm a hardy lass," she agreed. "Comes of bein' shot-up, and such." They were both detectives at Scotland Yard, and Doyle had experienced more than her share of gunshot wounds.

As he broke the bread with his fingers, Acton's eyes rested on her for a thoughtful moment. "Can you tell me what is bothering you, Kathleen?"

Trust him to know something was amiss; he knew her better than she knew herself, sometimes. With a small frown, she drew a fingertip along the crisp linen tablecloth, and chose her words carefully. "I don't know, Michael; I'm feelin' as though this may not be the best idea, just now—to go adventurin' off to Ireland."

"Oh? I would like to see where you lived."

She smiled, as this was true. What was also true—but remained unspoken—was that he wanted her well-away from whatever was going forward back home, at the Met. She didn't know what it was, but that something ominous was unfolding seemed a given; she knew the signs.

He continued, "And a visit to the new orphanage would probably be in order."

"Aye—we've got to let the nuns know that we're keepin' an eye on 'em; no funny-business allowed." This would, in fact, be a welcome diversion—to see St. Brigid's again, and the orphanage that she and Acton had founded at her old school. Doyle had lived a hard-scrabble life until she'd mustered up the courage to apply to the Metropolitan Police force in London in the hopes of becoming a detective. Promptly upon graduating from the Crime Academy, she'd been assigned to be Chief Inspector Acton's support officer—which was something of a surprise, since the much-renowned DCI had a reputation for being reclusive, and for not suffering fools.

The reason behind this unlikely assignment soon became clear, however, because Doyle's superior officer proposed marriage out of the blue, and—unable to come up with a plausible excuse—she'd accepted. As a result of this impetuous decision, she was now Lady Acton, riding in a first-class railway car on her triumphant return to Dublin, and never having to look at another fish-eye again. Life was a crackin' wonderment; truly.

"I can't put on airs at St. Brigid's," she warned. "They know better."

"There will be no airs of any kind," he assured her, and decided to have another slice of bread.

"Reynolds can't come, then," she teased, trying to shake off her uneasiness. They were traveling with Reynolds, their butler, who tended to be more cognizant of Lord Acton's rank and importance than Lord Acton himself, and it was doubtful

3

that the servant could downplay this exalted status, even if he were so inclined.

"Just the two of us will go, then."

This was welcome news, as—aside from Reynolds—they were also traveling with Mary, Edward's nanny, Mary's daughter Gemma, and Trenton, who acted as security. It seemed that upper-class traveling necessarily involved bringing a great many people along, and Doyle had feared she'd have little alone-time with her husband. "I'll bring Edward to St. Brigid's, too—I imagine they'd like to see him. I can manage, since he tends to sleep all the time, anyways—I'll put him in that chest carrier."

"Don't let him squash your new bosom."

"Edward's just as concerned about that as you are, believe me."

The soup was served, and they ate for a few minutes in companionable silence, until he asked, "Is it anything in particular, Kathleen, or just a general feeling?"

She paused to consider the remains of her soup bowl— she hadn't managed to throw him off the subject then, which came as no surprise since he'd a fine-tuned radar when it came to her. "No—nothin' in particular, Michael; I'm just a bit fashed, and for no good reason. Mayhap it's my hormones, runnin' amok."

Doyle had a rare gift—well, if one could call it a gift—in that she was what the Irish would call "fey"; she had an extraordinary perceptive ability which mainly meant that she could read the emotions of the people in her vicinity, and could usually tell when lies were being told—a very useful tool when one was a detective, even though no one really knew of her abilities, save Acton. The other detectives at the CID only knew that she was top-of-the-class in interrogation technique, but bottom-of-the-class in everything else—except for marrying one's superior officer, of course. In that, she'd carried off the palm.

It also meant that she didn't like crowds, or traveling—faith, this trip was sounding less and less like a good idea—not to mention she'd a husband who was well-familiar with her abilities, and so was being careful to hide from her whatever-it-was that he was up to.

That he was up to something seemed a given; beneath his correct, public-school demeanor—so much-loved by the citizenry—lurked a rather bloodthirsty vigilante who did not hesitate to take justice into his own hands, up to and including manipulating evidence so that the right people went to prison or were simply murdered, if it seemed that manipulating the evidence wasn't going to turn the trick.

And she couldn't just ask him outright about his latest schemings, because he'd be reluctant to tell her on the fear that she'd try to spike his guns—she was probably the only person on earth who could persuade him to spike his guns. He was a complicated man, but he was devoted to her—sometimes overly-devoted, truth to tell—and because she loved him in return, she spent a great deal of her time and energy trying to save him from himself.

Pausing with this thought, she gazed at the passing scenery for a moment, because she'd the sense—she'd the sense that Acton wasn't exactly *up* to something; instead, Acton wanted her well-away from whatever was going forward, back home. It couldn't be a coincidence, that her mobile phone was suddenly having service problems. And—although he was a busy DCI and running a huge caseload of major crimes—he'd not been checking in at all; or not that she'd noticed.

Another flippin' crisis, she thought with resignation, and hoped that she could handle whatever-it-was in forty-five-minute intervals.

Acton checked his watch. "An hour or so, until Holyhead."

"Then comes the ferry-ride," Doyle added brightly, trying to sound enthusiastic. On the ferry-ride to London she'd been a bit seasick, and was rather dreading a repeat performance.

"We'll stay away from the crowds," he assured her, and reached to take her hand.

Touched, she pinned on a smile to reassure him. Truth to tell, he didn't like this any more than she did; he wasn't much for traveling, either—faith, Acton didn't like being amongst other human beings as a general policy. Unfortunately, this was yet another indication that he was bound-and-determined to take them away from London, for the nonce, and for reasons which were unknown but which could probably not withstand the light of day.

I wonder what's happening back home, she thought, as she dipped a surreptitious fingertip into the butter, and then brought it to her mouth. Hopefully, the Met would still be standing when they returned, although when Acton was involved one never knew.

She was startled out of her thoughts by Mary, Edward's nanny, who suddenly came through the dining car door, holding Edward in his chest-carrier and looking a bit wild-eyed. She was accompanied by Trenton—Acton's private security person—and as Doyle rose, she noted that Trenton met her husband's eyes with some sort of message.

"Why, Mary—whatever's happened?"

Blushing, the young woman swallowed, and glanced up at Trenton. "I feel so foolish, Lady Acton—and to think I may have—I may have—"

Doyle stood, and reached to ease Mary into her chair at the table. "Sit yourself down, Mary, and we'll call for tea. Here, let me take Edward." This, mainly because Doyle wanted to make sure the baby was all right, but he was sound asleep, and made no protest when his mother pulled him into her arms.

Acton was sitting quietly—although Doyle knew he was on high alert—and she recognized the interview technique; oftentimes a detective had to be patient with an agitated witness, because agitated witnesses tended to over-explain. Eventually, the facts would come out; it would just take a bit longer.

Doyle shifted Edward to her other arm and reached to pat Mary's hand. "Tell us what's happened, Mary—no harm done, after all."

The stricken nanny lifted her face. "Oh—oh, but Lady Acton; when I think—"

"The vestibule door came open," Trenton interjected. Not being a police officer, Trenton had no patience for interviewing techniques.

Doyle tried to tamp down her alarm. The vestibule was the enclosed area between the train carriages, and the passengers had to negotiate the vestibules as they walked from one carriage to another. "Truly? The emergency door opened?"

"I must have knocked the lever," Mary confessed. "I was so very foolish, Lady Acton—I was trying to find better reception for my mobile, and I wasn't paying attention. Then suddenly I could feel the wind, rushing by, and I stumbled—"

"Was there anyone with you, in the vestibule?" Acton's voice was calm, and matter-of-fact.

Doyle was so surprised by the implication behind the question that she caught her breath, but Mary saw nothing amiss, and confessed, "Oh, yes—there were people going in and out, and jostling a bit. I shouldn't have stopped to fiddle with my mobile—I'm so sorry." She paused, then glanced up at Trenton in gratitude. "Mr. Trenton pulled me back, and then another man slammed the door shut."

"No harm done, Mary," Doyle repeated firmly. "And Edward's due for a feedin' anyway, so I'd best go back to our compartment and do the deed before we get to Holyhead."

"Oh—yes; I'll go with you; I'd like to check on Gemma."

They all rose and made their way out of the dining carriage, Doyle holding the baby and noting that Trenton walked before her, watchful and alert, as they made their way through the vestibule and back to their train carriage.

As soon as Mary was dropped off at her own compartment, Doyle cast a glance over her shoulder at Acton, who was navigating the narrow hallway behind her. "Tell me what it is you're thinkin', husband."

Acton held their compartment door for her as she passed through, and then Trenton firmly closed it from the outside. "It may be nothing, Kathleen. But it seems unusual that the automatic alarm didn't sound."

Much struck, she considered this as she sank into the upholstered seat and unbuttoned her blouse. "Oh—oh, of course, it should have." With a small frown, she thought about this unexplained failure, but finally shook her head to express her doubts. "Faith, I don't know, Michael; it seems unlikely that anyone would make an attempt on Mary—or even Edward, for that matter—by hopin' to get a chance to shove them out a train door."

"Yes; a very unreliable means and mode." His unreadable gaze rested on the baby, and she knew that his mind was turning over possibilities. Interesting, that his attention had been caught, and not in a good way.

She glanced up at him, as she gently jostled Edward so that he didn't fall back to sleep, which he was wont to do after taking the first hearty gulp. "Should we have a look at the manifest—to see if there's anyone of interest?"

"Already accomplished."

This only made sense; as a result of his chosen profession, Acton had a basketful of enemies and so he'd be very cautious when venturing away from their security flat in Kensington. In a way, it reassured her; Acton would take no chances, and Acton was no fool. It must have been a dereliction by the train personnel—the alarm wasn't functioning—and they were unlucky, at most. As she'd said to Mary, no harm done.

Thinking about it, Doyle ventured, "I imagine Mary was tryin' to ring up Howard, and shame on you, for muckin' up the phones. Let this be a lesson." Mary had recently become romantically involved with one of Acton's acquaintances, and it seemed clear they were both well-smitten—not a good time to be away from home and discover that one's mobile was not working.

He didn't deny this accusation, but instead rested his thoughtful gaze on the baby. "I thought it would be a welcome change to remain incommunicado."

Doyle took a guess at what "incommunicado" meant, and chided, "That won't wash, husband; you're one who's got a finger in every imaginable pie—you'd no more go off the grid than you'd fly to the moon." She paused, and then decided she may as well take the bull by the horns. "What is it, then, that you're not wantin' me to find out?"

He did not disclaim—he knew she'd know if he told an untruth—and so he thought carefully about his answer for a moment. "Only that there have been some very distasteful spite murders coming onto the docket, lately. It is my preference that neither one of us is assigned to those cases."

"Done," she agreed willingly, knowing that what he'd said was true, but also knowing that this was not exactly the reason he wanted her well-away. Spite-murders were always distasteful, as they were the result of the killer's raging fury; the motive tended to be personal, and the crimes were messy— often involving multiple stabbings, or mutilation. However, the excuse didn't really hold water, because the illustrious Chief Inspector could pick and choose his own assignments and his support officer was currently dossin' about on maternity leave.

Taking a guess, she ventured, "I think that one or two of the blacklegs from the Health Professions Council has managed to get himself spite-murdered." The Council had been deeply implicated in a recent corruption scandal—a nasty conspiracy that had involved blackmail and sex slavery. However—as yet—there was no direct evidence that would support a charge, and so the prosecutors hadn't gone after any of the members. As a practical matter, you couldn't arrest someone in such a high-profile position unless you had an airtight case.

"I'd rather not comment."

She glanced up at him, and then decided she was in for a penny, in for a pound. "Is it you, doin' the spite-murderin'?"

"No," he replied steadily. "It is not."

This was nothing more than what she'd expected—the last thing Acton would do, one would think, would be to involve himself in a spite-murder; he was too well-bred, and would probably shrink from the idea of having to scrub blood-spatter off his shirt-cuffs.

She brought her gaze down to Edward again. "Then fine, husband; I've no objection to stayin' off the grid, for a bit. Although please let poor Mary phone Howard on occasion, else he'll be droppin' whatever he's doin' to come and join our wretched tenirue."

He smiled, and put a finger within Edward's little fist, where it rested on her breast. "It is 'retinue', but good attempt; I am impressed."

"You should be; I never thought I'd have a retinue in the first place."

"We'll keep our travels low-key," he soothed, lifting his finger to see if the baby would hold on, which he did. "No need to attract unwonted attention."

With a sidelong glance at him, she offered, "Well, the first order of business is to keep Trenton from fallin' in love with Mary; the woman's a hazard, is what she is."

He smiled in amused acknowledgment. "It is rather surprising." The soft-spoken nanny had acquired no shortage of admirers before she'd met Howard, even though it never seemed as though she was making the least push to beguile them.

Doyle teased, "Faith, Michael; she reminds me of you—an out-and-out honey-trap. Always attractin' shirt-tail admirers left and right—although hers aren't crazed, which is a point in her favor, I think." Due to his title and public status—not to mention his handsome face—Acton had been a target for the lovelorn, some of who'd been willing to commit major crimes so as to achieve the object of their affections.

"I am not certain how I can answer such a charge without sounding insufferable."

Laughing, she met his gaze. "Well, it's not exactly a secret, husband. Hopefully Tasza is not gearin' up to shoot me, herself." They'd recently tangled with a female MI 5 officer who seemed to have an out-sized interest in Doyle's wedded husband.

"Death before dishonor," he promised, and leaned across the baby to kiss her.

Quirking a corner of her mouth, she lifted Edward and began patting his back. "I don't think it will come to that, my friend. You're an old da, now, and the only crazed admirer left standin' is your poor wife, whose bosom is only temporary. It's time to face the sad facts."

"Consider the facts faced."

With great contentment, they sat together and watched Edward doze, whilst Doyle tried not to notice that Trenton hadn't budged from his post outside the door.

Chapter 2

The stupid fool botched it. Bloody, bloody hell.

Doyle stood out on the forward deck of the Holyhead ferry, wrapped tightly in her coat with her hands on the rail as the vessel skimmed across the choppy seas. She'd forgot to bring along gloves, and was a bit worried that her hands would soon no longer respond to direction—faith, it was cold—which was something else she'd forgotten; how cold it could be. Despite this unhappy state of affairs, she was semi-grateful for the bracing wind in her face because she felt a bit queasy, and the cold air seemed to help somewhat. That she'd never again be able to draw a comb through her hair seemed a small enough price to pay.

They were on the high-speed ferry to Dublin; originally, they'd signed up for the more leisurely crossing because it offered better amenities, but Acton had decided to change their booking to the high-speed crossing after Doyle had confessed her tendency to seasickness.

"It may be rougher ride," he'd explained, "but it will be over much sooner."

In silent sympathy, he now stood beside her on the rail as they bumped along the waves, the white spray pluming out from either side. It was too cold for the baby—or for anyone else, for that matter—and so his staunch presence by her side was a true measure of his devotion.

She leaned toward him to say, "I'll be all right, Michael; go inside. And anyways, if I disgrace myself it would be best if there were no witnesses."

"No matter," he replied. "Here, allow me to lend you my gloves."

"No, Michael—I'll never learn, else. Instead I'll put my hands in my pockets, if you'll let me lean against you."

This was accomplished, and as she stood within the circle of his arms as he held the railing, she managed to flex her stiff fingers in her pockets. "Mother a' mercy, but it's cold and miserable. And to top it off, I must look as though I've been dragged through a hedgerow backwards."

He bent to say near her ear, "If you'd rather not talk, I don't mind, Kathleen."

"No—let's keep talkin', it helps to keep my mind off it." That, and she knew that the incident with Mary on the train was bothering him—he was making a mighty effort to conceal it, but he was wary. Upon exiting the train, he'd held a low-voiced conversation with Trenton, and both men had a serious aura about them, ever since. Try as she might, though, Doyle couldn't think it was truly a serious matter; her time at the CID had taught her a thing or two about homicides, and death-by-open-train-door seemed a very sketchy mode of operation.

"It shouldn't be much longer," he said.

"Good, this may be a close-run thing, and I'll do my best to give you a warnin', if there's nothin' for it—I don't want to ruin your coat."

"You may ruin my coat any time you wish. I've only to blame it on Edward."

She mustered up a wan smile. "At least I'm not houndin' you for sex—there's that." In a strange twist of hormones, Doyle had found in recent days that she'd an out-sized desire for her marital rights; making up for lost time, she was.

"You may hound me for sex any time you wish, also. Only perhaps not just now."

Lifting her face against the wind, she closed her eyes and took a deep breath—mind over matter; not much longer, now. If only the wretched ferry would stop bucking and diving like a fish on a string; it was a wonder that anyone could bear it, let alone sit in the stuffy cabin and eat greasy things.

Don't think about the greasy things, she warned herself in a panic as her stomach lurched; don't, don't don't.

"There—you can see landfall. It may help to keep your eyes on the shoreline."

She opened her eyes to see the dim outline of the dark coast on the horizon. Ireland, she thought, surprised by how moved she felt; isn't it grand, you look?

He bent to take an assessing look at her pale face. "All right? How are you faring?"

She watched the shoreline get closer. "I think I would sell my soul for a hot shower."

He spoke near her ear. "You'll have one. We'll spend the rest of the day settling in at the hotel, and then tomorrow we will reconnoiter at our leisure."

Without taking her gaze from the shoreline, she replied, "Of course, we will—never doubt it."

She could sense his amusement. "It means we'll have a look 'round."

"And here I was hopin' it was some sort of sex-thing."

With a small chuckle, he rested his chin on her shoulder. "That, too."

"Best study up then; I'll be puttin' you through your paces, husband."

As they approached the harbor, the ferry slowed, and Doyle began to feel cautiously optimistic that she was going to complete the journey without casting up her accounts. "It looks the same as the day I left." She glanced up at him. "Have you ever been?"

"Once," he replied easily. "I quite look forward to another visit."

Doyle turned back to watch their arrival and smiled to herself, having forgotten that his prior visit was no doubt when he'd come—all secret and stealthy-like—to falsify the records at St. Brigid's Church. Doyle's parents had never married—her father had abandoned Doyle's mother when Doyle was a baby—but when she'd confessed this unfortunate fact to Acton, he'd assured her that the registry at the Dublin church showed a valid marriage between the two.

Fondly, she leaned her head back against his chest, and breathed a mental sigh of relief as the ferry entered the calmer waters of the harbor. The fact that he'd gone to such lengths to board-up the Doyle family skeletons was one of her first clues that the man she'd married was a bit nicked—and that was putting it mildly. Time and time again, she'd been a first-hand witness to Acton's maneuverings; if he didn't like the facts on the ground, then he'd change those facts to suit his fancy and the devil take the details. It would be quite the change of pace, in fact, to see how Acton behaved when he was forced to let go of the reins, so to speak. Hopefully, the poor man wouldn't go stir-crazy in Dublin, because opportunities to exercise his masterminding skills would be few and far between—or at least one would think.

The waves abated as the ferry maneuvered toward its berth, and—now that her stomach had settled—Doyle thoughtfully fingered her husband's coat sleeve. Come to think of it, it was rather out-of-character for Acton to pack up and leave when there were nasty spite-murders brewing back home; in the usual course of events he wouldn't hesitate to swoop in—like that Nemesis fellow—and knock some deserving heads together. Which left her with the rather disquieting notion that her renegade husband had no particular objection to these spite-murders, even if he wasn't the one behind them.

I'll have to look into it, once we're home again, she decided. I imagine there's good reason that Acton doesn't want me anywhere near these particular homicide cases—he's worried I might actually solve them, which wouldn't do at all. After all, spite-murders usually have an element of vengeance to them, and Acton was the sort of person who'd no problem at all with a hearty dose of home-brewed vengeance, if it was justified. This philosophy was, in fact, a bit alarming—since the illustrious Chief Inspector was supposedly sworn to uphold the law—and it meant the fair Doyle often found herself on the horns of a dilemma, where on one hand she was trying to contain the Acton-fallout so as to save her husband from himself but on the other hand, she was sworn to uphold the law, too.

They disembarked at the dock, and—since they'd got there more quickly than anticipated—distributed their party amongst the queue of cabs waiting along the quay, rather than avail themselves of the limousine service that had been hired.

Doyle was not at all surprised when Acton casually squeezed her into a cab along with Edward and Trenton, as it was apparent her husband was still on high alert, and taking no chances. The cab ride, however, was uneventful—save for Edward's taking great exception to the fact that Doyle's forty-five minutes was up, and the food-wagon had best get crackin'.

Their hotel in the posh area of town proved to be just the type of establishment that Acton most liked; a renovated Georgian townhouse—understated and elegantly appointed—with the staff showing a great deal of polite deference to the new guests and not betraying by the flicker of an eyelash that there was a squalling infant in their midst.

As the concierge discreetly ushered them toward the waiting lift, he mentioned to Acton that there'd been a note left by the local constabulary, who'd asked that it be delivered to him as soon as may be.

They'll catch cold at that, thought Doyle with amusement, as she jostled Edward in a vain attempt to keep him quiet. The last thing Acton wants to do is pose for promotional photos with the local coppers.

But in this, apparently, she was mistaken. Acton nodded, and then paused as the man handed over an unmarked envelope. Whilst Doyle tried to soothe the restless baby, she watched her husband open the message and briefly scan the handwritten lines before tucking it into his inner jacket pocket.

She'd the impression that whatever-it-was, it wasn't an invitation to glad-hand, and so once they were in the lift, Doyle eyed her husband and prompted, "What is it that they're wantin', Michael?"

"I don't know," he replied, and it was the truth. "But the local Inspector has asked that I stop by the Garda station-house at my earliest convenience."

"They're goin' to arrest you," she decided. "Bring your toothbrush."

"Unlikely." He drew a soothing hand over Edward's unhappy head. "But I doubt they'd bother me unless it was important."

"May I come?" she asked, as the lift doors slid open. "It was my old station-house, and the desk sergeant there helped me fill out my application for the Yard. I wanted to thank him—if he's still there, that is."

"By all means."

She was rather surprised that he'd acquiesced—she knew that he wasn't best pleased about this unexplained request for a police visit—but on the other hand, he was still unhappy about the incident in the train, and no doubt wanted to keep her within arm's length for the next day or two.

As they walked down the hallway, Doyle raised her voice so as to be heard over the baby's cries. "Everyone else on the floor will hate us with a seethin' rage, if the boyo keeps this up."

"No matter—we've booked the entire floor."

With mock-relief she teased, "Of course, we have—what with the retinue, and all. Do I get to have a dressin'-maid? Because there's nothin' I'd like more."

He granted her a small smile, but his watchful gaze was on the hallway before them, and he took her elbow so as to check her progress. "We'll wait for a moment, so as to allow Trenton to do a quick sweep."

This seemed overly-cautious, and—due to the screeching banshee strapped to her chest—Doyle was fast losing patience. "Are we expectin' trouble? Because I think I'd rather take my chances in a shootout than listen to this child for another moment."

Still holding her elbow, Acton watched Trenton move from room to room down the hallway. "Just as a precaution, Kathleen—only another minute or two."

Trenton finally gave the all-clear, and then Doyle made a bee-line toward the settee in their elegantly-appointed suite, lifting her blouse for the hungry baby with no further ado. "I'm nothin' but a pack of udders to this child," she complained as she sank down into the soft upholstery. "And to you, too."

"Surely not," he protested, and ran a fond hand over her hair as he reviewed the room. "You have many other fine qualities."

"Well, all other fine qualities play second fiddle to these two fine qualities, my friend, and now I know how the bell-cow feels when she's bein' herded into the milkin' barn."

He laid his coat over the back of the settee, and loosened his tie. "Perhaps the bell-cow could be tempted by a room-service meal."

She lifted her brows. "Now, there's a fine idea; but the shower's first—I need to get the sea spray out of my hair."

"I'll have Reynolds order something for afterwards, then. And he can unpack the bags while you shower."

Doyle tilted her head so as to rest it on the back on the settee and look upside-down at her husband. Although he was making a mighty effort to disguise it, he was still all on-end, and—bing as she'd plenty of experience in such things—she knew just how to smooth the poor man out. Reaching to take his hand, she asked, "Join me in the shower?"

"Reynolds can wait," he decided, and bent to bestow a lingering kiss on her neck.

Chapter 3

She'd get her nails done and consider her next move.

"You can see, sir," the Irish Inspector said to Acton, "why we have some concerns."

"Yes," Acton agreed, in his reserved, public-school way. "It is alarming, indeed."

This seemed an understatement, and Doyle was hard-pressed to hold her tongue even though—although he'd not said anything to her—she knew that Acton wanted her to hold her tongue.

They'd arrived at the Garda station-house that morning to meet with Inspector Geary, an ox of a man in the best tradition, whose head seemed to be resting directly upon his burly shoulders. He was new since Doyle had been there, and in his understated way, he'd expressed his great pleasure in making their acquaintance before ushering them into the interview room, and carefully closing the door behind him. In a measured voice, he'd informed them that a gentleman had come by the station, two days previous, asking for Acton's contact information, and demanding to know at which hotel he'd be staying.

"He was that insistent," the Inspector related, "but he refused to identify himself. Of course, we gave him nothin', and sent him on his way. I asked the desk sergeant to give me the head's-up if he ever came back, but he seemed harmless enough—not a brawler."

"And now," said Acton, "he has turned up dead."

"Not a pretty sight," the man agreed. When he'd produced the photo, Doyle had struggled mightily not to gasp aloud. The body of a man was lying face-up, splayed on the very steps of the Garda, where apparently the victim had been fleeing to find refuge. It seemed probable that the cause of death was a dagger through the eye, since the hilt of the weapon remained embedded therein for all to see. That the victim had been aware of his impending doom also seemed evident; his mouth was opened in horror, and even rigor mortis couldn't disguise the terror in his expression as he faced his last moments on earth.

"The victim is a priest," Acton disclosed. "Father Gregory Brown, late of Holy Trinity parish, in London."

The other man didn't hide his surprise, and lifted his shaggy brows. "A priest? Now, there's a wrinkle. Not wearin' a Roman collar, for starts."

"No," Acton agreed. "And no doubt he was traveling incognito for good reason."

"Oh?" asked the Inspector with polite interest. "Never say he was a stalker?"

Acton inclined his head. "No; instead, he was a suspect. We believe he was one of the players in the forced-prostitution enterprise; the one which was connected to the corruption rig at the Met."

Leaning back, the man whistled softly. "Is that so—a priest, of all things? Was he ever indicted?"

"The prosecution continues to gather evidence—it was a far-reaching enterprise—but I am not certain whether they decided to finally go after him. As you know, oftentimes the victims are reluctant to testify in a sexual abuse prosecution, and so it is difficult to build a solid case."

The other man nodded slowly. "It's lucky, we are, that he came in here askin' for you, or we may have never made an ID—we had 'im in the morgue as a 'John Doe'." He lifted his chin to contemplate the opposite wall for a moment. "Strange, that we couldn't find his prints anywhere in the database."

Acton remained silent, and Doyle blinked in surprise as this was indeed strange—in fact, there was an additional database for clergy that existed aside from the general database. Perhaps Father Gregory wasn't truly a priest? That seemed far-fetched, though; it wasn't as though RC priests were thick on the ground in England, and the other seminarians of his age would surely have known if he were only posing as a priest. Not that he was much of a priest to begin with, of course; anyone who could prey on the helpless didn't deserve the privilege in the first place.

I suppose I should pray for his soul, she thought, as her gaze strayed again to the grisly photo, and wished she could muster up a bit more enthusiasm at the prospect. On the other hand, she'd best add another layer of prayer for Acton's soul, because—despite the way he'd carefully couched his answers—he knew more about this than he was letting on.

Careful not to give anything away, she shifted her gaze to the battered wooden tabletop for a moment, wondering why the dead priest had been so desperate to seek out Acton—and face-to-face, too—considering that the last time they'd seen the man he was fleeing Acton's confirmation reception with all speed. Acton had recently converted to Roman Catholicism—Doyle's influence, of course—and what should have been a tedious punch-and-cake reception after the religious ceremony had turned out to be fraught with high drama. Mary-the-nanny had met her Howard—even though he was engaged to another woman, at the time—and their friends Timothy and Nanda had openly quarreled, which was very out-of-character for them.

But all these other unsettling events paled in comparison to the sudden and unexpected death of Acton's fellow Chief Inspector, DCI Drake, who'd been hip-deep in the corruption-and-sex-slavery rig, and who'd died in dramatic fashion next to the punch bowl.

At the time, Father Gregory—who'd also been attending the reception—had been clearly terrified by his fellow-conspirator's death, and now—with hindsight—it seemed that the priest had been terrified with good reason.

Doyle frowned slightly, because it would be an easy thing to conclude that this particular murder was by Acton's hand, save for the fact her husband would never stoop to go about knifing people in the eye. When Acton went into vengeance-mode he was fearsomely efficient, and always set-up the evidence so that there was not the smallest chance that a trail would lead any determined investigator back to the renowned Chief Inspector.

Therefore—assuming Acton didn't do it—he must know who did, but he wasn't going to offer any insights to the Irish Inspector, for reasons which were unclear.

Rather shocked by this conclusion, Doyle nevertheless reassured herself that in the end it hardly mattered, because the crime should be an easy one to solve; spite-murders were bloody, messy affairs, and the odds were good that a print or shoe impression had been left somewhere in the carnage. Or—failing that—they could probably trace the dagger's purchase; it looked to be rather unusual, and not the typical edged-weapon that was usually plied by the villains they ran across.

"I have to ask," Inspector Geary said apologetically, "if you could disclose your whereabouts for the early morning hours yesterday, sir."

Doyle lifted her head in astonishment, as the soft-spoken man apparently had big brass ones, to say such a thing to Acton.

But her husband was not at all discomfited. "Of course. I was not yet in Ireland, as we were traveling by train to Holyhead. If you would like, I can produce the receipts, and the station will have surveillance tape."

"Not at all necessary, sir—your word is good enough."

Oh-oh, thought Doyle with some surprise; this fellow's suspicious, despite his reassuring words. This did not bode well, since the fair Doyle was herself suspicious, and with better reason.

She decided she shouldn't sit like a stump, but instead should show some detective-like curiosity, and so asked, "You don't have the victim's electronics, sir?" It seemed obvious that they didn't, if they were unable to identify him.

"We don't," the other man admitted. "He wasn't carryin' a blessed thing—not even a coin. But now that we've an ID we'll have a look at last contacts, to see what there is to see."

"If you would, please keep me informed," said Acton.

"Of course, sir," said the Inspector, who had no intention of doing so.

Oh-oh, thought Doyle again, trying with little success to tamp down her alarm.

Since Acton had made it clear that the subject was now closed, he turned to address Doyle. "I believe you wished to take this opportunity to look up old friends, Kathleen."

"I do," she agreed, happy to change the subject. "Is Sergeant O'Shaughnessy about? I wanted to say hallo."

"He is indeed, and if you wouldn't mind takin' a moment, the staff was hopin' to meet with you."

"Oh—oh, yes; I suppose that would be fine." With a mental sigh, Doyle acknowledged that the bridge-jumping incident was about to rear its ugly head yet again, and no matter where she went she couldn't seem to escape it, which was apparently God's little joke and shame on Him.

"This way." The Inspector smiled in a friendly fashion as he ushered them out of the interview room, but Doyle wasn't fooled, and devotedly hoped that the good Inspector wasn't about to put Acton even more on-end than he already was. Between the train incident and Father Gregory's getting himself spite-murdered, it didn't seem that their holiday trip was starting out on a very relaxing note, and that was before you added in the fact that Acton was busily trying to pull the wool over her eyes with respect to whatever was going forward back home.

I need a holiday from my holiday, she thought crossly, and pinned on her best company-smile.

Chapter 4

It was for his own good, of course. She'd made him a laughingstock.

Inspector Geary led them down the narrow hallway—
the building hadn't been renovated lately and looked very
much as it had at the time Doyle was there—and then they
emerged into the situation room, where the on-site detectives
conducted their serious business in their cluttered cubicles.
The dedicated atmosphere was remarkably similar to that at
the CID in London and probably everywhere in the world—the
sense that one was fighting the good fight, against almost
overwhelming odds.

Doyle harbored mixed emotions, and found that her
memories of the place weren't exactly fond; instead, she was
reminded how nervous she'd been about applying to the Crime
Academy in London, even though she'd hardly started here as
a uniformed officer. And—although Sergeant O'Shaughnessy
had openly expressed his doubts that it would amount to
much—the man had willingly provided her with a reference
and had made suggestions to help her with the process.

Faith, when she looked back at it now, it was a shrine-
worthy miracle that she'd persisted; she'd never set foot
outside of her own neighborhood, and she wasn't one to put
herself forward in the first place. On top of that, she'd also had
her mother to think about—no question that if the fair Doyle
wound up moving to London her mother would come along,
too, and leave everything that was familiar behind. I was that
determined to be a homicide detective, Doyle realized, so as to
put these abilities of mine to the best use possible—even

though I had to steel myself to do it. Good on me, and let this be a reminder that I should stick with it, come what may.

Upon their entry, the various personnel in the room paused in their work so as to rise and greet her with genuine good will—and out of politeness, they all shook Acton's hand with a palpable lack of enthusiasm.

Oh, Doyle belatedly realized; I'm shown to have misjudged the situation—these people couldn't care less about the famous DCI Acton, instead, he's the one who's the interloper, here, and they've all closed ranks against a common enemy.

The desk sergeant had come back to join the group, and Doyle greeted him with sincere affection. "Hallo, sir."

"The prodigal returns," Sergeant O'Shaughnessy said to Doyle in a mock-jovial manner. "Well done, missy."

There was a slight edge to his words, and Doyle hurried into speaking, so that it didn't linger in the air. "I was wantin' to thank you, sir. You were very generous, to help me to transfer out after I'd just got started here."

The sergeant shrugged and confessed, "I'll tell you the truth, lass; I'd no clue it would work out the way it did. But I knew that your father was livin' in London, and I thought it would give you a chance to look 'im up."

Doyle blinked, as this was entirely unexpected, and she could feel her color rise. "Oh—oh, well; whilst that may have been a fine idea, sir, I never knew my father, and wouldn't have known how to look him up in the first place."

The man was unfazed, however, and jutted out his chin a bit. "Your mum must have known of his whereabouts, though; I thought I'd try to put the family back together."

Doyle could sense that Acton was made very unhappy by the man's clumsy remarks, and so yet again, she tried to diffuse the situation with a smile. "Well, the best-laid plans, as they say, sir. We never did run across each other, and I'm afraid he's met with a bad end."

To her dismay, it seemed to Doyle that the sergeant was winding up to inquire about the particulars but unexpectedly, the young intern who'd been hovering in the background spoke up and changed the subject. "Do you mind if I take a snap, Officer Doyle? I have followed your career with great interest."

"We all have, and that's a fact," Sergeant O'Shaughnessy quickly seconded, and Doyle knew he was trying to retrench from his awkward opening. "Faith, a commendation for bravery is nothin' to sneeze at."

"Two," offered Acton. "Two commendations."

The intern hurriedly intervened again. "It would just take a moment, Officer Doyle."

With some relief, Doyle readily moved aside to stand next to the girl, who appeared to be Middle Eastern—Pakistani, perhaps—and presumably a first-year intern, as she was wearing civilian clothes. Doyle asked kindly, "Are you hopin' to become a detective trainee?"

"I am, ma'am," the other girl replied politely, as she held up her mobile. "I enjoy this work very much."

"Yes—well, it's a bit more peaceful, up here in Dublin," Doyle offered, as the girl took a snap. "It took some gettin' used to, seein' what there was to see in London after bein' stationed here."

"We did have the murder yesterday," the girl noted.

"Of course—now, there's somethin' that doesn't happen every day, even in London. Nothin' like a body showin' up on the doorstep to catch your attention."

After checking the snap on her phone, the other girl turned her dark eyes to Doyle. "Did you know the victim, ma'am—the man who'd been asking for your husband?"

"Yes; well, not well—I knew *of* him, I suppose is more accurate, because he was the priest at a neighborin' parish."

Doyle could sense the girl's strong surprise. "The victim was a Roman Catholic priest?"

"Indeed, he was, and—although I shouldn't speak ill o' the dead—he was a blackleg, through-and-through."

With a knit brow, the young intern hesitated for a moment, and then asked, "Was he a missionary, ma'am?"

This seemed an odd assumption, but Doyle answered readily, "Not that I'm aware, but I doubt it. He was a soft sort of priest, and rather spoiled, I think—the missionaries tend to be hardy specimens, and burnin' with a righteous fire."

"Of course," the girl replied politely.

Doyle belatedly realized she'd blundered, and hastened to explain, "Not that they're deliberately tryin' to stir up trouble—the missionaries, I mean. Or not usually, leastways." She then decided to snabble it, before she got caught up in the sort of comparative religions argument that tended to end in open warfare.

"I was not offended," the girl assured her, and thankfully, this was true. "What a sweet little baby."

They both peeked into the chest carrier at Edward's fuzz-covered head. "He's a brick," Doyle agreed, happy to change the subject. "I've no idea what I'm doin', and thankfully he doesn't seem to care much."

A young DC who'd been standing nearby stepped forward. "Do you mind if I take a snap too, Officer Doyle? My daughter will be that thrilled."

Dutifully, Doyle stood next to the young man, and as he grinned into the mobile, his voice reverberated next to her head. "If I may ask, ma'am; what were you thinkin', when you jumped off the bridge?"

"I was just thinkin' that I had to help my friend," Doyle replied by rote, having been asked the question many a time before. Much of her renown—and one of her commendations for bravery—stemmed from the fact she'd jumped off Greyfriars Bridge into the Thames, even though she didn't know how to swim, so as to rescue a fellow detective. "It was nothin', truly."

Everyone laughed, and Doyle had to join in with them.

"Our lass gave you a heart-attack, I'll bet," said Sergeant O'Shaughnessy to Acton, in an overly-jovial manner. "Didn't know she was the type to take the bit between her teeth, did you?"

"I did not," Acton agreed in a deceptively mild tone.

"Acton was there to help fish me out, though," Doyle offered quickly. "Lucky for me."

"Indeed, very lucky," the intern said, trying to pour oil on troubled waters. "And at no small risk to yourself, sir."

"No risk to myself, actually," Acton corrected.

"It was DS Williams, who jumped in," Doyle was forced to explain. "Williams was first on the scene."

She paused, surprised, because she could feel a strong jolt of emotion coming from the young Pakistani woman. "Thomas Williams?" the girl asked.

"Why, yes—d'you know him? He's an Inspector, now."

"Oh, no—no." The girl unclasped her hands in a disclaiming gesture. "I have only seen the name."

"Then this Williams fellow is deservin' of a medal, too," the sergeant proclaimed. "I suppose they thought it would look better in the newspapers if they just gave it to you, lass."

"Yes; well—we should probably go," Doyle announced apologetically. "We shouldn't interrupt your work, and anyways, we're due at St. Brigid's." This was not exactly true, but Doyle was itching to leave; she didn't like the cross-currents of emotion—what with Sergeant O'Shaughnessy clomping about like a cow in a cornfield, Acton on a low simmer, and the Pakistani intern puzzling over something behind her soft brown eyes.

As he ushered them out, Inspector Geary made generalized one-ranking-officer-to-another conversation with Acton, and then the two shook hands, very civilly, as they parted before the entry door.

Acton offered, "I will inform the Met of the priest's murder, and ask that they assist you in every way possible. If you have need of any resources, please do not hesitate to ask."

"It's an odd case, and that's a fact," the Inspector conceded. "But if he was involved in the Met scandal, that puts a whole different light on it." Bowing his head, he added, "I appreciate the ID; now at least we have somethin' to work with."

"Indeed," said Acton politely, and Doyle wished she didn't have the sense that swords had been crossed.

Chapter 5

They weren't using the limousine service, so that was frustrating.

"Sorry," Doyle said immediately, as she emerged with Acton onto the Garda's front portico. "That was crackin' awkward."

"Not at all," he replied, and took her arm to assist her down the stone steps. "It was only to be expected."

But Doyle found that she was annoyed on his behalf, and retorted, "Well, I didn't expect it—Mother a' mercy, why was everyone so willin' to give you the side-eye?"

But he was philosophical, and didn't seem at all put-out. "There will always be a certain amount of tension between different jurisdictions. It goes with the territory."

She made a wry mouth. "Not to mention you used to rule their territory, back in the day."

"There was that, too. Again, it can't be helped."

"Well, no one should be rude to you," she insisted. "Not on my watch; I've half a mind to go back in and dress them all down."

"I am not certain," he replied in a mild tone, "that such a course of action would be beneficial."

She had to laugh, because he was taking it all in good part—no doubt because he wanted to spare her feelings, since Acton was not someone who'd submit meekly to insult. In keeping with his wishes, she decided to let it go, and instead paused to lift her face, and breathe in. "I'd forgotten what the streets smell like, here—there's nothin' like a scent, to bring back a memory." The clouds had cleared away to reveal a gloriously sunny day, with the remnants of the rain sparkling on the pavement as people began to go about their business.

Acton checked his watch. "We have a bit of time; shall we visit your old lodgings, and tour the neighborhood? I would like to see where you lived."

"It's not much to speak of," she warned. "You'd have to duck your head, to get through the door."

"I am forewarned, then."

There was a small silence. "Mayhap not just yet, Michael. We've a busy day planned, today."

He lifted his head to gaze down the street. "Then shall we walk for a bit? We're not due at the orphanage for another hour."

This was unexpected—Acton was not a walker-about, but she could sense that he was trying to soothe her, and she decided that she was more than willing to be soothed. "That would be grand, Michael—although if Edward wakes up, we'll need to find a dry bench, somewhere."

"We'll hail a cab, if he wakes, and you may feed him on the way to St. Brigid's."

"We don't have a car-seat," she reminded him.

"We'll have to manage without, then."

Meeting his eyes in mock-astonishment, she teased, "Holy Mother—who *are* you, that you're so willin' to lower yourself to public transportation?"

He lifted his gaze to contemplate the street ahead and tucked her hand into the crook of his elbow. "It's rather a relief to be spontaneous, for a change."

"That's you," she agreed with heavy irony. "'Spontaneous' is your middle name."

"Unfair," he protested, as they made their leisurely way down the pavement. "Our wedding was nothing if not spontaneous."

She made a sound of extreme disbelief. "Doin' it too brown, husband; you'd been layin' the groundwork for weeks. Instead, it was a stealth campaign—by way of ambush, and deceit."

He lifted a shoulder in admission. "Of necessity; the element of surprise was of paramount importance."

With a fond smile, she rested her cheek against his arm. "And done to a fare-thee-well, my friend—although I'd expect nothin' less. I'm the one who's spontaneous, to have been so roped-in."

"You were delightful," he declared, and leaned down to kiss her head. "And you continue delightful."

They walked along for a few minutes, Doyle very much appreciating the pains her husband was taking to coax her into a better mood. Unfortunately, she'd have to venture back into bad-mood waters, and there was no bunkin' it. "Best be careful, Michael; the Inspector is suspicious, behind his kind words. Thinks you're an eye-stabber of the first order."

But Acton did not seem discomfited by this revelation, and only nodded. "I am unsurprised; it is a troubling sequence of events."

"I wonder what he wanted to talk to you about—Father Gregory, I mean." She glanced up at him, sidelong.

"I suppose we may never know."

Stubbornly, she persisted, "His electronics aren't goin' to show much, I imagine. If he was that desperate to speak to you in person—comin' all the way up here—he must have wanted whatever-it-was to be kept on the quiet."

"I would tend to agree," Acton said. "Which would also suggest he was aware that he was soon to be murdered."

"I was tryin' to get to that point in a more roundabout way," she admitted. "But there's the nub of it—why did he think you'd lift a finger to save him?"

"It is puzzling indeed."

As her husband was carefully guarding his words, Doyle ventured, "Was he hopin' to force your hand, in some way? Did he have somethin' to threaten you with?"

"Not that I am aware."

She breathed out a mental sigh of relief, because it was the truth, and she'd been worried. Father Gregory shouldn't have been seeking help from Acton—of all people—so he must have been trying to threaten him, or bargain with him, or otherwise leverage his way out of his doom. But if this had been the case, it would raise the unwelcome specter that Father Gregory knew a thing or two about Acton's many misdeeds—things that may now be unearthed by the Irish Inspector's murder investigation. Hopefully, Acton was right, and they'd never find out why the panicking priest had tried— so desperately—to track him down.

Still and all, she should give him fair warning. "Watch your step, husband; it's not like home, here—they'll be only too happy to throw you in the nick, and the fact that you're an English lord will only add to the general sense of satisfaction."

"I wasn't going to mention that aspect," he admitted, "out of deference to your feelings."

"I up and married a *sassanach*," she lamented. "Shame on me."

He smiled. "I can always explain to them that you weren't given much of a choice, if you think that would be of help."

She laughed—as he'd intended—and squeezed his arm fondly. "Don't encourage them—they shouldn't have been so bristly, and I'm that ashamed for my countrymen. Although the Pakistani intern was civil, even though you've had a boot on her neck for centuries, too."

"She probably wants a job at the Met."

Doyle laughed again. "I hope not; she's kind and smart, and wouldn't fit in at all."

There was a small pause, whilst they walked a few more paces in silence, and Doyle thought over the uncomfortable scene at the Garda. "I'm truly sorry, Michael; I never think about these things—these stupid tribal allegiances—and I wish everyone would just get over it."

"It is often a motivation for crime," he noted, in a massive understatement.

"Exactly," she agreed, warming to the topic. "Why can't people just start their lives with a clean slate, instead of inheriting the same pack of grudges their ancestors hauled around with them? It's medieval, is what it is."

"I cannot disagree."

"And it's not only the ancestors that matter, either—any sort of tribe will do, as long as one has a ready-made enemy to resent and scheme against."

"I didn't take it personally, Kathleen."

She sighed in disagreement. "Oh—you were annoyed, my friend; mainly, you were annoyed on my behalf, but you were annoyed all the same, and I'm that sorry you had to put up with it."

With a regretful tilt of his head, he replied, "I am more annoyed that I let you see that I was annoyed."

In sympathy, she squeezed his arm. "Not your fault, Michael; it comes of my bein' a crackin' tunin' fork—especially when it comes to you."

He glanced toward the trees for a moment. "I will admit I was tempted to rebuke the good sergeant."

But she only shook her head. "I'm glad you didn't, Michael—he's that unhappy about somethin'; that's why he was bein' so bristly."

Acton turned to regard her with interest, and then gave a guess. "He is jealous of you, perhaps?"

"Perhaps," she agreed, although she knew it was something else—the man had been a bundle of conflicting emotions. "But to the good, he's definitely not lookin' for a job at the Met."

"A shame," he teased. "We need every hand."

Edward began to make the little mewling sounds that were the warm-up for the big wailing sounds, and she stroked his head, gently. "There we go—the boyo's gettin' hungry."

Acton glanced toward the street. "I'll hail a cab, then."

She feigned astonishment. "Do you even know how to hail a cab? Mayhap you should ring up Reynolds, and ask for instructions."

"Nonsense. I need only put my mind to it."

"You have to lift a hand, and look harassed," she warned. "There's a strict protocol."

But as it turned out, Acton only needed to turn his head toward the oncoming traffic, and a cab immediately pulled over, the driver rolling down the window. "Yes? You need a ride?"

"St. Brigid's," said Acton, striding over to open the door for Doyle. "But no hurry, please; we must feed the baby."

"Yes: I am very careful—very good driver," the big man assured them, his smile flashing white against his dark skin. Incongruously, he wore a plaid tam o'shanter, and Doyle decided that it was only in keeping that they'd run across an African cab driver who wore a plaid tam o'shanter; it was shaping up to be that kind of a day.

The reason Acton normally avoided public transportation was soon made clear, as the driver did not hesitate to strike up a conversation, craning his head around in an alarming fashion—alarming because it seemed unlikely that he was able to watch the road at the same time.

37

"You are going to church, yes? A big church, very nice."

"We are," Doyle agreed, thinking to bypass all explanations about wealthy benefactors. "It was my old church, when I was growin' up."

"Very nice," the man said enthusiastically, and then turned to take a passing glance at the busy road ahead.

Doyle smiled to herself, because he was clearly humoring the customers—one of whom was wearing a very expensive suit—even though there were assorted fetishes hanging from his rear-view mirror. He practiced Santeria, perhaps, but whatever-it-was, he was definitely outnumbered, here in Roman Catholic country.

"You do not live here, now?" The grinning man craned his head around, yet again.

"We are visiting from London," Acton informed him. "And I believe the light is changing."

"Oh—yes, yes, thank you." With a jerk, the man halted the cab at the intersection, and was seen to hesitate a moment, as though debating what to say. "Do you know of the dead man?" He turned again to face them, this time with a more somber expression. "A dead man, this morning. A holy man."

"Yes," said Doyle, when Acton remained silent. "We did hear. Terrible, of course."

The man sighed hugely, and tapped his thumbs on the sun-faded steering wheel. "You try to get away from the troubles, but the troubles find you anyway."

"A very sad state of affairs," Doyle agreed, thinking that this fellow seemed very well-informed. On the other hand, a body on the Garda steps was not something that happened every day, and word on the street tended to get 'round fast, with the cab drivers probably picking up information faster than most.

As they started up again, Acton spoke into the silence. "Perhaps we could find a quiet place to stop for a few minutes;

my wife would like to finish feeding the baby before we arrive at the church."

"Good-good," said the driver, nodding enthusiastically. "The baby must eat. Here is a street that is a good, quiet street. Very nice." He then swerved so that Doyle had to brace herself against the door, and they turned onto a residential street, lined with spreading trees and relatively peaceful at this hour of the mid-morning.

They parked, and almost immediately Acton opened his door. "I should check in," he said to Doyle, "to ensure there will be no interruptions during our visit to the orphanage."

And so, Doyle sat in the back of the cab, feeding Edward and thoughtfully watching her husband as she listened with half an ear to the driver's lengthy description of his extended family, who could not be convinced to move to Dublin.

"They are afraid to change," the man declared, holding up his pale-colored palms in bewilderment. "They are tied to their old ways, and to their village. But there is no money, and I tell them, come here—here you can have as many jobs as you want."

I do miss working, Doyle thought, as Acton spoke in quiet tones on his mobile, his head bent and his manner serious. But I've a feeling that I'm slated to have plenty on my plate, this visit—not to mention a baby who eats as though he has a hollow leg.

When Acton slid back into the cab, she lifted Edward to her shoulder, and began to pat his back. "Everythin' all right?"

"A few odds and ends," he replied. "Nothing that can't be handled."

She gave him a look, as this last statement wasn't exactly true. "Lucky, it is, that your mobile's workin'."

"Indeed. Shall we go?" said Acton to the driver.

"Good-good," the man said cheerfully, and gunned the engine.

Something's up, Doyle thought for the hundredth time, and then was certain of it, when Acton massively over-paid the driver, and asked for his card.

Chapter 6

He was too polite to say it, but of course he regretted marrying her—how could he not? And now he was stuck in Dublin.

St. Brigid's was an old church in a working-class neighborhood; a brick-and-stone structure that had been expanded over the years to include a convent and a small neighborhood school. As was often the case with such old, established churches, many of the parishioners lived their entire lives in its shadows, never venturing outside the parish boundaries until they were eventually buried in its churchyard. Indeed, if Doyle hadn't decided to pursue a law enforcement career, she'd no doubt be living there still, and with her mother buried in that very churchyard. It was a strange thing to contemplate—that she'd be marking her days doing something other than solving major crimes, and married to someone who was not Acton.

As was the case in the Garda, Doyle found that she felt uncomfortable rather than nostalgic, and almost wished they hadn't come—which was nonsense, of course; this was her tribe, after all.

The taxi pulled up to the curb, and they alighted to be greeted by the three nuns that awaited their arrival outside the school's front door. The convent's Mother Superior—Sister Mary Theresa—was new since Doyle had graduated, but the head nun was flanked by Sister Margaret, who'd been the school's principal when Doyle attended St. Brigid's School for Girls. Both women were joined by a younger nun—younger being mid-forties—who identified herself as Sister Roseline, and who was serving as the Mother Superior's Second.

The three nuns greeted them warmly, in the universal manner of dedicated people who nonetheless must rely on generous benefactors.

"How wonderful to see you again, Kathleen," said Sister Margaret, who'd never really spoken to Doyle before, except to remind her to stand up straight. "I hope your journey was a pleasant one."

"It was, ma'am," said Doyle. Best not to mention any attempted pushings-out-of-trains, and a husband who'd been noticeably spooked, since then.

Sister Mary Theresa gestured them through the massive oak doors. "With your permission, we'll take a tour of the facilities, and then have a presentation—along with a luncheon—in the common room. Sister Roseline—" here, she nodded toward her Second, "has prepared a power-point presentation."

"I am quite looking forward to it," said Acton, who'd sat through innumerable presentations by the bureaucrats at the Yard, and therefore knew to a nicety how to sound as though he were truly interested.

"I hope you didn't put yourselves out," said Doyle, who wished she didn't feel as though she should curtsy, every time she spoke.

But Sister Roseline smiled warmly, and assured her, "Not at all, Lady Acton. We are blessed to have you here, so that you may witness what we have accomplished with your generosity."

Acton's mobile pinged, and he glanced at the ID. "Excuse me," he apologized. "I should probably answer this one. I promise I will make it fast."

"Please—use my office." As Sister Mary Theresa led Acton away, the other two sisters took the opportunity to watch him in retreat, as even nuns have a healthy appreciation for a handsome man. Sister Margaret turned to Doyle. "Such a charmin' fellow."

Nonplussed, Doyle wasn't certain how to respond, since she had never heard this particular adjective applied to her husband before.

"How did the two of you meet?"

"Oh—oh, well; as for that, he was my superior officer. Technically, he still is."

Sister Roseline smiled. "How wonderful, that you fell in love. It's rather like a fairy tale."

Dutifully, Doyle nodded. "Yes—like a fairy tale." Best not to mention the murder and the mayhem.

"And Sister Mary Theresa tells me he has converted to the faith."

"Yes, he had his confirmation ceremony only just recently." Again, best not to mention the murder and the mayhem.

"Glory be," said the Second, and meant it. With a broad smile, she then quoted, "*Love hopes for all things, and rejoices with the truth.*"

"Not always," Doyle disagreed immediately. "Sometimes love doesn't hope for all things, and instead rejoices over wrongdoing." She then paused in acute dismay, amazed that she'd said such a thing. Her scalp began prickling—as it did when her intuition was making a leap—but she ignored it, and offered quickly, "I am so sorry; faith, I don't know why I would say such a thing—I must sound like a jaded copper."

"Well, you've had a different life experience than we have, my dear." Sister Margaret was doing her best to smooth over Doyle's strange gaffe, despite the fact that the woman's inclination was to give her former pupil a taste of the ruler.

Sister Roseline offered gently, "If love rejoices over wrongdoing, then it is not love. I think that was the Apostle's point."

"Of course, it was," said Doyle hastily, and then—trying to redeem herself—she quoted in turn, *"Love bears all things."*

No, it doesn't, Doyle's intuition immediately responded, but the nuns—now re-joined by Sister Mary Theresa—were nodding in approval, since things were back on polite-conversation-track. What? Doyle asked herself, bewildered. Of course, love bears all things—although—although Acton would be the exception, since his brand of Doyle-love tended to go scorched-earth—

"A beautiful baby," Sister Mary Theresa pronounced, using a finger to pull at the carrier's edge and peek in at Edward. "I think he'll be another red-head."

"D'you think so?" Doyle made a show of regarding him with fond maternal pride, whilst in reality she was trying to organize her bewildered thoughts. There was something here; something ominous—although how a nun quoting from First Corinthians could be ominous remained to be seen. Nevertheless, Doyle knew—in the way she knew things—that it was somehow important; somehow tied to Acton's sudden desire to engage in phone calls where no one could hear what was being discussed, especially the wife of his bosom.

Hard on this dismaying thought, Acton returned and apologized for the interruption, whilst Sister Mary Theresa clasped her hands and assured him that they understood the necessity. "We are grateful you took this opportunity to visit; we know you are particularly busy, just now."

This seemed a diplomatic reference to the unfortunate fact that the Yard was mired hip-deep in scandal, and Doyle was surprised to intercept a jolt of emotion from the calmly-standing Sister Roseline. Hard to believe, that an African nun socked away at St. Brigid's knew anything about the Met's unholy corruption scandal, but it did seem as though the woman was struggling to hide her reaction—guilt, perhaps? But why on earth would the Second feel guilty about the Yard's troubles?

As Doyle tried to make sense of it, Sister Mary Theresa shepherded them toward the portion of the convent that had been renovated to house the new orphanage. "We are still building," she explained. "The laws are strict about square-footage and such, but by next month we should be able to take on five more children." She counted on her fingers. "At present, we have the six babies who were abandoned last year, and seven more children —three of whom are special needs."

The woman paused to nod in grateful acknowledgment to her Second. "Fortunately, Sister Roseline assisted in a Rwandan orphanage when she was a postulate, and so her experience has been enormously helpful."

"Very helpful," Sister Margaret agreed with sincere enthusiasm. "I don't know how we'd have done it without her— she has a knack."

"You are originally from Rwanda?" Acton asked the Second.

"I am, sir," Sister Roseline answered readily.

"You must have been in the thick of it, then," he offered, with a show of sympathy. "An unfortunate state of affairs, at that time. Were you finally forced to flee?"

"I was indeed, sir," the nun replied in an even tone, and offered nothing more.

Doyle shot him a grateful glance; it was very unlike Acton to show an interest in anyone—unless he was interrogating them, of course—and she was pleased that he was making an effort to be civil, since there'd been no nuns in Acton-world, up to now, and they must seem like a strange and exotic species to an English aristocrat.

The tour continued as they were escorted through the nursery, followed by the preschool area, where a layperson was reading to the assembled children from a story book.

As they stood in the doorway, Doyle looked on the children—sitting cross-legged on the rug—and had a sudden recollection of sitting thus, trying not to fidget and hoping they weren't going to have fish sticks again for lunch.

"I think the baby is gettin' a bit restless," she announced suddenly, even though Edward was slumbering peacefully. "Just as a fair warnin'."

Sister Mary Theresa turned to her with a smile. "Oh— then we'll take a break, Kathleen, and find a quiet room so that you may feed him. When you're finished, we can adjourn to the common room for the presentation."

Thank you," Doyle replied, and felt her color rise as she turned aside from the tableau before her, and followed the Mother Superior away from her memories.

Chapter 7

He was desperately needed here, and it was all her fault.

The Mother Superior escorted them into a small receiving room—where the nuns received visitors—and then closed the door behind them with an indulgent smile. Settling into her chair, Doyle jostled the surprised Edward awake, and the baby was only too happy to partake in the unexpected boon of another meal so hard upon the last one.

Acton pulled up a chair and leaned forward to rest his forearms on his knees as he watched Edward. After a moment, he offered, "If you'd like, I could say I have an emergency, and we will make our excuses."

Trust him, to sense that she was uncomfortable—he had his own brand of intuition, especially when it came to her. "No—no, it's all right, Michael." She glanced up at the crucifix, hanging on the otherwise bare, white wall. "It's only—it's hard to explain, but it makes me anxious to be here. It shouldn't, but it does."

He bent his head, as he considered this. "Perhaps you miss your mother."

"No—I always miss my mother. But here, I just feel—I suppose I feel that I've taken a step backward, somehow. This chapter's been closed, and I don't want to be openin' it up for a re-read."

He lifted his head to meet her eyes and nodded. "Yes. I understand completely."

Of course, he did; he had his own chapters that he kept firmly closed, after all. She watched Edward for a moment, feeling a bit foolish for wanting to duck out, like a naughty schoolgirl. "It's got nothin' to do with them, though; they seem to be workin' wonders."

"Yes," he agreed. "Do you mind if I make a call, Kathleen?"

She quirked her mouth. "Not a'tall."

He pulled his mobile, pressed a tab, and then lifted the phone to his ear. After a moment, he said simply, "Acton." He listened to the voice on the other end—it sounded like the low tones of a man's voice, but more than that she couldn't say—and after a few seconds, he rang off without saying anything else.

Running a fond finger over Edward's fuzzy head, she asked, "Are you goin' to tell me about whatever-it-is, husband?"

He bent his head, and contemplated his hands, clasped between his knees. "I am afraid not."

She glanced up to consider him. "I always seem to find out, you know. May as well save us both a bit of thrashin' about."

Hesitating, he chose his words carefully. "It would be for the best. At least for the time being."

With some impatience she reminded him, "You and I aren't in charge of 'what would be best', my friend—and that's a lesson you never seem to learn, if I might make mention of it. At least tell me whether this is an old disaster heatin' up, or a new one altogether." It seemed a bit alarming that he was keeping such close tabs on whatever-it-was—she'd the sense that he'd been distracted, ever since their cab ride.

"A bit of both," he replied, and it was true.

She ventured, "Are we worried about the Inspector? Is he hot on the trail?"

But her husband didn't appear to be at all dismayed by this suggestion. "If he isn't yet, he soon will be."

This seemed a strange thing to say—it was much more likely that Acton didn't want the Inspector to get any bright ideas, so as to unearth whatever-it-was that Acton didn't want him to unearth. But there was little point in quizzing him any further—she recognized a brick wall when she saw one—and so she turned her attention back to Edward, knowing that there was more than one way to winkle a bit of information from her sphynx-like husband, and that he wasn't the only one who could be wily.

"Keep your secrets, then, but try not to throw a spanner in the wheel of good works that's goin' on here, if you please. If there are dire events unfoldin', promise to keep them well-away from poor St. Brigid's."

"It is impressive, that so much has been accomplished, and in so short a time."

Doyle smiled. "That's nuns for you—they're focused like a laser-beam on savin' the world; that, and makin' sure you have good posture."

She'd noted with no small alarm that her husband had sidestepped a direct answer to her question, and so she took a different tack; waiting for a few moments, and then making a show of idle curiosity. "What was goin' on in Rwanda, that Sister Roseline was forced to flee?"

"A civil war—although it was more along the lines of a genocide."

Doyle took a guess at what 'genocide' meant, and ventured, "Faith, that sounds grim. I hope they managed to get the orphans out."

His chest rose and fell. "Perhaps, although many were murdered, and of all ages. She is lucky to have escaped."

Doyle glanced at him. "She's a long ways away from home, up here—although I suppose if so much has changed, it wouldn't seem much like home to her, anymore."

"Rather the same way you feel," he offered, and reached to draw a commiserating hand down her arm.

"Rather like me," Doyle agreed thoughtfully, and then decided she truly couldn't say much more, else he'd realize that she'd twigged on to the fact that there was something here—something in the way the African nun had answered Acton's questions, and in the way he'd answered Doyle's, just now. Although what a long-ago germicide—or whatever the word was—had to do with the new Irish orphanage was unclear. On the other hand, it was clear that Sister Roseline had landed on her feet—no matter how terrible her past—and good on her; she exhibited the same kindness-laced-with-efficiency as Sister Mary Theresa, and was no doubt slated to be the next Mother Superior when that worthy nun retired.

"Shall we cut our visit short, Kathleen? We'd have time to walk over to your old neighborhood, if you'd like."

Doyle made a face. "No—we can't possibly duck out, and I'm that ashamed of myself, Michael; I'm a bigger baby than Edward. They're makin' such an effort, and—to the good—no one is sendin' snide remarks your way, like they were at the Garda. I think I'm just a bit down-pin, and out-of-sorts."

"All right—but only say the word."

With a small smile, she tried to lighten the mood. "Only if the power-point is worse than the one from diversity training, last fall."

"Impossible," he decided, with his own answering smile. "Although that bar is indeed very low."

Laughing, she moved Edward to her shoulder. "And don't forget that I've yet to recite the bridge-jumpin' story; it wouldn't be any sort of proper visit without that."

In a mock-serious manner, he cocked his head. "Perhaps—with hindsight—it would have been wiser to leave Officer Munoz to drown."

She stood, and he helped her slide Edward back into his carrier. "Don't think that hasn't occurred to me, my friend."

With a show of resolution, she smoothed back her hair, and lifted her chin. "I don't know why I'm stewin' like a barleycorn, Michael, and I beg your pardon fastin'."

"Only give me a signal, if you'd like to leave."

"I'm fine," she insisted, pronouncing it "foine" so as to tease him. "I'm over-mopey, just now—what with my hormones, runnin' amok." This was only true; she'd been a bundle of emotions ever since she'd set foot on Irish soil, and she needed to get back to being her steady self. Unless she very much missed her guess, there was a disaster or two that were brewing, and the fair Doyle needed to stay sharp.

"Shall we go?" He reached for the door.

"Lead on," she agreed. "Hopefully, they'll be feedin' us sometime soon."

Chapter 8

*The baby was the problem, of course. He couldn't leave
her, even if he wanted to.*

After re-joining Sister Mary Theresa in the hallway, they
were escorted into the common room, where the cook had
served up a buffet luncheon—Doyle noting thankfully that
there was nary a fish stick in sight—and they were introduced
to several other staff members, including a few teachers who
remembered Doyle from days gone by.

As Doyle greeted each, she listened with an inward
smile to their polite reminisces; she hadn't been an exceptional
student, and the bright little girl they described—who was
clearly destined for great things—didn't jibe with her own
memories. Until, that was, she was re-introduced to Sister
Luke, her former mathematics teacher.

Sister Luke was very aged, and sat in her wheelchair in
the hunched manner of someone who'd already survived a
stroke or two. A shell of her former self, she was a far cry from
the stern, imposing nun who'd tried to teach the young Doyle
her sums—a thankless task, and one much lamented by Sister
Luke at the time.

Doyle bent, and kindly took the old nun's hand. "It's
that grand to see you again, Sister."

The woman scowled, and rasped, "I'd have never
believed it, if I hadn't seen it with my own eyes. Never thought
you'd amount to much."

While the sentiment was not a polite one, Doyle had discovered, in the course of police work, that the very old tended to say whatever they wished to say with little regard for the proprieties. Therefore, she was not offended. "I still haven't mastered long division," she teased.

Rather than acknowledge this sally, the old woman made a derisive sound, and Sister Margaret offered in an embarrassed aside, "Sister Luke is a bit outspoken—do forgive her."

"Tell the truth and shame the devil," the elderly nun insisted—making it obvious that her hearing was as sharp as ever.

"A lesson for us all," offered Sister Roseline, trying to smooth over the awkwardness. "Perhaps we should be seated—"

"Your mum's dead?" the rheumy old eyes considered Doyle with a sharpness that was unexpected, and tended to remind her of long-ago classrooms, and nervous little girls.

"Yes, ma'am. She was gathered-up a few years ago."

The elderly nun regarded her shrewdly for a long moment. "You don't have the look of her much, do you?"

"No," Doyle agreed, and wished they'd change the subject.

Irritably, the nun shrugged a thin shoulder. "Then she won't leave much of a trace, will she?"

"Shall we eat?" Sister Margaret intervened. "Cook has set a fine spread."

Thus rebuked, Sister Luke leaned back in her wheelchair, and smoothed her long sleeves. "Well, I hope your mum's sins were forgiven her—I wasn't sure they'd even allow you in here."

There was a collective gasp of horrified dismay, and Doyle was so taken aback that she couldn't find her tongue for a moment.

Acton however, suffered from no such paralysis, and strode forward to place a hand on each arm of the wheelchair, bending to face the old nun in his best threatening-policeman manner. "You will apologize to my wife."

There was a moment of profound silence. "I dinna mean anythin' by it," the woman grumbled. "Thin-skinned *sassanach,* is what you are."

But the elderly nun had committed the one unpardonable sin in Acton's world, and he only repeated in a voice of steel, "You will apologize to my wife immediately."

The aged gaze skewed over to Doyle. "I'm sorry, then."

"It's nothin'," said Doyle, who rather wished the floor would open up and swallow her whole. "I loved my mother, and I love her still."

"Of course—as did we all," Sister Mary Theresa said briskly. "If you would, Sister Margaret, please take Sister Luke back to her room." She then turned to Doyle as the wheelchair was quickly pushed away. "Oh, dear; please accept our apologies—I'd no idea she'd try to embarrass us in this way."

"It's nothin'," Doyle repeated, and smiled to reassure them that no damage had been done. "She was always a bit crusty, that one."

But Acton stood ominously silent, and so Doyle decided she'd try to diffuse the situation as best she could, lest the good sisters worry that the Acton-gravy-train had decided to leave the station. Laying a soothing hand on his arm, she said, "She's from a different generation, Michael—where such things were much more important. I truly didn't take it personally."

Taking his cue, Acton laid a hand over hers. "Of course. And I must offer my own apology in turn—I should not have lost my temper, no matter the incentive."

Much relieved, Sister Mary Theresa began brightly expounding on the cook's talents, as she led them toward the cold supper. Doyle nodded along, but nevertheless noted that—despite his conciliatory words—Acton was itching to throat-punch someone, and that the female hearts that surrounded them were made all a'flutter by this masculine display. Just crackin' grand, she thought, as she defiantly scooped up a double-helping of butter. I hope my masterful husband doesn't make everyone re-think their holy vows—not to mention that I'm dyin' to take him to bed myself, but that doesn't seem likely to happen any time soon, more's the pity.

The confrontation with Sister Luke began to fade as they listened to Sister Roseline's presentation—well put-together, and not too lengthy—showing the progress that had been made in establishing the orphanage. They were treated to a virtual tour of the infant nursery, along with some candid views of the older children, cheerfully lining up in their neat uniforms to attend the adjacent school.

They're happy, Doyle realized, and one of the reasons they're happy is because they're all in this together, and they have each other. Watching them, she was suddenly reminded of how it felt to be the only student in the school without a father. Stop, she commanded herself; you're letting Sister Luke's nastiness make a dent, and you mustn't.

As their visit concluded, Sister Mary Theresa expressed her gratitude. "It was lovely to have you both, and I hope Sister Luke didn't make you re-think your religious conversion, Lord Acton."

"I'm afraid that I over-reacted," he admitted. "Please convey my sincerest apologies."

The Mother Superior smiled and lowered her voice in a confiding manner. "I don't think anyone has ever dressed her down, and—perhaps—it was past due."

"She's a corker," Doyle agreed cheerfully. "Back and edge."

"Please feel free to visit at any time," the nun continued. "And thank you again, for your extraordinary generosity."

As they emerged out on to the front steps, Doyle breathed a sigh of relief. "Well, that's over with, and not a moment too soon, I might add. I don't know how you nobs bear it, frankly—all that bowin' and scrapin'. I'd so much rather be a nobody from nowhere."

He paused to survey the street before them. "I am almost reluctant to point out that the title is not nearly as important as the funding, in this instance."

"Oh," she said, much struck. "I suppose you're right. Mayhap you should donate some huge sum of money to the Garda, so that they'll be inclined to treat you better."

"An interesting experiment to consider."

Laughing, she took his arm as they began to walk down the pavement. "Meaning there's not the smallest chance, and small blame to you, husband—they've ruined all their chances at hittin' the jackpot, and let this be a lesson to them." Only half-teasing, she glanced up at him. "And speakin' of which, d'you need to make another mysterious call?"

"No more for today," he replied easily. "But tomorrow, perhaps."

Exasperated, she shook her head. "That's just crackin' grand—somethin' to look forward to. Although I suppose I can't nag at you like an archwife anymore this fine day, because you defended my honor in spectacular fashion. Thank you, Michael—I truly appreciate it."

"Hardly a worthy adversary," he demurred.

"Whist, she was the meanest teacher at the school, and everyone in the room was secretly applauding you."

He glanced down at her. "You don't know the half of it. I took the Mother Superior aside, and told her that it upset you too much to speak of the bridge-jumping incident, and asked if she could see to it that the subject did not arise."

She halted in her tracks, and stared at him in incredulous amusement for a moment. "No—did you truly?"

He bowed his head. "I did, indeed."

Laughing, she took his arm and resumed walking. "Mother a' mercy; why haven't I thought of that before?"

"Because you are honest to a fault."

"It is my burden to bear," she agreed. "And yours, too— hence the need for mysterious phone calls."

She eyed him, but he ignored this probe, and instead looked toward the street. "Shall I call a cab? I believe I've mastered the process."

Chapter 9

So, the baby had to go.

Upon their return to the hotel, the wooden-faced concierge said to Acton in modulated tones, "When you have a moment, sir."

Just crackin' grand, thought Doyle, as they both entered the lift; whatever-it-was, the man didn't want to broach it in front of all and sundry, which was truly no surprise a'tall, when you considered her husband's strange and recent predilection for secrecy and stealth.

As the lift doors slid closed, she asked with no small irritation, "Now what's afoot, Michael? I was hopin' to squeeze in five minutes of dedicated bed-work, between Edward's feedings and the next crisis."

Thus prompted, he bent to bestow a lingering kiss. "Hold that thought; I honestly don't know what he wants, but I promise it won't take long."

Mollified by the sincerity and tenor of his kiss, she guessed, "The Inspector from the Garda wants to grill you about Father Gregory. They've lifted your prints from the dagger, and an indictment is in the works as we speak."

He smiled. "I don't think that's it—they would not inform the concierge, if that were the case. Much better to show up without warning, in an attempt to catch me off-guard."

She blew out a derisive breath. "Well, good luck to them, even if they tried to pull such a move, you're not one to get rattled—smooth as ice, you are—and they'd only learn it the hard way."

"You rattle me," he teased. "All the time."

"No—clearly, I do not." She gave him a meaningful look that made reference to his recent secretive behavior.

He bent to kiss her again—trying to soften her up, he was. "I disagree; you rattled me to the core on Edward's birthday."

She returned the kiss, being as she could only concede this point; Edward had been born in a helicopter, because at the time Doyle was in the process of being evacuated from a prison riot. "That exception only proves the rule, my friend."

He raised his head, as the lift had come to a stop. "Let's not repeat the experience."

"Never say never," she teased, and they stepped into the hallway. In a way, it was a good sign that he was joking about that day—he didn't like talking about it, because Acton was one who needed to feel as though he were in control, and it was made crystal-clear, on that particular occasion, that he wasn't. Fortunately, all was well that ended well, and there was no lasting harm done—his dark hair had gone a bit gray at the temples, was all.

After having seen her settled in the suite with Edward, Acton returned downstairs to speak to the concierge, but as it turned out, Doyle was to discover what was behind the concierge's concern before Acton did.

"Madam," said Reynolds, hovering in the suite's doorway. "May I fetch a refreshment?"

Reynolds normally didn't like to disturb her whilst she was feeding the baby, but the servant was bristling with suppressed outrage, and so Doyle immediately decided that there must be a connection between the concierge's desire to speak privately to Acton and the servant's upset sensibilities. So as to draw him out, she teased, "Where's our Mary? Never say the two of you have quarreled?"

Since Mary was not a quarreler, this was meant in jest, but Reynolds nonetheless reposrted, "Miss Mary has taken Miss Gemma to the corner grocer's, to look for plums. Mr. Trenton has accompanied them, at Lord Acton's instruction."

"Oh-oh," said Doyle, with mock-concern. "Trenton had best guard his heart."

"I believe," Reynolds offered in precise tones, "that such an eventuality is unlikely, madam. In fact, I am informed that Miss Mary's fiancé will soon make an appearance."

"Well, that's crackin' grand," said Doyle crossly, and wondered how people with retinues ever managed to have sex.

Reynolds continued, "I am given to understand that Mr. Howard is concerned about the incident on the train and will be visiting for a few days. Rest assured, madam, that I will endeavor to keep Miss Gemma entertained, so that Mr. Howard and Miss Mary may spend some time together."

Doyle smiled to herself; they'd discovered lately that little Gemma—an orphaned child, taken in by Mary—was actually a long-lost Romanov, one of the last few remnants of Russian royalty. Upon making this astounding discovery, Reynolds had humbly devoted himself to the little girl, and the two had become very close. "Thank you, Reynolds, I'm sure it will be much appreciated."

After mulling this development over, Doyle plucked up somewhat; perhaps this wouldn't turn out as badly as she'd thought—if the courting couple were together, and Reynolds was off somewhere entertaining Gemma, presumably she and Acton would manage some alone-time themselves—in forty-five-minute intervals—which should be plenty of time to get the deed done.

As the servant paused to straighten a picture frame that was not askew, Doyle was recalled to the fact that he was emanating a strong sense of discreet outrage, and that she'd best soothe him or she'd wind up having to handle both Gemma and Edward without an assist, and all her sex-plans would lie in ashes and ruin.

"Can you tell me what's afoot, Reynolds? The concierge is all up-in-arms about somethin'." The concierge, of course, was not an up-in-arms sort of person, but Doyle decided she needed to get the ball rolling, and so pretended that she knew more than she did.

Happy to have been given an opening, the servant turned to her. "Indeed, madam. I was called down to the desk this morning because a woman had come in, insisting that she was Lord Acton's girlfriend. She claimed he'd given her a key to his room, but that she'd lost it."

Doyle stared at him, amazed. "Truly? Now, there's some brass for you."

The servant indicated his strong disapproval of such a vulgar subterfuge. "I sent her about her business, of course. A newspaper reporter, no doubt."

But Doyle found the whole thing rather amusing, and countered, "I must say I'm a bit disappointed in you, Reynolds. What if she was truly Acton's girlfriend? You'd think the Butler's Rules of Conduct would require that you check with him first, before you go tattlin' about it to me."

The servant thinned his lips in disapproval—let it be said that he did not always appreciate Doyle's sense of humor—and he replied in measured tones, "I can assure you, madam, that Lord Acton does *not* have a girlfriend."

"As far as you know," she corrected. "He's very wily, Reynolds—I'm just sayin'."

But the butler replied in a dampening tone, "If I suspected such a liaison, madam, I would do everything in my power to convince him to disengage."

Quirking her mouth, she turned her attention back to Edward. "Good luck with that, my friend. The only person with any influence on the man is me, and there are plenty of times when I fall well-short of the mark."

"Precisely. Which is why I feel certain such an unfortunate situation would never arise."

Doyle considered this. "Good one, Reynolds. That's some good, roundabout logic."

"Thank you, madam," the servant replied with a brisk nod. "I shall consider the subject closed."

Doyle glanced up in alarm. "Faith, not yet—we haven't covered the good parts. What did she look like?"

Reynolds crossed his arms and considered this. "An attractive blonde lady—well-bred, which is why the concierge was uncertain, I imagine."

"Not Acton's taste at all," she teased. "Unless she's got a better bosom, that is."

Not quite knowing how to respond to this sally, Reynolds retreated behind correctness. "I sent her about her business, and the concierge warned her not to come in again, or they would contact law enforcement."

"Good one," she said again, and decided not to reveal that local law enforcement did not seem much inclined to come to the aid of the *sassanach* Chief Inspector, no matter how busty the blonde.

Then, because Doyle was truly desperate, she ventured, "Would you mind seein' to it that Acton and I have some privacy, for an hour or so? I'm longin' for a bit o' quiet."

If the servant was aware that the "bit of quiet" would involve wrestling the bedclothes onto the floor, he gave no indication, other than to say smoothly, "Of course, madam. Allow me to put Master Edward down for his nap."

And so, when Acton returned from speaking with the concierge, it was to find his naked wife propped atop the bed pillows, and doing her best to strike an enticing pose.

"Here's a surprise," he said, pausing on the threshold.

"Just hurry up," she responded impatiently. "The retinue clock is tickin'."

"Ever the romantic," he observed, and with no further ado, crawled forward on the bed to kiss her, without even taking off his shoes.

Giggling, she pushed his jacket off his shoulders, and then broke away from his mouth to instruct, "You have to take off your tie, Michael—it only gets in the way."

"And I should hang my jacket, or Reynolds will be unhappy."

But she only hooked her arms around his neck in a death-grip, and refused to let him rise. "No, he won't— Reynolds is an aider and abettor."

"Then he'll have to wait his turn," was the muffled reply, and all conversation came to an abrupt and happy close.

At the conclusion of a frenzied session of lovemaking— one had to regrettably skip the slow parts, when one had an infant who could wake at any moment—they lay content on the bed, Doyle nestled in the crook of his arm. "Reynolds likes me better," she teased.

"I am unsurprised. Everyone likes you better."

"Not Sister Luke," she reminded him, pulling gently at the hair on his chest.

He considered this. "I think Sister Luke should be called a draw—she doesn't like either of us."

"Then pull back some money from the Order's retirement fund, 'til she mends her wicked ways."

He lifted a lock of her hair and ran it through his fingers. "How did you find out about the retirement fund?"

"Sister Mary Theresa let it slip. Which should be a lesson to you; nuns are very loose-lipped. Priests are much better at holding a secret, bein' as they've had lots of experience."

"I will keep it to mind," he replied, "when next I am reciting my secrets."

"Well, you have a secret girlfriend, I understand—a blonde, no less."

He didn't disclaim, but bent an elbow behind his head, to prop it up. "I am as surprised as you are."

She eyed him. "D'you know who she was? Are we worried?"

Absently, he rubbed a thumb along her wrist, where she was resting in his arm. "Not particularly—it may have been an attempt at a burglary, since she waited until we were absent. I have asked for surveillance tape, and I will see if I can find a match in the database."

"No rest for the weary," she teased. "And speakin' of which, can you muster up enough strength for round two?"

"Let's test it out."

Giggling, she climbed atop him, and then kissed him soundly whilst her hair fell all around his face.

Chapter 10

She needed to come up with another plan. It was a shame that the last one missed.

That night, Doyle had one of her dreams. She had them occasionally—vivid, intense dreams where—unlike most dreams—she was aware that she was dreaming, and at the same time marveled at how real they seemed.

Usually, the dreams involved someone who was no longer alive and who was urging her to perform some necessary task, or solve some necessary puzzle. The dreams tended to be a source of frustration, because Doyle was not one for reading-between-the-lines, and her appointed task never seemed to be clear—as though the normal rules of communication didn't apply. Nonetheless, Doyle always tried her hardest to understand the roundabout message as best she could, since there was no denying that the dreams were important. Indeed, they'd saved her life, once.

This one was no different; Doyle was aware that she stood in a desolate, outdoor location with the wind blowing about her but—strangely enough—she couldn't feel it against her skin, as though she were in a different dimension altogether. She didn't have much time to consider this paradox, however, because the scowling person hunched before her was entirely unexpected.

"Your husband's up and killed me," Sister Luke said accusingly.

"That's a lie," Doyle scolded. "Shame on you."

The elderly nun grumbled, "Well, he'll not be sorry that I'm dead."

Doyle retorted with a great deal of meaning, "His opinion is not the one you should be worried about, just now."

The old woman grimaced, her mouth nearly disappearing amongst the network of deep wrinkles. "I did my best. A lot of wickedness, in the world."

"My mother," Doyle retorted, barely holding on to her temper, "was *not* wicked."

The nun shrugged. "Robbie gave her a black eye, but you can hardly blame 'im."

Doyle blinked in surprise. "Who's Robbie?"

But she was suddenly awake, and staring into the darkness of the suite's bedroom, listening as her heartbeat echoed loudly in her ears.

"All right?" Acton murmured sleepily, as he groped for her. "Did you have a dream?" Acton was well-familiar with her dreams, and even tried to help her decipher them, on occasion. In a strange way, he seemed to respect her intuitive abilities almost more than she did, which was a huge relief, all-in-all, in that it meant she could speak to him about it without worrying that he'd be gathering kindling the next day so as to burn her at the stake.

"Aye, that," she whispered into the darkness, and then debated whether or not to tell him the news. "Sister Luke's dead."

He considered this in surprised silence for a moment, as he absently drew a comforting hand down her back. "A good riddance."

"You mustn't speak ill of the dead, Michael. She deserves our prayers, instead."

"If you say," he replied with no real conviction.

"I do say," she countered in a firm tone, and then wondered why her scalp prickled.

"You, first," he suggested, and then drew her against him as he settled back into sleep.

She brushed his arm with her fingers, absently, and frowned at the wall as she tried to make sense of it. How strange, that Sister Luke had died today of all days, after the embarrassing confrontation in the common room. Had she been murdered? Doyle considered this possibility; sometimes, the ghosts she met had been murdered, and sometimes they hadn't, but they were always trying to warn her to do something, or trying to get her to right some sort of wrong. It seemed very strange that crotchety Sister Luke was a ghost-candidate, but there was no mistaking that there was something here the fair Doyle was tasked to do, even though she hadn't the first clue as to what it might be. Learn long division, perhaps.

I need more information, she decided, and smoothed the corner of her pillow; I've got to find out who "Robbie" was, since that was the gist of the message. And wasn't it just like the old battle-axe not to be clear—I could never make heads-nor-tails of what she tried to teach me at school, either. After turning her face to press it against Acton's arm, she then slept soundly throughout the rest of the night.

The next morning, they breakfasted in the suite, seated at the linen-clad table whilst Reynolds ably commanded the hotel wait-staff, who uncovered a variety of silver platters with quiet efficiency. Doyle watched them, thinking over her dream and trying to decide if she knew of anyone named Robbie—and not just any Robbie, but someone who'd haul off and smack people.

Robert, she decided; his given name must be Robert. And he was someone who'd taken an interest in her mother, obviously—even if that interest was a violent one. A relative, perhaps? Doyle could think of no relatives named Robert, which came as no surprise, since her mother never spoke of any relatives in the first place. And why anyone would haul off and smack a gentle, self-effacing person like her mother was almost incomprehensible. Although, of course, she'd got herself pregnant, and—even in this day and age—such a thing was not tolerated well amongst the church-Irish. Just have a look at the late and unlamented Sister Luke, as a prime example.

Apparently, her preoccupation had not gone unnoticed, because as soon as the staff left them alone, Acton gave her an assessing look. "Everything all right?"

"Just thinkin'," she admitted. "Can you smell the wood burnin'?"

With a small smile, he unfolded his napkin. "Shall we do something for Sister Luke? Send flowers?" Apparently, her take-no-prisoners husband had decided he'd been a bit too harsh the night before.

"Faith, no," Doyle replied, with a definitive shake of her head. "Remember, we don't officially know she's dead, and I imagine they'll not want us to know, for fear you'll think you drove her to into the grave."

"I'd be very remorseful," he agreed, and bit into his toast.

She gave him a look, as she reached for the jam jar. "Did you have a chance to warn Trenton about our blonde burglar? Can't have dangerous blondes runnin' about, willy-nilly." She paused in surprise, because her scalp had started prickling. What was it? Something about dangerous blondes? Something about Trenton?

"I will brief him." He glanced at his watch. "I'll need an hour or so to get into the database, and then—if you are so inclined—we could take a tour of the city."

"How will you manage to look into the database?" she asked around a mouthful of slathered toast. "Where can you get your fingers on it, up here in the back of beyond?" The Met's classified databases had to be accessed from a secure location, for obvious reasons.

"I'd thought to go over to the Garda. They're closest to hand."

This gave her pause, although it shouldn't have—that Acton had no hesitation in going back into the lion's den for a second round just went to show you that he was not the sort of person to be intimidated, unlike his bride, who'd been thoroughly intimidated by the cross-currents of unsettling emotions at the station-house.

Taking her fearful self in hand, she stoutly advised, "Then I'm goin', too—you'll need back-up, in case they try to wrestle you into the nick."

She rather expected a protest—he was carefully choosing his words, which is what he did when he didn't want her to discover something—but he only replied mildly, "I'd appreciate it."

"Just let me hand Edward off, and then I'll be ready in two shakes." Mainly, she wanted to hold on to Acton's coat-tails; there was something afoot—something he didn't want her to see, and unless she very much missed her guess, it had to do with Father Gregory's grisly death; that, and—strangely enough—a cab driver who wore a jaunty tam o'shanter.

Chapter 11

The baby must be sick, or something. That would explain why they weren't using the service to drive anywhere.

It was with no real surprise that Doyle beheld the cheerful African cab driver, parked at the curb and grinning at them as they exited the hotel.

"Hello-hello," he called to them, one fleshy elbow resting out the window. "Where is that baby?"

"I've lost him, somewhere," Doyle replied, knowing that this would appeal to the man's sense of humor. "I'll have to take a look-round."

"Ha!" The driver watched with a benign eye as they saw themselves seated—he was not the sort of fellow who'd emerge to hold the door for his passengers. "The Garda," he announced without prompting, and then took a perfunctory glance at oncoming traffic before pulling out into it with a touch of bravado coupled with nerves of steel.

Doyle hung on to the strap, and duly noted that Acton must have hired the man to ferry them around Dublin—not to mention the driver had the satisfied air of someone who was taking gross advantage of a situation—and she remembered that he'd done the same when they were first married; Acton had handsomely paid an African cab driver to ferry the fair Doyle about, because she'd been too self-conscious to take the limousine service to work.

Her scalp prickled yet again, and she frowned slightly, wondering why it would. It was a coincidence, of course; Acton was gun-shy about transportation, here in Dublin, after the incident with Mary on the train, and this fellow was as harmless as they came—faith, he'd have a hard time sitting upright without help. So—why was her instinct acting up? Aiki—her driver from home—had been murdered, of course, but that murder had nothing to do with Father Gregory's murder, surely? Or with Acton's sudden desire to be mysterious, and to keep her in the dark about whatever was going forward?

These troubling thoughts were interrupted when her husband leaned his head next to hers and took her hand. "Edward will be all right, and we'll be back soon."

"Oh—oh, yes; I've no reason to be so worried." Making a show of being a concerned mother, she decided she should pull her mobile to text Mary.

"Mary does not have her mobile," Acton explained—although he didn't offer an explanation for this explanation. "But Trenton is with her, and I can contact him, if necessary."

This was alarming, and Doyle met his eyes as she leapt to the obvious conclusion. "You don't want anyone to be able to trace her whereabouts."

"No," he admitted. "Purely as a precautionary measure."

Doyle eyed him with dismay. "D'you think she's in danger?"

"No—at least I do not believe so," he replied, and it was the truth—although this didn't make a lot of sense; if he didn't think Mary was in danger, then there'd be no reason to take her mobile away, one would think. Perhaps he didn't want her phoning Howard, for some reason?

Doyle hung on as they darted between two slow-moving lorries, and tried to decide if she should make another sleeveless attempt to winkle more information out of her tiresome husband—strange, it was, that he'd taken the nanny's mobile away in an excess of caution, but had no problem subjecting them to the tender mercies of this death-defying cab driver.

Before she could think of another question to ask—it was hard to be subtle, when one was clinging for one's life—the cab driver craned his head around to address her. "Where did you live when you were here—what street? Me, I know all the streets." He grinned proudly.

"Oh—oh, I lived on Highbury."

"Highbury? Yes—over by the church, yes? Good-good; I will take you there, and you can visit the old days, later."

There was a small pause. "We'll see how the day goes."

"I believe," said Acton, "that our destination is fast approaching."

"Yes." The driver seemed unfazed by this observation, and rested an arm on the seat back to address Acton, rather than watch the road. "I will park in the back, yes? It will save me the meter."

"Oh? So you're comin' in?" Doyle teased, lifting her brows at him. "Never say you're goin' to report me for misplacin' my baby?"

"Ha!" He laughed loudly as he swung across all lanes to turn into the station-house lot, the tires screeching as he deftly pulled into a space. Setting the gearshift with a victorious gesture, he observed, "I must tell the police what I know. I must help out, and not keep secrets." The whites of his eyes showed as he slid Acton a sly glance of acknowledgement.

"The police need all the help they can get," Acton agreed. "Any lead could be useful."

"What lead is this?" asked Doyle in confusion.

"Mr. Mensah may have information that would cast light on Father Gregory's murder," Acton offered smoothly.

"Is that so? Did you drive the murderer to the station-house?" Doyle was only half-joking; she didn't have the sense that the jovial cab-driver had any connection to the murder whatsoever, and it seemed too much of a coincidence that his testimony was suddenly being proffered up by her exasperating husband.

"The information addresses possible motive," Acton explained. "Mr. Mensah hears a lot of things, in the course of his day."

The driver turned off the ignition and nodded so that his chins wobbled. "Many, many things—yes. Much of it I cannot tell you." Laughing, he waggled a finger at her. "You would be very shocked, so I cannot say."

"No doubt," agreed Doyle, who'd seen many a shocking thing in the course of her police work. But she also recognized an Acton-style diversion when she saw one, and so as they walked into the station-house, she took the opportunity to ask in a low voice, "What's afoot, husband? Do I need to know my lines?"

Acton held the door for her, and said only, "Mr. Mensah made mention of something that could shed light on the murderer's motivation. I'd rather say no more, because I would rather you were not involved in the case."

Since both these statements rang true, she concluded, "Then you must truly think this murder is related to the corruption rig, and the spite-murders back home."

"I do," he agreed.

This was also true, and she decided—rather crossly—that it was all of a piece; they'd come all the way to Dublin on holiday because Acton wanted her well-away from London for some undisclosed reason, and now it seemed that they were unexpectedly hip-deep in something ominous whilst they were here. Something complicated as well as ominous, since her husband seemed to be juggling a lot of balls in the air to keep his wedded wife from finding out whatever-it-was he was hiding from her.

And it was lucky for Acton that he was fast on his feet; she'd the sense that whatever-it-was had been entirely unexpected, and that he was making up his strategy on the fly. As a case in point, she knew down to the soles of her shoes that Acton didn't want to make a return visit to the Garda, but that for some reason he was compelled to.

With a show of sympathy, she remarked, "Poor you—it's a busman's holiday, you're havin'," and then was not at all surprised when her scalp prickled, yet again.

Chapter 12

He'd gone grey at the temples, thanks to her.

It seemed clear that Acton had already alerted the police staff that he'd be by to access the database, because after checking in with Sergeant O'Shaughnessy at the front desk, Inspector Geary promptly appeared, civilly shook hands, and then escorted Acton into a back office.

Doyle hovered in the waiting room for a moment, wondering whether her husband would physically bar the door if she tried to wiggle her way into the secure room with him, but before she could test it out, her attention was claimed by the Pakistani intern who requested, very deferentially, if she could ask Doyle a few questions, so as to post an interview in the station-house newsletter.

"Of course," said Doyle, and then resigned herself to reciting the stupid bridge-jumping story again—or perhaps the stupid prison-riot story instead, just because that one was even more annoying, if such a thing was possible.

But as they were seated in the battered wooden chairs, it seemed that the questions were slated to be of a different nature. Instead, the girl began to ask about the challenges Doyle faced in dealing with the various ethnicities that abounded in London. "I would think it is an important consideration, for a law enforcement officer who must operate in such a diverse city."

This was unexpected, and Doyle thought about her answer for a moment. "I think we're all so steeped in it—the variety of people, I mean—that it's somethin' of a given. You have to be careful not to offend anyone, of course. And there's an element of distrust, which is why the Met tries to make certain they send the right officers out into the field, dependin' on where the call originates, and whether a different language might be spoken by the locals—you'll hear a lot more of interest if the witnesses feel they're talkin' to one of their own."

She paused, and then offered, "It's a huge city, and so people tend to draw themselves into groups—and I don't mean groups by language, although there is that, too. Everyone is protectin' their own interests, whether they're immigrants, or businessmen, or church-people, and each group tends to view outsiders with a great deal of suspicion—although everyone seems to distrust the police, so at least they all have that in common."

The intern smiled along with Doyle, and then Doyle continued, "It's not like here, where there aren't as many different ethnic groups—and what groups there are tend to be much smaller. Faith, I should be interviewin' you about it— you're the goat in the sheep pen, around here."

Almost immediately, Doyle froze in horror at her own clumsiness—some fine day she'd learn to hold her flippant tongue. "Mother a' mercy; that didn't come out right—"

"Please—I was not offended. Officer Doyle." The girl glanced toward the doorway, and Doyle had the sudden impression that there was a method to this line of questioning—there was something here that was above and beyond an interview for the newsletter.

The girl turned her gaze back to Doyle. "You mentioned Inspector Williams, who came to your aid when you leapt from the bridge. He is a friend?"

Gamely, Doyle strove to keep up with this unexpected change in topic. "He's a dear friend—the very best."

The girl's fathomless eyes held hers for a moment, a slight frown between her brows. "He—he is not English, perhaps?"

This seemed a feeble attempt to create diversity where there was none, and Doyle had to smile. "He's as English as the day is long, I'm afraid. With a name like Thomas Williams, there's no denyin' it."

"Yes," the other said thoughtfully, her gaze drifting to contemplate the wall. "That is what I thought."

Before Doyle could follow-up on this rather disjointed tangent, they were interrupted by Inspector Geary, who appeared from the hallway and, with a brisk nod, dismissed the intern. He then pulled up a chair so that his imposing bulk sat nearly knee-to-knee with Doyle, and with a grave expression, he began, "I was wonderin', Officer Doyle, if you could shed some light on a problem I've encountered."

Mother a' mercy, Doyle thought in startled surprise; he's using basic interrogation tactics on me—invading my space, and trying to catch me off-guard. And—unlike Acton— I'm the sort of person who's very much inclined to get rattled, and gabble off any panicked thought that might dart across my mind.

The man continued, "Now, I don't want to be causin' a ruckus, Officer Doyle, but there are a couple of things that are head-scratchers about this Father Gregory murder, and that's the truth. We think his entry in the database may have been erased in the days just before he was killed—done purposefully, so that it would be difficult to identify him. Our intern is good at that sort of thing—she's a Paki, you know— and she thinks his information was there, but that it had been erased."

"Never say you think DCI Acton would do such a thing?" Doyle asked in all surprise, and then hoped that she wouldn't be struck by lightning on the spot.

Infinitesimally, the Inspector leaned closer. "Now, why would you be sayin' that?"

But Doyle didn't flinch, and retorted with all scorn, "Because you asked for his whereabouts at the victim's time o' death, and I was that embarrassed for you, I might add." Let it be said that Doyle knew a thing or two about counter-interrogation technique, and putting the questioner on the defensive.

The counter-tactic appeared to be successful, and the man retreated, leaning back slightly, and shrugging in chagrin. "I don't mean to offend, but I can't ignore the fact that the victim was tryin' to contact him, just before he was murdered. He was that fashed about it."

But Doyle would grant him no insights. "Perhaps he was seekin' my husband's help, and that's why he was so fashed."

The Inspector eyed her for a moment. "If that was indeed the case, your husband didn't offer any reason as to why that would be. Quite the opposite, if I may say so."

Doyle leaned in a bit, herself. "Perhaps you should ask him about it, then. Would you be askin' these questions of me if he were an Irishman?"

Blowing out a breath, her companion ran a hand down his chin. "I'd like to think I would be chasin' the truth, no matter where it led."

"Then—unless I'm in custody, sir—I'll bring this chase to a close."

Immediately, the man pushed back and away. "Of course, you're not in custody, Officer Doyle. I'm sorry—I didn't mean to offend."

This was not true, but that was not a surprise—the whole point of his gambit had been to make her feel pressured so as to spill the murderous-husband beans. Fortunately, she didn't have anything to tell him in the first place, except that his questions had made her suddenly realize why the intern had been asking the questions she'd been asking Doyle about the worthy DI Williams.

Inspector Geary exited into the hallway, and—after waiting a minute or two—Doyle walked over to the front desk, and asked Sergeant O'Shaughnessy if she could leave a note for the intern. "I should finish up my interview with her, for the newsletter." After rapidly calculating her forty-five-minute window of time for the following morning, she wrote: *Tomorrow 9 am Hotel Longbourn lobby* and hoped the girl could get away.

"I'll see she gets it, Officer Doyle," the man said, as he reviewed the note. It's kind, you are, to sit for an interview."

Again, there seemed to be the slightest edge of malice in the sergeant's tone, and Doyle wondered why it always seemed to be there. In an effort to be friendly, she offered, "Well, I remember what it was like, when I was just a baby here, myself. You were very helpful to me, and so I'm tryin' to follow in your footsteps."

"Brilliant," he replied, not-quite-sarcastically.

I wonder why he's such a bundle of unhappiness, Doyle thought, but then caught sight of Acton approaching down the hallway, and decided she'd like nothing better than to get away from this place. "Are we ready?" she asked brightly.

"We are." Acton cordially thanked the Inspector and the sergeant, and then steered her toward the entry door with a hand on her back.

Just before the door closed behind them, Doyle heard the Inspector say to Sergeant O'Shaughnessy, "We've a cab driver who has a theory on the Father Gregory murder, and he'll need to be doxxed. So, when you have a moment, Robbie."

Chapter 13

She was very demanding; he never had a chance to work late anymore.

Doyle's thoughts were all a-jumble as Acton escorted her down the steps of the Garda station-house. So—Sergeant O'Shaughnessy's name was Robbie; was he the "Robbie" who'd smacked her mother? They'd be approximately the same age, although Robbie was a common name, after all. That, and it seemed so unlikely; one wouldn't expect a policeman to be the violent sort.

Hard on this thought, the violent policeman who walked beside her spoke up. "What's happened, Kathleen?"

She sighed, and wished she was as good as her husband at hiding her thoughts. "The Inspector buttonholed me the moment your back was turned and tried to make me confess your many sins."

Interestingly enough, instead of wheeling back to confront the man, Acton chose to be amused, instead. "And did you?"

"No—and I accused him of bein' prejudiced against you, just to brush him back."

He smiled. "Did you indeed? I appreciate it."

"No one holds ancient grudges against you, my friend. Not on my watch."

They walked a few steps in silence, and then she ventured, "The Inspector's no fool, Michael."

"No," he agreed.

Since he offered nothing further, she prompted, "So, are we fleein' on foot, or just takin' another walk-about? Whichever it is, I hope it doesn't take too long; my prodigal bosom is startin' to wonder where that baby is."

With an easy gesture, he pulled her hand through his arm, so that it rested in the crook of his elbow. "I thought we'd walk for a few minutes, and then catch a cab back to the hotel."

Having decided she'd been patient enough, Doyle decided she'd cut to the nub. "Are we waitin' for our cab driver to tell them whatever it is he's tellin' them?

"We are," he agreed, without a trace of self-consciousness.

"What was his name, again?"

"Mr. Mensah. Or at least, that is what his card says."

There was a small pause, whilst she contemplated the flower beds that lined the side of the pavement. "You are goin' to drive me barkin' mad, Michael."

He lifted her hand from where it rested on his arm and kissed its back. "Surely not. Although I regret to inform you that our retinue is about to expand."

"Howard," she guessed, remembering what Reynolds had said. "The poor, besotted man can't stay away from our Mary."

"No—although I would not be at all surprised if Howard made an appearance, and soon. Instead, it is McGonigal who will join us."

This was a surprise—and not an unpleasant one, for a change. Dr. Timothy McGonigal was perhaps the only person on earth who Acton considered a friend; an old university schoolmate who was as kind and cheerful as Acton was not. It was that "ying and yams" thing, Doyle decided; they were very different people, yet they seemed to get on well together—not to mention that McGonigal had been involved in more than one House of Acton crisis, and had shown many-a-time that he could be trusted in a tight corner.

"That's grand, Michael—happy to have him join the crew. Will Nanda be comin', too?" A Rwandan refugee, Nanda had been a nurse at the same free clinic where McGonigal volunteered his surgical skills, and the two had fallen deeply in love. It was a wonderful testament to keeping faith, because poor Nanda had been abruptly widowed, and was struggling to support herself and her small son when Timothy had stepped into the picture. Indeed, it was doubly-wonderful, because Nanda's dead husband had been Doyle's friend Aiki, the cab driver whom Acton had hired in London to ferry her about. Doyle was grateful that—after surviving such a tragedy—Aiki's widow and child had managed to land on their feet, with the prospect of marriage to a well-respected surgeon signaling a bright and happy future.

Acton explained, "Timothy did a Fellowship at Trinity College, and he has spoken of making a return visit whenever he could get away for a day or two. It seemed an opportune time."

Doyle nodded without comment. Her husband was—yet again—sidestepping the question, and this time it was not hard to guess at the reason. In the usual course of events, Timothy and Nanda were inseparable, but as of late Doyle had the sense that they were having a lover's tiff. And—if that was the case—it may be just the thing, to separate for a short space of time so as to re-commit to the romance; with any luck, absence would indeed make the heart grow fonder.

Such a thing wouldn't work with Acton, of course; Acton liked to have her within arm's reach at all times, and so the last thing he'd allow was anything resembling a lover's tiff. Instead, Acton was devoted to her happiness, because her happiness was his happiness.

Hard on this thought, her scalp prickled, and she decided to ignore it, because there was no point in getting such a barrage of signals if one had no clue what it all meant, and she was almost hoping for another visit from stupid Sister

Luke to explain it to her, which only went to illustrate the extent of her exasperation.

Acton's voice broke into her thoughts. "Is there any place you'd particularly like to visit, in town? Shall we see the Guinness storeroom, or have you been too many times already?"

Doyle had to hide a smile at the idea of Acton taking a gander at the local brewery, and willingly mingling with all the other tourists. "I've never been, actually—my mum didn't drink, and I don't think it ever occurred to either one of us to visit the storeroom." Not to mention that the bus fare alone would have taken up the milk budget for the month, but that was not something Acton would factor-in, and small blame to him as he no doubt had a fleet of cows milling about at his beck and call.

She tried to decide what sounded most appealing, and suggested, "Stephen's Green is a pretty place to visit—we used to go feed the ducks, there."

"We will go, then, and I will see if we can meet up with Tim for lunch, afterward."

It suddenly occurred to Doyle that the whole reason they'd visited the Garda—to look up the blonde burglar—had not yet been mentioned, which seemed a bit strange. He's hoping I've forgotten, she realized; a shame, it is, that the poor man's wife is constantly mucking up his well-laid plans. "So, who's the blonde woman? Did you find out?"

"I did," he replied. "It is rather surprising."

There was a pause, whilst she eyed him sidelong. "Unsnabble, then."

"It was Lady Abby."

The name was familiar, and Doyle frowned, trying to place it. "Remind me who that is."

"She was Howard's fiancée, before he met Mary."

Doyle came to an abrupt stop, staring at him and trying to assimilate this astonishing news. Howard had been engaged to a pretty, vivacious member of the aristocracy until that fateful day when he'd attended Acton's confirmation and had promptly fallen head-over-heels in love with Mary. In short order, he'd broken off his engagement and now it appeared that Lady Abbey was not one to take such an insulting turn of events lying down.

"Holy *Mother*, Michael—what d'you suppose she was about?"

"Nothing good," he said succinctly. "I will have to go speak with her."

This seemed a good idea; that the woman had attempted to do something so brazen was nothing short of alarming, but Acton was a master at assessing the correct pressure points to apply—depending on the situation and the person being pressured—so as to cool everything down, and make the person think twice before continuing on their questionable course of action. A great deal of his perceived influence sprang from his status within his tribe, of course—he came from an ancient line of leaders—and, whether that status was deserved or not, people tended to respond.

"Well, I hope a stern talkin'-to will turn the trick—just don't let her practice her wiles on you, and convince you that you should have married another nob instead of me."

He bowed his head. "I will do my best to hold fast."

Doyle squinted up at him. "What's her bosom like?"

"I regret to confess that I don't remember."

She nodded in satisfaction. "Well, if it's not memorable, I've probably nothin' to worry about. Speakin' of which, I'm startin' to leak a bit, so we'd best get back."

"Very good—here's our driver."

The grinning driver pulled up to the curb and tugged on his cap in a conspiratorial way at Acton. As Doyle slid across the back seat, she thought, poor Acton; this fellow's not at all the type of co-conspirator he'd prefer, but—for reasons unknown—Acton has tapped him as such. I imagine it would behoove me to find out why.

With a roar of the engine, they darted out into traffic.

Chapter 14

DI Williams called to tell her he needed to come by. Time to re-apply lipstick.

Rather than plan for lunch at a restaurant, Doyle decided they should procure a picnic basket from the concierge and go to Stephen's Green, so as to eat outdoors. The park was in the center of the old city and boasted acres of beautiful trees, as well as a small lake. The weather was holding fine, and that way they could bring everyone along; Gemma could feed the ducks, and Reynolds and Mary could enjoy a bit of freedom, too. Besides, Timothy McGonigal was the sort of person who'd enjoy a picnic, himself, and if he felt self-conscious about his love-troubles, he needn't feel obligated to speak of them in such a crowd.

That McGonigal was troubled seemed evident, even to someone without Doyle's perceptive abilities. They'd met up at the Green—he had other lodgings, but Acton hadn't mentioned where—and the poor man looked a bit ragged around the edges when he greeted her.

"Timothy," she smiled. "It's that grand to see you." It was one of those awkward moments where you didn't know whether to mention the Nanda-troubles or ignore them, and so Doyle—knowing how she'd feel, in the same situation—chose to ignore it. If he wished to speak of it, he could bring it up, but otherwise she'd respect his privacy.

"And you too, Kathleen." Almost hungrily, he lifted baby Edward from her arms. "And this fellow is thriving. Tell me your secret."

"The secret is this; he's a food-hound, and best not stand in his way."

The baby, on hearing her voice, turned his head to attempt a smile in that muscles-aren't-quite-under-control-yet way that small babies have, and they both laughed. Bleak, she thought with some surprise; McGonigal's situation was bleak, apparently. Poor man; Nanda was his first foray into a relationship with the opposite sex, and he'd been smitten hard. A shame, it was, that he was apparently to have his heart broken as a result—he was a man who deserved better, but Doyle had observed, in her dealings with humankind, that kind people were just as likely to take their lumps as unkind people, which didn't seem fair but there it was. In all things, give thanks.

With an attempt at heartiness, McGonigal turned to address Acton. "He looks to be a redhead, Michael—you're surrounded."

"I'll willingly surrender."

Doyle teased, "You already have, my friend. I can't imagine that you've attended many picnics-in-the-park, and never with such an assortment of characters in tow."

Timothy chuckled, and Acton tilted his head in acknowledgement. "No one could have foreseen, certainly." He then met Doyle's eyes for a moment.

Oh—he wants me to make myself scarce, she realized; Acton wants to talk to McGonigal, and that's probably a good idea—a man-to-man discussion could be just what was needed, although it's not as though Acton's had many female-troubles, himself, so his advice might be a bit suspect.

"Give over that baby, Tim—he has to learn how to feed the ducks, and his father wouldn't know the first thing about how to go about it."

Doyle carried Edward down the grassy bank to join Mary and Gemma where they were standing with Reynolds at the lake's edge, and paused for a moment to take in the morning. It was good to come here, she told herself firmly; you've many happy memories and it's a lovely place—not to mention the bell-cow needs a bit of exercise.

Glancing back at the two men, she saw that Acton was speaking quietly to McGonigal, who was nodding as he listened, his gaze fixed on the grass at his feet. Why, they're planning, she realized, as she turned back toward the lake; Acton's not commiserating with McGonigal as much as they're planning something—something rather grave. Hopefully, they're not planning to murder Nanda.

Startled, she shifted her grip on Edward and took herself to task, wondering where that unwelcome thought had come from. McGonigal would never harm Nanda—she knew it down to her bones—but there was something here that was more than a lover's tiff; something serious. McGonigal wasn't just suffering from heartbreak—it was something else, something powerful. Shame, perhaps?

She didn't have much chance to dwell on it, though, because she'd joined the group at the lake, where Reynolds was teaching Gemma the fine art of casting bread upon the waters. "Only one piece at a time, Miss Gemma; too much at once and it will sink, rather than be eaten."

"They're grossly fat," Doyle offered, as she observed the proceedings. "It would serve them right to go without, for once."

"They do seem a bit spoiled," Mary agreed with a smile. "Spoiled, and aggressive—stay back, Gemma; don't let them nip at your fingers."

"But the one over there—the one with the striped head." The little girl indicated with the stick she held. "The others aren't letting him have any bread."

Doyle could muster no sympathy. "Ducks are not known for sharin', I'm afraid—it's every man for himself, in duck-world."

"Perhaps I can toss one his way," Reynolds suggested, and suited action to word.

Whilst Gemma exclaimed with satisfaction, Doyle noted, "It's soft-hearted, you are, Reynolds; mayhap he's done somethin' deservin' of bein' iced out."

"A black sheep," Mary offered, teasing. "Known only for his many sins."

"And he's a different sort of duck, with that striped head," Doyle pointed out. "Mayhap they're all prejudiced against him—he's not of the tribe."

"What does 'prejudiced' mean?" Gemma asked.

And here's a perfect example of why I should watch my tongue, thought Doyle. "It means that you're angry with someone, but for no good reason."

With a knit brow, the little girl thought about this. "Like the lady who yelled at my mum."

"Oh, Gemma," Mary said hurriedly. "That's over and done with."

"What's this?" Doyle asked in surprise. That anyone could be angry with Mary was hard to imagine.

"Oh, Lady Acton—it's nothing, and it's so embarrassing—"

"It was Lady Abby," Doyle guessed, having put two and two together and come up with one blonde burglar. "When was this—and what did she do?"

Her cheeks turning pink, Mary stammered, "She was unhappy that Nigel—well, that she'd been thrown over. She waylaid me at Gemma's school and—and was rather nasty."

"Was she violent?" This was the first thing the police always sought to find out, since the angry-jilted tended to get themselves into confrontations on a regular basis, and the wheat had to be sorted from the chaff.

With some reluctance, Mary confessed, "The school security had to restrain her, and send her on her way. I should have told you, Lady Acton, but I was so embarrassed, and I didn't want Nigel to have to speak with her—"

But Doyle cut her off. "Never mind that; I've got to tell Acton that she may be dangerous—she's here in Dublin, somewhere."

Mary opened her mouth in horror. "She *is*? Oh—oh, dear—so is Nigel."

Doyle blinked in surprise. "Howard is already here?" She shouldn't have been so surprised, though; Reynolds had hinted as much, and Reynolds was one who kept an ear to the ground.

"I'm so sorry, Lady Acton, but he was insistent, and said he'd make certain he didn't interfere with my duties—"

Again, Doyle rather ruthlessly cut her off. "Nothin' to be sorry about, Mary—but I've got to go warn Acton; you stay here with Reynolds—don't stray away from him."

Doyle put the baby to her shoulder and traipsed back up the bank, of two minds because she didn't want to interrupt whatever was going forward betwixt Acton and McGonigal, but knowing that Acton must be warned that Lady Abby's attempt to grift a hotel key from the front desk was actually the second hostile action, after an earlier angry confrontation. In the Crime Academy, they taught you that escalating hostile actions did not bode well and shouldn't be ignored.

Acton saw her coming, and excused himself to McGonigal as he stepped down the hill to meet her. "What's happened?"

He was on high alert, of course, and so she assured him, "Nothin' major, but I thought you should know that Lady Abby confronted Mary at the school before we left, and had to be restrained."

His hands on his hips, Acton looked over toward the lake and made an impatient sound. "Right then; I'll have Trenton track her down, and I'll speak with her today."

Doyle could not be easy about this proposal, and warned, "Be careful Michael; she sounds a bit desperate, to go to such lengths. D'you think she's dangerous?"

But he didn't seem overly-concerned, which was reassuring, since Acton was a fairly good judge of who was dangerous, and who was not. "I will have to assess. I hope not—I'd rather not be asking any favors of Inspector Geary." He signaled to Trenton, who'd been stationed on the perimeter whilst they picnicked. "Allow me to take care of this, and I'll join you in a few minutes, Kathleen."

So, she thought; I've been roundly dismissed, because he doesn't want me to hear the discussion with Trenton. No doubt he wants to handle Lady Abby with kid gloves—she's part of his tribe, after all—and besides, he'll also want to save Howard and Mary from the embarrassment of any possible police action. With any luck, he'll be able to dissuade the woman from her chosen course, and she'll go home to lick her wounds in private.

Shifting Edward yet again, Doyle began the walk back toward the lake.

Chapter 15

Williams gave her a packet. Acton had run into a spot of trouble, and she was to wait for word.

As Doyle retraced her steps—faith, but she hadn't expected quite such a workout—she thought about thwarted love, and the ugly turns it could take. They saw a lot of it, in their business; more often than not, any and all potential homicide suspects could be plucked from the ranks of those who should love the victim best, which was a sad, sad testament. The Apostle had said that love bears all things, endures all things, and hopes all things, but the unfortunate reality often fell well-short of such lofty goals. Women in particular were often murdered by their own menfolk, and sometimes for the most trivial of reasons—jealousy being a prime mover. Although in this particular case, a woman was jealous of another woman, and wanted to exact revenge on her rival.

Frowning, she paused to catch her breath for a moment, because she'd the sense that this was important, for some reason, and she tried to think why this would be. Lady Abby was jealous of Howard's affection for Mary—no surprise there; she'd been engaged to an important man, after all, and it must have been a cataclysmic-sized disaster to watch another woman steal him away, literally in the blink of an eye.

And now the cast-aside woman was stalking them to cause trouble—although the extent of the trouble remained to be seen. It was a bit more unusual—for a woman to go violent revenge-mode, as opposed to a man—but it did happen, oftentimes when the woman was very prideful and couldn't bear with having been rejected, or when—as was the case, here—when it meant her imagined life of status and ease was to be usurped by an interloper. Which was important, for some reason—

Unable to catch at the elusive thought, Doyle mentally shrugged, and then resumed her progress down to the lake, thinking about how terrible it all was for poor Mary, who was caught up in the cross-fire through no fault of her own. In these types of cases—where love turned into something nasty, and vindictive—Doyle always felt sorry for the poor victims who tried to go about their daily lives, all the while knowing that someone was lurking in the shadows, wanting to do them harm. The police could only react after a crime was committed, and so, aside from obtaining a civil restraining order—which was oftentimes ignored by a determined stalker—there was little a potential victim could do. Move to a different locale, perhaps, and change one's identity. All in all, it seemed grossly unfair.

It was a different thing altogether, of course, if the victim was someone like Father Gregory—not that he deserved to be murdered, of course—but he was presumably deserving of every anxious moment he'd experienced, before his untimely death. After all, the wages of sin were death, as they say. And you couldn't help but appreciate the ironic aspect; whilst he'd been panicking—and aware that he'd a target firmly on his back—he couldn't tell the local police who was after him, or why. Instead, he'd been desperate to seek out Acton, because he couldn't let the Irish Inspector know why he was slated to be murdered, and by whom.

But Acton knew. It seemed very clear that her husband knew all about Father Gregory's spite-murder and had little sympathy to spare for the victim—especially if the priest had truly been involved in the sex-slavery rig. Faith, the disgraced priest would have been barking up the wrong tree, if he'd been hoping for a dose of mercy; not a tender-hearted creature, was our Acton.

Doyle shifted Edward and paused again to rest for a moment—faith, but she was out-of-shape—and wished she'd brought along the stupid chest-carrier. Struck with a thought, she knit her brow and wondered if it was possible that Lady Abby was somehow connected to the eye-stabbing of Father Gregory—mayhap that was why Doyle's trusty instinct was acting up so much, and for apparently unrelated reasons. This seemed unlikely, though; Doyle had barely met Lady Abby, but she'd not gained the sense that the woman was capable of knifing anyone, much less a full-grown man who was capable of defending himself—albeit in a priestly manner.

Which—come to think of it—brought up a very good point that she should have realized straightaway, if her detective-skills hadn't been as rusty as her stamina. Because there was no indication that the priest had been bound, it stood to reason that the killer had aiders and abettors, since no one was going to stand quietly by and take a dagger to the eye.

Much struck, she re-positioned Edward and considered this rather strange aspect—that there must have been other perpetrators who were involved in this nasty spite-murder. After all, if the priest had been drugged or tied-up into submission, he'd not have been killed literally as he was fleeing up the Garda's steps. Someone else—probably more than one someone-elses—had held him down, whilst the dagger was brought home. It rather flew in the face of the usual rationale for spite-murders—that someone was enraged, and not behaving rationally. Hard to believe that three or four were all behaving irrationally in a coordinated fashion.

But try as she might, Doyle couldn't come up with a working theory for this puzzle. She was reminded that the Pakistani intern had her own, rather alarming theory, which only went to show that the fair Doyle had best shake her stumps and find out why the girl felt the way she did—and the sooner, the better.

Mother a' mercy, but we're not having much of a holiday, Doyle thought crossly, and then was almost unsurprised to hear sounds of alarm from the lake's edge.

"Oh—oh, *please*—"

With a gasp of dismay, Doyle spotted Mary, holding her hands out in a beseeching gesture toward another, blonde woman whose back was to Doyle—Lady Abby, presumably— whilst Reynolds stood beside Mary, holding the distraught nanny back with one hand as he held a pistol on their attacker with the other. He dared not use it, however, because Lady Abby held Gemma before her in a tight grip, using the little girl as a shield.

Her voice hoarse with venom, Lady Abby shouted, "I'll make you pay—you *ruined* my life—"

Doyle's first instinct was to rush forward so as to provide reinforcements, but almost immediately Acton called out, "Hold, Kathleen," and so she froze in place whilst he strode down the hill so that he was clearly visible to the enraged woman, with Trenton quietly circling around toward Lady Abby's flank side.

"You—you *Jezebel*," Lady Abby raged. "How *dare* you—"

"Oh, Lady Abby, *please*—"

"Enough of this, Victoria," Acton commanded in his best public-school voice, as he halted a small distance from Mary and Reynolds. "Stand down; you are embarrassing yourself."

The blonde woman jerked her head around to regard Acton, and—a bit wild-eyed—was seen to clutch the girl even tighter, as she backed away a step. "No—no; Lord Acton, you don't understand—"

But as it turned out, Gemma had had enough, and shifted to the side so as to turn and shove the stick she held directly at the woman's face.

With a cry, Lady Abby staggered back, a bright red gash showing on her cheek, as Gemma thrust the stick at her a second time, so that the frantic woman stumbled backwards to avoid being stabbed again. As Trenton ran in to tackle the woman to the ground, Gemma brandished the stick at her, her little face a mask of cold fury. "You are not to yell at my mum."

Chapter 16

It was gratifying, that he needed her help. He knew he could count on her.

"Brawlin' on Stephen's Green," Doyle observed in a dry tone. "I'm definitely back in Dublin, again." She sat beside Acton on the picnic table, their feet resting on the built-in bench as Edward peacefully slept on Doyle's knees.

Acton smiled. "It is hard to imagine, that you were involved in any brawls."

"You never saw my co-workers at the fish market, my friend. Loved a good tussle, they did. Had to step lively, to stay out of the way."

Trenton had escorted Lady Abby from the premises, with McGonigal accompanying them so as to examine the woman and apply stitches—or a sedative—if needful. Mary had phoned Howard with Doyle's blessing, and now the two sat on a bench beside the water, the nanny's head on his shoulder as she recovered from her traumatic experience. Gemma had resumed the duck-feeding expedition with Reynolds, walking along the water's edge and not portraying by the flicker of an eyelash that she'd wielded a stick with all the blood-lust of a raging Cossack.

"I'm glad Gemma's in our corner."

"A very interesting display of hidden depths," Acton agreed. "Apparently, it is in the blood."

But Doyle shrugged. "I don't know if it was that, as much as she was just defendin' her mum."

He smiled slightly, watching the servant as he pointed something out to the small girl. "As you defended yours, to Sister Luke."

But Doyle blew out an amused breath. "I can't hold a candle, my friend. I yelled at a nun in a wheelchair, which is nowhere near the same as stabbin' an evildoer with a stick. My hat's off to her."

There was a small pause, and Doyle ventured, "Why won't you tell me what's goin' to happen to Lady Abby, husband?"

He dropped his gaze and contemplated the sleeping Edward for a moment. "Because you may not approve, and I fear you will come after me with your own stick."

But Doyle wasn't much surprised, and only sighed. "We're sweepin' it all under the rug, then."

He nodded. "Due to Lady Abby's status, there would be unwonted publicity if this incident made its way onto the police docket. It could turn very unpleasant, both for Howard and for Mary."

Doyle could actually see the wisdom in this. "The local press would have a field day, what with all the English-nobs-behaving-badly."

He nodded. "I would rather not garner unwanted attention, particularly when there is a potential that someone may delve into Mary's past—or Gemma's, for that matter."

She added fairly, "Not to mention that Reynolds was wavin' an unregistered firearm about."

"And Reynolds has an unregistered weapon," he agreed. There was a small pause. "I note you are not wearing yours."

"Guilty as charged," Doyle confessed. "I'm that sorry, Michael."

On their first date—if it could be categorized as such—Acton had given her a lightweight pistol, complete with a Velcro ankle holster, and it was one of her first clues that her husband wasn't much for the protocols, since the weapon was illegal and Doyle wasn't trained to carry a weapon in the first place. At his gentle insistence, she'd worn it ever since, and—as it turned out—he'd been right to insist, since she'd been forced to put it to good use a time or two.

"I feel a bit foolish; I suppose I thought I'd be safe, what with the retinue, and all."

"You must think of Edward too, Kathleen."

It was the closest he would ever come to remonstrating his wayward bride, and she ducked her head in apology. "I'm that sorry, Michael," she said again. "And I'm sorry that you had to tell me to stay back; I think the copper-instinct kicked in when the mother-instinct should have."

"No harm done, but if you would be a bit more circumspect in the future, I would appreciate it."

"Yes, sir," she said, and hung her head like a good penitent.

To soften the scolding, he ran a hand over the back of her head, and then pulled it toward him to briefly kiss her temple. "I don't think we'll have any more trouble from Lady Abby, but I have asked Williams to join us for a few days, as extra security."

For reasons which were unclear, Doyle found she wasn't at all surprised by this unlooked-for turn of events, even though it didn't seem, at first blush, to be the wisest course to take. "Faith, husband; if you bring Williams into the mix, aren't you worried that you're throwin' another matchstick atop the fire?" Williams had been a Mary-suitor, himself once; of course, it seemed unlikely that he'd be creating hysterical scenes, but one never knew—it all went back to that thwarted-love thing.

"Discretion is my first priority, just now, and Williams will be discreet."

This was true, and Doyle decided that she couldn't really argue with his point. That Williams had been given a role to play was a given; Doyle knew her husband too well. Perhaps he'd been tasked with drawing off Lady Abby's attention—although the woman didn't seem very distract-able, even by the likes of handsome Williams. Neither did Mary, for that matter; she and Howard were completely wrapped up in each other, sitting in the now-peaceful setting.

Doyle made a wry mouth. "Look at them, Michael; a couple of saps, bein' all sappy."

"We're not sappy?" he asked in mock-dismay.

"No. we're the opposite of sappy, whatever that is."

"You do hound me for sex," he reminded her. "It is somewhat exhausting."

But Doyle lifted a lip in scorn. "That's not the same at all, husband; that's just good, old-fashioned lust. I'd be that ashamed of you, if you made sheep's eyes at me like Howard makes at Mary, and I'd probably throat-punch you for good measure."

"To each, his own," said Acton mildly.

"Well, I like our 'own' much better. Remember when we had sex in the barn?"

He tilted his head in gentle correction. "Stables, rather than a barn."

"Honestly, Michael, the point is this; it never hurts to be a bit spontaneous, once in a while."

"We did have sex on my desk," he offered as a defense.

"That was my doin', not yours, and I'm amazed that you even remember, husband."

"Oh, I remember."

She laughed. "All right, when we're back in London, I'll make an appointment with your assistant to clear a half-hour, and ask her to clear your desk, whilst she's at it." This, said with a teasing glance, because Acton's assistant was not one of

Doyle's biggest fans, and—like so many others—was no doubt patiently waiting for Acton to come to his senses.

A half-smile tugged at his mouth. "I will call your bluff, you know, and then where will you be?"

"On the desk," she replied, and leaned to kiss him.

Chapter 17

She kept her phone with her at all times, waiting on his call.

In a marked change, when Doyle collapsed into the soft bed that night, she was almost eager to entertain a visit from the ghostly Sister Luke, despite the decedent's generally sour disposition. Therefore, when the ghost-nun did appear, Doyle addressed her without preamble. "Is the 'Robbie' you spoke of the desk sergeant at the Garda?"

But true to form, the nun was not going to allow Doyle to steer the conversation and ignored the question as though it hadn't been posited. Instead, the elderly woman groused, "Sister Roseline never liked me."

Diplomatically, Doyle decided to withhold a few home-truths, and instead made a mild reply. "Not everyone likes everyone else."

The nun snorted indelicately. "Well, that baluba doesn't fit in, and never has; I don't know what the Order is comin' to."

"You mustn't be so prejudiced," Doyle scolded, rather shocked that a nun would express such a sentiment. "Holy people come in all stripes and colors."

"Well, it's plain as a pikestaff she doesn't belong here. She knows it, too."

Reining in her exasperation, Doyle pointed out, "She's the Mother Superior's Second, and may well be the next Mother Superior. I'd say she fits in very well."

But the nun's sour expression evidenced her disagreement, as she lifted her chin slightly. "She was only promoted because she's a baluba. She'd be better off back in Africa."

Doyle decided there was little point in arguing with such an entrenched view—especially since its author was no longer earth-bound—and so reverted back to the topic at hand. "Why did Robbie hit my mother?"

Her companion eyed her for a moment, and then pursed her mouth so that the network of wrinkles in her face deepened. "He wanted to step in and be a father to ye, after that terrible business with Grady O'Brien."

Doyle stared, rather shocked, and momentarily unable to come up with a response.

The nun nodded in confirmation. "But she told him nay, the foolish girl." She shook her head, slightly. "Many of my girls were foolish; some more than others."

"My mother," Doyle retorted, "was not foolish."

But the old nun only made a derisive sound. "Fah—a' course she was; Robbie loved her—always had, from when he was a boyo. And he was a hard worker, and bright—first in his class, in mathematics."

Doyle frowned in puzzlement. "But he hit her, you said."

The nun lifted her thin, stooped shoulders in reluctant acknowledgement. "He liked the bottle a bit too much, back then—still does, truth to tell. And when he drank, he liked to use his fists. Your mum was leery—after she'd been done wrong by that evil Grady O'Brien—so it was Robbie's bad luck, to try to follow 'im up." Thinking about it, the nun's wrinkled brow clouded. "Now, Grady, that one was trouble, and I knew it from the start. Never trust a foreigner."

Puzzled, Doyle ventured, "My mum always said my father was from County Cork."

The nun stared at her in angry amazement. "Aye; like I said—a foreigner." She paused, and then intoned darkly, "A culchie."

"Oh," said Doyle.

Her companion continued, "She was sweet and soft, was your mum—ripe for the bad 'uns, and Grady O'Brien was an evil man. It's lucky she gathered up the gumption to pack it up and leave 'im."

Surprised, Doyle exclaimed, "I always thought he was the one who left us."

Adamantly, the old nun shook her head. "No. She threatened to go to the police, but she didn't; didn't want to stir up more trouble for 'im—there was trouble enough."

"She was always a bit naïve," Doyle acknowledged, trying to assimilate these revelations.

"Didn't trust her own judgment, after Grady. A shame."

But Doyle lifted her face, and said with all sincerity, "I don't think it was such a bad decision, all-in-all. We were very happy, just the two of us—despite everythin'."

The nun regarded her from aged eyes that were sunken into her skull. "Aye, I think you were. No divisor was needed nor necessary."

Frowning, Doyle ventured, "A divisor?"

Impatiently, the old nun recited, "The dividend is divided by the divisor to get the quotient. D'ye remember *nothin'*, girl?"

"Truly, not very much," Doyle confessed. "I was never very good with numbers; I've always been able to sense things, rather than puzzle them out."

Her companion nodded in reluctant acknowledgment. "Well, that's true, and I'll give you that. And it seems to have turned out well-enough for you. You've a good husband—won't treat you ill, that one."

Doyle had to smile at this unexpected accolade. "Even though gave you a brow-beatin'?"

"Nothin' to fault, in a strong man," the nun declared. "Nice-lookin', too."

"It's off to confession, with you," Doyle teased.

"Oh, I'm there. I'm there." The nun pursed her lips thoughtfully, so that the network of wrinkles appeared again, and she seemed lost in thought.

"The baby's gettin' hungry," Doyle ventured. "I'll have to wake up, soon."

"Never missed havin' a baby," the nun proclaimed. "I had my girls, I did." And then she was gone.

Doyle's eyes flew open, and she contemplated the dark hotel room for a moment before she carefully slid from the bed so as not to disturb Acton. After she'd settled into the chair with Edward, she thought over what she'd learned from the old nun—not much, it seemed. Although it was interesting that the unhappy emotions she'd sensed emanating from Sergeant O'Shaughnessy were apparently because he was remembering her mother, and lost chances. She'd probably be more sympathetic toward him if he hadn't sunk those very chances by giving the object of his affections the back of his hand—he'd only himself to blame.

Lifting the baby to pat his back, she leaned back, and frowned into the darkness. But what was the point? Doyle knew—in the way she knew things—that there was indeed a point—there always was, when she had these dreams. There was always some sort of task that she was slated to perform, but since her mother was long dead—and her mother's past troubles were water well-under the bridge—it was unclear just what that task might be. And—and then there was that strange reference that seemed out-of-place; the divisor, the nun had said—something mathematical, but as Doyle wasn't very mathematical to begin with, she wasn't certain what was meant.

With a mental sigh, she concluded that—yet again—she hadn't enough information, and it was maddening that none of these night-visitors ever seemed capable of simply telling her straight-out what was needful. So, she'd just have to trust that events would work to show her—they always had, before. In the meantime, she'd a baby to soothe—and a husband, for that matter; best get some sleep.

But as it turned out, the night's dreams had not yet ended because she was soon to have another, hard on the first one. To Doyle's astonishment, the ghostly figure standing before her was the bishop from back home, the Nigerian man who'd presided over Acton's confirmation. He looked to have been involved at the receiving end of a nasty knife attack, with multiple stab wounds featured prominently on his face and neck.

"Your Excellency," she breathed in horror, "Holy *Mother*—what's happened to you?"

"I am not a pederast," he retorted, furiously. "I am not a vile sinner—it is the rankest calumny. You! You must remedy this!"

"Oh—oh, yes, sir; I will try." If only she'd the first clue what he was talking about.

"Grant me justice," he continued, gazing on her with an infuriated expression.

"I am on maternity leave, just now," Doyle ventured. "Sir."

"Grant me justice!" he commanded again, and then he was gone, leaving Doyle staring in abject dismay at the dimly-lit bedroom wall, her breath coming in stifled gasps.

Chapter 18

She hoped he'd phone in soon.

The next morning, they breakfasted in their suite whilst Doyle tried to decide what was her best course of action, now that she knew the reason Acton wanted to keep her well-away from any contact with the London CID. The bishop back home had been cruelly murdered, and Acton didn't want her to know about it, much less get involved. Another spite-murder, it seemed—they taught you that there was usually a lot of pent-up emotion behind multiple knife wounds; the killer was enraged, and beyond rational thought.

She could confront Acton about it, but she was reluctant to do so without a bit more information—there was something here; something she didn't understand, and she should tread carefully. It might be best to do an on-the-ground assessment, first—although what she could do here in Dublin remained a mystery; it was not as though she could march into the Garda and demand access to the database. Acton could, of course—and already had—but for some reason, she was reluctant to let the illustrious Chief Inspector know that she was on to him.

Her scalp prickled, and for a moment she entertained the horrifying thought that the aforementioned Chief Inspector had up and murdered a bishop. No, she decided almost immediately, he wouldn't—no matter the incentive—because he'd be worried that she'd find out, and that she'd finally pack it up and leave him; he'd never take that chance. And again, it looked to be a spite-murder, which wasn't Acton's style at all. Although—although he definitely knew something about Father Gregory's spite-murder, and here was yet another one,

106

hard on the first. Mother a' mercy, but the clergy were dropping like flies, and the common thread seemed to be her newly-Roman-Catholic husband.

Her scalp prickled, and with a show of casualness, she asked, "What does 'pederast' mean. Michael?"

He raised his brows at this unexpected question. "A pederast is another word to describe a Section Five. A pedophile."

Doyle blinked in surprise. "Oh." This was alarming, and small wonder that the bishop was upset, if this was the accusation being lodged against him. And it was rather strange, too; she'd never heard the slightest whisper of scandal attached to the bishop, and if such a thing were suspicioned, it would certainly have been on law enforcement's radar.

Acton's thoughtful gaze rested on her. "Where did you hear the word, Kathleen?"

She met his eyes, and noted with some surprise that he was suddenly wary, although he was hiding it—behind his relaxed manner, he was very alert.

Turning up a palm, she explained, "I overheard it in a conversation, is all. I could tell it was somethin' bad, but I didn't know what it meant." So as to avoid further ghost-explanations, she added, "I think it was in reference to the corruption scandal, which makes sense. The sex-slavery rig featured some nasty pedophiles, if I remember my miserable villains aright."

"Indeed, it did."

Interesting, she thought, as she dropped her gaze to her plate; he's relieved that I'm far afield, and on the wrong track. Which leads to the startling assumption that someone is a pedophile, and that Acton is covering for him.

No, her instinct told her immediately; don't be daft, lass.

Trying to make some sense of it, she fingered the hem of the linen tablecloth. Then what? Acton undoubtedly knew the bishop had been murdered, but he didn't want his sidelined bride to ferret out this unfortunate fact—although he must know that she would definitely find out, sooner or later.

So—why the secrecy? Perhaps he didn't want to ruin their holiday with the grim news? Although it was not as though she was fond of the bishop—she hardly knew the man—and this truly wasn't much of a holiday to begin with, what with all the various disasters that had been striking, and what with the local constabulary casting a predatory eye toward her blue-blooded husband.

Reminded, Doyle lifted her face to his. "I'm to meet the Garda's intern in the lobby this mornin', so as to finish up my interview for the station-house newsletter. It shouldn't take long."

Acton signaled to Reynolds that they were finished. "Right then; but wait for me before you go anywhere, please."

Easily, she pulled one of her legs up beneath her and leaned back in the chair. "More like wait for Edward; I'm tethered to that boyo like a boat to a buoy."

With a smile, he rose to kiss her head, and then headed off to shower. Thoughtfully, Doyle watched him go, and then turned to address the servant. "Reynolds, if you were speakin' about mathematics with someone, what does the 'divisor' do?"

If the servant was surprised by the question, he made no betrayal of this fact, and instead straightened up, thinking. "I believe, madam, that the divisor is the number that is to be divided into the dividend."

Doyle considered this rather crossly, thinking that someone should have thought up better and less-confusing names for things, but mathematics people weren't the best explainers to begin with, and so it was only to be expected. "The 'dividend' bein' the bigger number?"

"Yes, madam—the bigger number."

This was said in the tone of one speaking to a small child, and she groused, "I hated division—just talkin' about it gives me the ravin' willies."

"Many feel as you do, madam."

After considering this information, Doyle stared out the window, and frowned. "Is 'devisor' related to 'devious'?"

But this theory appeared to be a dead end. "I do not believe so, madam. It simply means 'that which divides'. Indeed, there is a 'harmonic divisor'—which would be far from devious, but I will have to refresh my memory as to what the term means."

Doyle slowly nodded, since she knew that this was the right track for whatever-it-was she was supposed to be understanding. When the nun had used the word, it meant something—something having to do with Doyle's task. Was it Acton, who was the harmonic divisor? Although Acton's actions weren't very harmonic; instead he tended to divide evildoers from their evil doings—not to mention divide them from the land of the living—but why a deceased Irish nun would take such an interest remained unclear.

"Makes no sense," she mused aloud. "Have no idea what her angle is."

"Did you say something, madam?"

She sighed. "This holiday's been hard on my husband, is all I'm sayin'."

Reynolds paused in surprise. "Oh? If I may say so, madam, Lord Acton seems quite content."

"Yes," she agreed absently. "That's how he seems."

The wait-staff came in to clear the dishes away, and as Reynolds directed these efforts, Doyle moved over to the settee, content to have a few minutes with absolutely nothing to do. Having a baby was a crackin' wonderment, but it definitely took up all one's spare staring-into-space time.

After the hotel's servants had exited, she duly noted that Reynolds seemed reluctant to make his own exit, and was emanating a low-level anxiety behind his unruffled façade. Now what's amiss? she thought crossly. Mother a' mercy, but I hate having a retinue.

"Have we a schedule for the day, madam?"

Doyle turned to him with suspicion, since Reynolds was not one to suggest that Doyle get herself organized, knowing it for a hopeless cause. Perhaps he was looking for some time off, and she felt a pang of guilt that she'd never considered arranging for it. "I don't think anythin' is set in stone, Reynolds, so if you'd like a half-day to take a look 'round, you've only to say the word."

"I only wondered," the servant offered, hovering by the windows so as to straighten an already-straight curtain-tail, "if Mr. Howard's addition to our party might impact the schedule."

Hiding a smile, Doyle raised her brows and considered him. "Well, our Mary will be head-in-the-clouds, and that's goin' to have an impact on everyone else, I suspect. Should we grant her a boon, and tell her you're willin' to watch Gemma for a half-day? And then I can handle Edward—that way the two of them can spend some time together."

"An excellent idea," the servant said briskly, his spirits rising considerably. "A very kind offer, madam."

In a solemn tone, Doyle continued, "As long as Gemma's not too much trouble, Reynolds—she can be a bit bloodthirsty, as we know to our sorrow. Here's hopin' she doesn't turn on you."

But as it happened, Reynolds was too preoccupied to respond to this sally. "Do we know, madam, if Mary will be leaving us, shortly?"

So; here was the nub of it, and Doyle hastened to assure him, "I don't think she's plannin' such a thing, whether it works out with Howard or not. She's very loyal, Reynolds."

The servant suppressed his relief, and nodded in his correct fashion. "Very good, madam. I was only thinking of staffing considerations."

With a gleam, she replied, "Not to worry—Gemma's here to stay. You'll be givin' her away at her weddin', my friend."

But the butler thinned his mouth at such a ridiculous suggestion. "Perhaps it is not a joking matter, madam."

"Sorry," she offered, with an inward smile. "Now, let me feed that baby, and then I'm off to go get interviewed. I'm expected to sound brave and useful, so wish me luck."

"Certainly, madam."

Because, thought Doyle as she reluctantly pulled herself up from the comfortable settee, I'm going to need more than a spot of luck, if what the Pakistani intern believes is true.

Chapter 19

He hadn't phoned, yet, but he'd need to get away from his stupid wife for a moment, which was probably not easy.

It turned out that the intern had come to the lobby a few minutes early, and so Doyle was treated to the sight of the concierge closely questioning her, flanked by two security officers.

Can't blame them, Doyle thought, as she approached to assure them that all was well. Not after the Lady Abby incident; and the intern was definitely a foreign type of foreigner, and not to be confused with someone from County Cork.

The two girls settled into the upholstered lobby chairs, and Doyle opened by asking the intern's name.

"Naziha," the girl replied with her soft smile. "But I am called Nazy."

Doyle nodded. "Well, Nazy, I don't have a lot of time, since I'm between feedings. Tell me why you think Inspector Thomas Williams killed Father Gregory."

If the girl was surprised by the blunt assessment, she didn't betray it, but only replied steadily, "I am not certain that is the case," and it was true.

With a knit brow, Doyle stared at her. "Whyever would you be thinkin' such a thing in the first place?"

Slowly, the girl confessed, "I believe it was Inspector Williams who erased the victim's identity from the database."

This was also true. Unfortunately, since Doyle was already aware that Acton knew more about this than he was letting on, this was actually not beyond the realm of possibility—that Williams had erased Father Gregory from the database—and so the fair Doyle had best tread carefully, so as not to betray those who were near and dear to her. With feigned surprise, she replied, "Oh. Well, there's a wrinkle."

Fairly, the girl offered, "Although it may have been someone trying to make it appear as though it was Inspector Williams, using his log-in and his IP address. It is possible to manipulate such things."

Doyle considered this, on the off-chance that her wretched husband's fingerprints weren't all over the dead man's missing data which was truly a faint hope. "Yes; perhaps that's the case—that it was faked to make it look that way—and I say that mainly because Williams surely has a cast-iron alibi for the time o' death, since he's bein' run ragged back at the Met. We're horrendously short-handed, and his caseload is as long as your arm."

The girl nodded. "Oh—I see. Then it would be easy to establish an alibi, if that is the situation, and he'd be NFA."

Doyle paused. "Remind me what that means."

"No further action," the girl supplied, and then leaned forward to confide, "I am trying to memorize all the codes."

Doyle said kindly, "Yes—well, that is excellent, and the codes are very fun in a secret-handshake sort of way, but you'd be better served by learnin' about how to establish a timeline. Have they explained about how important that is? It's the first thing you do as a detective, so as to see the victim's last hours, and who had opportunity."

Listening with a serious expression, the girl nodded. "Yes—I see. If DI Williams was not in Dublin for the murder, he didn't have opportunity, and so some other explanation must exist for the database tampering."

Doyle cast about for an alternate theory—one that didn't involve law-breaking on a major scale by her better half and his trusty henchman. "Well, Father Gregory was one of the suspects in the massive corruption rig—although he seems to have been missed, in the first wave of arrests—so I'd not be surprised if DI Williams was indeed investigatin' him, and so was lookin' him up in the database. Mayhap Williams erased the victim's data by mistake." Best not mention that Williams was not the sort of person who would make such a monumental mistake; she was doing her best to come up with a pretend-working-theory, here.

But the intern only shook her head. "I do not believe that is what happened. Instead, I believe the erasure was deliberately done; perhaps not by DI Williams, but by someone with the foreknowledge that the victim was going to be murdered. It was an attempt to hide the victim's true identity from law enforcement."

Eyeing the other girl's calm certainty, Doyle prompted, "You'll have to tell me why you believe whatever-it-is you believe, Nazy. I've a husband and a baby who are goin' to hunt me down at any minute, and not necessarily in that order."

The girl met Doyle's gaze, hesitated for a moment, and then revealed, "I believe the murderer was from my country. In my culture, a dagger through the eye has significance—a significance that others, from other cultures, would not recognize."

Puzzled, Doyle regarded her with a doubtful expression. "It looks like a spite-murder to me; nasty thing to do—stick a knife through someone's eye."

"No, Officer Doyle—instead, it is a vengeance crime. A dagger through the eye connotes vengeance."

Doyle considered this. "Vengeance, as in 'an eye for an eye'?"

"Very similar. It has been understood as such for hundreds of years."

But Doyle was having trouble accepting this alternative working theory, and therefore allowed her skepticism to show. "I don't think Father Gregory had any connection to Pakistan, though. So, I'm not certain that we can connect those particular dots."

But as it turned out, the intern had one more trump to play. "The dagger was from my area of the world, also. It is ceremonial—Damascan steel, with a carved rosewood handle."

"Oh," said Doyle, very much surprised. "Then I suppose that tears it."

"Yes. It is very clear to me that such is the case."

Doyle, however, found this comment a bit damning. "You've kept this interestin' little fact under your hat, though, Nazy."

The girl pressed her lips together for a moment. "I would like to know who did it, and why it was done, before I make any judgments."

Another example of these wretched tribal allegiances, Doyle thought with no small exasperation; if the deed was done by one of hers—and for a good reason—she's fine with it. In a scolding tone, Doyle declared, "You can't let people go about murderin' other people, no matter how 'just' you think the cause. There's no such thing as an honorable murder."

"Of course," the girl hastily agreed, and it was not true.

Frowning, Doyle thought it over for a moment, mainly to consider the surprising fact that the motive for the murder didn't seem to be in any way connected to Williams—or Acton, for that matter. "All right, then; let's do our jobs, and try to make some sense of it. I can see now why you were wonderin' about the missionary angle, and I suppose that's the best place to start—to try to find out if the victim had some background connection to Pakistan. And mayhap you can keep your ear to the ground with respect to the Pakistani community here; they may be willin' to give you a hint, since you're one of them, yourself."

But the intern shook her head slightly. "It is unlikely anything is known; Inspector Geary believes the only reason the victim was here was because your husband was coming here—he does not believe there was any other connection."

Doyle admonished the girl gently, "You're not allowed to give out information about a pendin' investigation. Even to me."

"No—no, of course not," the girl stammered, embarrassed.

"And besides, the Inspector doesn't know what you know, and I'd urge you to tell him as soon as may be—it may change his mind about the motive behind the murder."

The girl's gaze faltered. "I will think on it, Officer Doyle."

Doyle smiled her encouragement, knowing that this was one of those "divided loyalty" situations, and the sooner you got over it—so as to follow the evidence, where ever it led—the better the detective you'd be. "It's always best to lay everythin' on the table; oftentimes someone else will look at the same evidence and come up with a different workin' theory, and then—like magic—the case will unravel. We all want the same end, after all, and there's a real danger that justice takes a back seat when the rank and file start to get territorial about what they know." She paused. "And besides, your Pakistani-vengeance theory lets my poor husband off the hook; the Inspector will be that disappointed."

The girl smiled. "That is true."

Rather relieved that it didn't seem as though the intern was going to call for Williams' immediate arrest, Doyle continued in a friendly manner, "So now that we're over that rough ground, d'you want me recite the bridge-jumpin' incident, chapter-and-verse?"

The other girl's smile broadened. "No—I think you are tired of that subject. Instead, I was going to ask you to tell our readers about the Irish community in London."

"We're outnumbered," Doyle replied immediately. "Surrender is our only option." She then thought about it for a moment. "Tell them that I long for the Isles, and that London can't hold a candle. That's what they'll want to hear."

Nazy unbent enough to laugh, and after they'd spoken on generalized topics for a few minutes, at the interview's conclusion they exchanged personal contact information. Doyle had the shrewd sense that she'd better keep tabs on what the girl was doing; the intern was no fool, and there was something here that Acton didn't want anyone to find out, ceremonial dagger or not. I've divided loyalties, myself, she thought with twinge of guilt; ironic, it is, that I'm lecturing the youngsters about it.

As she walked back toward the lift, Doyle thought over the intern's startling vengeance-theory, and then decided there truly couldn't be much to it—she'd bet a pound to a penny that the girl was wrong. Instead, someone probably found the knife in a charity shop, and happened to have it close-to-hand when the altercation escalated into murder. It made no sense whatsoever that Father Gregory was killed by some vengeful Pakistani, since he'd been a pampered priest in London his entire career. Instead it must be a coincidence about the knife—or even if it wasn't a coincidence, then it was a case of mistaken identity, or something. Or the killer could be doing a misdirection play—although that didn't make much sense either, since no one would even realize that he was trying to implicate a Pakistani, here in the land of the pale Irish—faith, even the fair Doyle was skeptical, and she'd been privy to the intern's theory.

So; very unlikely that it was any sort of tribal crime, and Doyle wouldn't think much more about it, save for the undeniable fact that her husband knew something, and had known it immediately upon viewing the decedent's grisly photo. Knew something he didn't wish to share with local law enforcement, or with the wife of his bosom.

And—to further complicate matters—the Inspector was a sharp one, and knew that Acton was playing his cards very close to the vest. With a mental sigh, Doyle pressed the lift button. Here's hoping I can keep my own little tribe out of trouble, she thought; I'd no idea that a nostalgic visit to the Auld Sod would wind up being such a crackin' minefield.

Chapter 20

There; he'd rung her up and he sounded thoroughly annoyed.

Doyle returned to the suite to find Acton alone in the main room, standing by the window and trying to soothe an agitated Edward.

Smiling at this unexpected sight, she walked over to relieve him of the hungry baby. "Have you no reinforcements, husband?"

"I thought you might prefer a little privacy, for a change."

"Is this about sex?" she asked hopefully. "We could stash Edward in the bureau drawer."

"As tempting as that sounds, I am actually expecting Timothy in a half-hour."

"Half-hour's plenty of time," she noted, as she drew a fond hand down his arm. "We could skip the preliminaries."

With his half-smile, he leaned to kiss her. "I'd be willing, but I don't see how you can feed Edward at the same time."

"Oh. Well, there's a good point—you'd be elbowin' each other out of the way."

As she unbuttoned her shirt, they settled in to the settee, and he placed an arm along it's back, behind her. "How went your interview?"

"Good. Better than good, actually—she's clever enough to know that I'm well-sick of talking about the stupid bridge-jumpin' incident—thank God fastin'. So instead I had to talk about bein' a stranger in a strange land, which is yet another tedious subject. You'd think everyone would get over this obsession with bloodlines, and who's-from-where."

He tilted his head slightly, in a disclaimer. "I am not the most sympathetic audience on the subject, perhaps."

She leaned her head to rest it on his shoulder. "No, you're not, and I meant no criticism, Michael. I suppose if I had all sorts of lofty connections, I'd be fightin' to preserve them, too."

In an absent manner, he stroked her shoulder with the hand that rested on the settee's back. "You know, strangely enough, I am not certain that is true. I think you are the rare exception to the rule."

She glanced at him, and teased, "It comes of havin' no connections to begin with, lofty or otherwise. And I wouldn't know the first thing about how to go about gettin' them, either."

But he only squeezed her slightly. "Which only proves my point, I think—that is exactly why you are the exception. It is an elemental instinct, to seek out connections so as to form an alliance. It is what helped the species survive; shared responsibilities, common goals—and a common defense, so as to protect those within the tribe."

"Everyone's fightin' for their own tribe, whether they deserve it or not," she agreed, thinking of the Pakistani intern. And—bringing the girl's theory to mind—it only went to show you that she must have it by the wrong leg, since the last thing Acton would do would be to aid and abet some sort of Middle Eastern retribution murder; it was not his tribe, and not his concern. No, there was some other reason that DCI Acton was hiding whatever-it-was he knew from the Irish Inspector.

"It is the way of it," he acknowledged. "But at least the allegiances are somewhat predictable, which is often helpful in solving a case."

"They're our bread-and-butter, the tribal-fights," she agreed. "We'd be out-of-business in two days if everyone just got over it." Much of the CID's homicide docket sprang straight from the fertile ground of ingrained prejudices, whether they stemmed from ancient grievances or modern ones, which—to Doyle's continuing amazement—often seemed to involve sporting events.

She watched Edward, who was regarding her with wide, solemn eyes as he ate. "Well, I suppose I'm in the wife-and-mother tribe, now, which is the best sort of alliance for that survival-species thing, when you think about it."

"I would agree." He leaned in to bestow a lingering kiss on her neck—regretting the lack of time, he was.

Reminded, she told him, "I gave Mary a half-day to spend with Howard; Edward's goin' to have to take his chances with us."

"We'll manage. Do you have any plans or preferences? Perhaps this is our opportunity to visit your old neighborhood."

She shifted in the seat a bit. "That's not much of a lark for Timothy, if we're tryin' to cheer him up. We should go have a look-round Trinity College, to remind him of better days. If we put our minds to it, mayhap we can bribe some pretty student to flirt with him."

"Or we could bribe Lady Abby, instead," he suggested. "She needs a distraction."

Curious, Doyle glanced at him. "What's goin' to happen with her? I'm a bit uneasy about unloosin' her on society."

"Williams is going to escort her home."

"Ah," she said, and brought her gaze back to the baby. "I was wonderin' why Williams was to be torn away from his duties. After all, if it's only extra-security you want, you can pick that up at the nearest pub by wavin' a fiver around."

"Yes; it is a delicate situation, and so it requires delicate handling."

To her surprise, Doyle's scalp prickled, and she realized there was something here—something about Williams, and the delicate situation. Was Williams in trouble? Could it be that the intern was right, and he'd up and murdered Father Gregory? But no; when Acton had said he'd sent for Williams as a security measure, it was true—not to mention that the last thing Acton would do would be to bring Williams into the Inspector's orbit, if he were indeed guilty of the murder—the Inspector was already suspicious enough. But wait—there was something here that didn't make sense. Trying to catch hold of the elusive thought, she lifted her head to stare out the window. There was something here that she was forgetting—

Acton's amused voice interrupted her thoughts. "I must give Williams fair warning to watch his back, in his dealings with Lady Abby. Hell hath no fury, after all."

Brought back to the conversation, she made a derisive sound. "If our Williams doesn't know how to outfox a conniving female I'll wash my hands of him. He's side-stepped many a lure, my friend."

Acton kissed her neck again and seemed regretful that the Edward-in-the-drawer plan had been so quickly scotched. "I am fortunate you didn't side-step my lure."

"Faith, husband; I was easy pickin's, and hardly worth the grapeshot. I don't know how much lurin' was needful or necessary."

"Timing was everything," he admitted, teasing. "If t'were to be done, t'were best done quickly."

Oh, Doyle thought, suddenly struck; oh—I'm roundly a knocker. Timing was indeed everything, and let this stand as a perfect example that having a baby tended to rust one's detective-brain. Acton was up to something, and the first thing the fair Doyle should have done was follow her own advice—for the love o' Mike—and establish a timeline. Because the operational events, thus far, didn't add up.

In the meantime, however, she'd an amorous husband to indulge. "I know somethin' else that can be done quickly. If you'll lock the door, I'll stash Edward, and he'll be none the wiser."

Clearly torn, he checked his watch. "Timothy is due."

"Then he'll have to wait his turn."

"He does need cheering up," Acton acknowledged, and rose to lock the door.

Chapter 21

His stupid wife had caused some sort of problem, and he needed the packet full of cash to be handed off to some government official. He sounded irritated, and apologized for the massive inconvenience.

Poor man, thought Doyle, as she walked beside Timothy McGonigal in the echoing hallway; he's been wound 'round the axle, and there's no mistaking.

They were wandering though the impressive library at Trinity College, Doyle carrying Edward in the chest-carrier and the two men discussing some famous display—an old book, of all things—but Doyle was awash in sympathy, and not paying much attention.

McGonigal was sunk in misery—although he was trying valiantly to disguise this fact—and he looked rather drawn, and not his sunny self at all. Neither she nor Acton had brought up the Nanda-troubles, but Doyle was wondering if perhaps this was not the right strategy—that it might be better just to let him rail and weep, rather than bottle it up inside. It was very English, to carry on without allowing one's emotions to show through, whereas the Irish were perfectly willing to blow off a bit of steam, with none to find fault when the broken glass had to be swept up.

Mustering up a small smile, McGonigal asked her kindly, "Have you visited the *Book of Kells* exhibit before, Kathleen?"

"No; I can't say as I have, Tim." Best not mention that she'd never come within hailing distance of this or any other college, and it was just as well; the place had its share of aggravating ghosts arguing about stupid, trivial-sounding things amongst the rafters. Who cared, I ask you, whether King Ecgfrith's wife was secretly plotting against the Anglo-Saxons, a million years ago? A pack of quarreling babies who threw around ten-pound words, trying to impress each other.

"There is a Yeats exhibit, over at the National Library," Acton suggested. "Perhaps we should have a look, Tim."

As he'd done at the park, her husband met her eyes briefly, and Doyle understood this to be a subtle suggestion that she withdraw, so as to allow the two men to spend some time alone together. She was perfectly willing to fall in with this plan, since she'd no idea what a "yates" was, and it didn't sound interesting in the least. And although McGonigal was a good friend, it was not an easy thing for someone like her to be around such bleakness—Doyle was feeling a bit bleak, herself, and didn't need any amplifiers.

So, having taken her cue, she made a show of pausing to stretch her back. "D'you mind if I take a pass, you two? I think I'll head back to the hotel, so as to rest-up for a bit." Not that she'd do any resting, of course—there was no rest for the weary, when one was a member of tribe-Acton. She'd started to cobble together a timeline, and in doing so had come into the sure knowledge that her husband was running some sort of misdirection play, and that she'd best shake her stumps and figure out what his object was because it was important, for some reason, that she figure it out. Sister Luke may think Acton was a handsome thing, but it was no coincidence that she was—just like in life—demanding that Doyle pay attention.

And so, when the two men escorted her over to Pearse Street, Doyle was almost unsurprised to behold Thomas Williams, checking his messages as he leaned against a rental car, obviously waiting for them.

All-in-all, he was a welcome sight. He wasn't going to tell her any Acton-secrets, of course, but on the other hand, he wasn't as wily as Acton in evading a straight answer, and so hopefully she'd gain an insight or two with respect to these latest strange and untoward events.

DI Williams could fairly be considered her best friend—not that she had many other friends, of course; it was not easy to have friends when you were someone like Doyle, which made her appreciate him all the more. And Williams was the only person save Acton who knew about her truth-detecting abilities—which was a measure of how much she trusted him. He'd attended the Crime Academy alongside her and had risen though the ranks to become an Inspector with lightning speed—no doubt helped to no small extent by the fact that he was allied with her husband as a doer-of-questionable-deeds.

Over the course of the various and sundry hair-raising events she'd experienced in her short marriage, Doyle had discovered that Williams shared the same alarming philosophy as Acton—that the justice system needed a push, now and again—and so his actions were often more in alignment with the Chief Inspector's wishes rather than with those of the bureaucracy at the CID. Despite this, Williams had always stood as a loyal friend to Doyle, and—because she often sought to curtail her husband's questionable activities—oftentimes he was caught between his own divided loyalties.

"Ho," Doyle called out. "Good to see you, Thomas; have you met Timothy McGonigal?"

"Briefly," Williams smiled, and as the two men shook hands, Doyle felt a flare of emotion from McGonigal—and not necessarily emotion that was warm and good. It was a little strange; Doyle didn't think the two men had interacted much at all—she wasn't even sure they'd met—and McGonigal wasn't the type of person to be stand-offish.

"Williams will see you and Edward back to the hotel," Acton said to Doyle, and then raised his head to look toward the oncoming traffic.

Almost immediately, their trusty African cab-driver swerved to the curb, his tam o'shanter set at a jaunty angle.

"Hello-hello," he called out, with a gleam at Acton. "You call, and I come."

Well, that's doubly-strange, thought Doyle, as she buckled the baby into the rental car's back-seat carrier. Underneath his bluff, jovial manner, the cab driver was actually quite grave. It appeared that no one was happy to behold Williams' appearance on the scene, but she'd hadn't the first clue as to why this would be.

Acton and McGonigal left with their driver, and Williams grinned at Doyle as he held the car door for her. "Are you surprised to see me?"

"No," she told him bluntly. "Everythin's upside-down, for some reason, so I've decided I can't be surprised about anythin', anymore. That, and Acton already told me that you'd be showin' up to lend a hand."

"I'd nothing better to do," he said with heavy irony, and shut the door.

She watched him with a considering eye as he came 'round to slide into the driver's seat. "You're the designated baby-sitter, I understand, and good luck to you."

He nodded in acknowledgement as he watched in the rear-view mirror for a break in traffic. "Acton thought it would be best if I provided an escort."

"Then it's a saint, you are. She's a handful."

With his lopsided smile, he glanced her way. "I've been forewarned; I have the pepper spray ready, and a Taser as back-up."

"Bring duct-tape," Doyle advised. "She's a howler."

He laughingly grimaced. "Wonderful."

As he pulled into traffic, she observed, "You've somethin' in common with her, though, so mayhap you could sympathize, instead. Faith, you could both pass the time away by stickin' pins into Mary-and-Howard voodoo dolls."

"There's an idea," he said easily, with no trace of self-consciousness. "It's a shame the Santero's shop has been closed down; it puts a crimp into my voodoo doll supply."

There was a small pause, whilst she watched the street ahead through the windscreen. "I wish I knew what was goin' on, Thomas."

He kept his gaze on the traffic. "What makes you think something is going on?"

She quirked her mouth. "I just do."

It was the reason she'd realized that she needed to set up a timeline; when Acton had gone over to the Garda to review the police database, his aim was supposedly to identify the blonde woman at the concierge desk. But if the hotel surveillance tape had shown Lady Abby, he would have recognized her immediately, and there would have been no need to spend an hour delving into the database. So, he'd gone over to do something else.

He's setting down some lures, she mused; I'll bet my teeth on it—there's a reason he's been so bristly with Inspector Geary, which is very un-Acton-like, no matter the incentive. He's picking a fight, and the fair Doyle had best find out why he would do such a thing so as to try to outfox him, which in turn is very un-Doyle-like. It's lucky, I am, that reinforcements have lately arrived.

Unsurprisingly, Williams changed the subject. "Edward looks bigger already."

"He's growin' like a crackin' mushroom. Faith, he's constantly hungry, and now I can see why they invented wet-nurses, because I'm ready to wash my hands of it."

He smiled. "Munoz sends her greetings, but mainly wants to know when you're coming back. We've been slammed."

"As soon as may be—I need to find a decent wet nurse, first. Any interestin' cases comin' in?" She eyed him sidelong, and didn't expect for a moment that he'd tell her about one homicide in particular—no doubt he'd been given strict instructions by his commanding officer.

He shrugged. "The usual, which is tough because we're so short-handed. A lot of them aren't getting the legwork they deserve—although more than a few have been pulled into the 'just cause' category, which may lighten the load, somewhat."

Distracted by this revelation, Doyle made a small sound of irritation and turned to look out the window. "Just cause" murders were those determined to have been committed for an excusable reason; "provocation", they used to call it. The argument would be first laid out before a judge, and if the judge determined that the murder qualified as a "just cause" homicide, then the burden of proof shifted, so that the prosecution had the burden of proving it *wasn't* a "just cause" murder, which oftentimes resulted in all charges simply being dropped.

"I'll never understand that line o' reasonin', Thomas; a judge shouldn't decide ahead of time that there was 'just cause' to kill somebody; that's what the jury's for."

But Williams wasn't as interested in the philosophy behind the defense as he was with the practical results. "It saves a lot of money, and it makes our jobs miles easier."

Crossly, she reminded him, "That shouldn't matter, Thomas."

He turned to grin at her. "Spoken like a DS on maternity leave."

She had to smile in response. "And on holiday, to boot; shame on me, for not havin' more sympathy for your poor wracked self. Has it been utterly miserable? Acton's keepin' me well-away from it."

He lifted his thumbs from the wheel for a moment. "That's how it should be, Kath. You've just had a baby and it's only fitting that you take a break. Not to mention that it gives Acton a chance to take a break, too, which—you have to admit—is well-deserved. I had to drop off a packet for his

129

assistant, yesterday, and she was fit to be tied; the brass wants to prioritize a stack of new homicides and she's having a hard time getting in touch with him."

Doyle blew out a breath in acknowledgment. "I can't blame her—he's gone completely off the grid for some reason, and I'm half-hopin' you'll tell me why."

Again, there was a small pause. "I imagine he's enjoying the novelty of a holiday, Kath. I don't think he's ever taken one, before."

Sighing, she turned away to watch out the window. "If you can't tell me, Thomas, then you can't tell me, and I'll harass you no more."

"I can't tell you," he admitted.

But Doyle was not one to give up so easily, and so she offered in an off-hand manner, "A bishop's been murdered, I understand."

There was a moment of surprised silence. "I didn't think you'd know about it, since Acton's off the grid."

Turning back to him, she confessed, "Well, he hasn't officially told me, Thomas, but such news travels fast, in certain circles. Who's workin' the case?"

She could sense that he was weighing how much to tell her, but he finally admitted, "I am, with an assist from Habib."

As this was entirely unexpected, she stared at him in surprise. "Habib? Never say that Habib's willin' to let you take the lead?" Detective Inspector Habib was ordinarily Doyle's supervisor, and he was the same rank as Williams—although they worked on different teams; it was the reason Habib most often supervised her work, instead of Williams. Habib was a very quiet and self-contained sort of fellow, but Doyle knew he kept a close and jealous eye on the company ladder—as did they all, of course; there was nothing like a massive bureaucracy to bring out the worst in competitive instincts.

"In this, he's been willing. A bishop's murder is high-priority, of course, and they thought it best if no one on the team was an RC. Munoz was assigned originally, but they took her off almost straightaway."

"I don't know if that's fair," Doyle protested. "Who's to say that the heathens will be motivated to do a decent job? At least the RCs would be out for bloody revenge."

He shrugged. "That decision's above my pay-grade, I'm afraid. I do what I'm told."

She allowed this comment to go unchallenged, because she'd the shrewd idea that the worthy DI Williams did as Acton told him, and not necessarily what the CID brass told him. "What've they got?"

"Not a lot, as yet." With a tilt of his head, he admitted reluctantly, "It may be connected to the recent unpleasantness."

This being a reference to the corruption-and-sex-slavery rig, and it was, of course, nothing more than what the decedent had told her himself, in his outraged insistence that she clear his name. So as not to let on that she knew more than she should, Doyle turned to stare at Williams in pretend-outrage. "Never say they think the bishop was a Section Five?"

He hastened to assure her, "No one's saying that, Kath; but there's circumstantial evidence that may indicate a tie-in. I can't say more, since we're keeping a tight lid on it."

Stoically, Doyle offered, "I wouldn't try to whitewash it, Thomas, even if he were a pedophile. The shame's on him, and on anyone who would try to protect him."

Williams offered a bit gravely, "There are those who would, you know."

Yes, she thought; there are indeed. And—interestingly enough—Thomas Williams was trying to throw dust in her eyes, and not let the fair Doyle know that the bishop's death was clearly a spite-murder, even though a spite-murder shouldn't be at all surprising, if the bishop were indeed a Section Five. Thinking to explore this strange and interesting fact, she asked, "What was the cause of death?"

But she was to gain no insights, as he explained apologetically, "We're keeping it locked down, I'm afraid. Naturally, we're getting some kooks who are confessing to the crime."

"Naturally," she conceded. It was what always happened, when a high-profile person was murdered, and Doyle always marveled that someone craved attention to the extent that they'd confess to a grisly murder. "Was he somewhere he shouldn't have been—can you at least tell me that?"

"No—it happened right after he'd conducted daily Mass, early Monday morning. It looks as though the killer was lying in wait, outside on the presbytery grounds."

It was actually rather a relief to hear this, as Doyle had entertained an uneasy suspicion—ridiculous, of course—that Acton was involved somehow in the bishop's murder, since that unhappy ecclesiastic was now showing up in her dreams and demanding that she right all wrongs. But now that suspicion—thank God fasting—was shown to be without basis, since Monday last was the day they'd traveled here, to Ireland, and the last thing Acton would do—or at least, one would think—would be to go off on holiday in the midst of masterminding a bishop's murder.

Which reminded her of a more pressing murder—in terms of present company—and a Pakistani intern's working theory. "Father Gregory Brown's been murdered, too." Pausing, she focused on him like a laser beam, watching for an unguarded reaction.

But—being Williams—he wasn't going to give her one, and only replied, "No one deserved it more."

"Shame on you, Thomas Williams; no one deserves to be murdered."

"Well, I suppose we've circled back to 'just cause' then; there's a reason that it's an ancient defense, Kath, and that's basically the theory—that the victim only got what he deserved."

Fortunately, she didn't have to try to refute this valid point, since they'd pulled up to the hotel's curbside valet service. As the staff came forward to assist, Doyle got out so as to fetch Edward from his car seat, but as she was unbuckling the baby, she heard a familiar voice and paused in surprise. Inspector Geary was purposefully approaching Williams, and hailed him from the pavement side of the vehicle

"Inspector Williams," said the Irishman, as he held up his warrant card. "I am Inspector Geary of the *Garda Siochána*, and if you wouldn't mind, I'd ask you to accompany me to the station-house, so as to answer a few questions."

"About what?" asked Williams in irritated disbelief, his brows drawn together.

"I'll fill you in once we're there. Come along, now."

Chapter 22

She made the travel arrangements and hoped that this was the last straw for him. It sounded like it was.

I wish I knew my lines, Doyle thought, as she sat in the Garda's waiting room. And I wish I'd thought to bring along extra nappies—you can never have too many, and let this be a lesson to me.

Yet again, it seemed that she was destined to cool her heels in the station-house waiting area, and yet again, she was wondering what was afoot, because that something was afoot seemed a given. Williams—upon being confronted by the Irish Inspector—had become a bit belligerent and testy, despite Doyle's best efforts to catch his eye in a warning to watch himself.

In addition to Williams' not acting at all Williams-like, Doyle was wracked with guilt because she hadn't had a chance to warn him about the intern's database-hacking theory, and so she'd promptly insisted on accompanying them to the station-house, so as to get a chance to do so—a chance that had never materialized, since Williams was escorted back to the interview room with no further ado. And to add to her frustration—although it shouldn't have been a surprise, truly—all attempts to raise Acton had been unsuccessful; the service wouldn't go through.

But the longer she'd watched Williams being all how-dare-you-I'm-a-Scotland-Yard-Inspector-by-God, the more she'd come to the realization that Williams was playing the arrogant Englishman and picking a fight with the Irish

Inspector in much the same way Acton had been picking a fight—although Acton didn't have to pretend to be an arrogant Englishman, of course—and that, for the *love* o' Mike, made no sense whatsoever. Especially because Williams knew better than most that when suspicious coppers starting asking questions of you, the best course of action was to assert your rights, button your lip, and ring up the best solicitor your bank account could manage.

So—Williams was following in Acton's footsteps and acting a lot like someone who had something to hide, but—unless they'd taken to killing clergymen, willy-nilly—they had, in fact, nothing to hide and were just being obnoxious for reasons unknown.

Doyle paused for a moment, because even through the walls she could hear the indistinct sounds of men's voices, raised in argument. It was all very strange, especially since Williams was slated to escort the fair Lady Abby away from these parts, and so he probably shouldn't be stirring up trouble with the local constabulary if he was hoping to keep that embarrassing episode on the quiet.

Doyle had passed the time by feeding Edward, who was now sleeping, and bent her head to mentally address his scrunched-up little face. Try not to take after your da, she directed; between the two of you I'd go utterly, rending-my-clothes mad.

"Officer Doyle?" Nazy hovered in the doorway, apparently poised to flee in the event Doyle decided to throw a chair at her.

"Come on over," said Doyle with resignation. "I can't be angry at you for followin' my advice, now, can I? Although Williams doesn't much like bein' grassed-out, it seems, and here's hopin' it doesn't result in an all-out donnybrook."

"I am so sorry for your friend," Nazy said as she slipped in the room. "They sound very angry."

Doyle made an impatient face. "Part of the problem is they're men who are both the same rank, so neither wants to back down—it'd be the same if they were tryin' to agree on lunch."

Nazy forgot herself enough to giggle behind her hand.

Doyle asked, "Whilst you were grassin' out Williams, did you tell the Inspector your theory about the weapon, too?"

The girl nodded. "I did, but he doesn't believe there is a Middle Eastern connection—"

"Ah-ah," Doyle warned. "Can't give away state secrets."

"Sorry." Quickly, the girl glanced at the doorway, and then lowered her voice. "But I feel I must—I feel I must tell you something; you've been so kind."

Oh-oh, thought Doyle; that doesn't sound good. Taking an educated guess—based upon her many and varied travails—she asked, "Does it have to do with my husband?"

Guiltily, the girl nodded.

Doyle considered this. "All right, then; all bets are off, and you should tell me as much as you can without bendin' the rules over-much."

The girl lowered her voice even more. "The Inspector asked that I do an in-depth analysis with respect to the deletion of the victim's information from the database—" She paused significantly.

Doyle filled in, "And you truly think it was Williams who was the guilty party, and not someone just tryin' to use his log-in." This seemed apparent, based on the hectoring that could be heard going forward in the back room.

But the intern only leaned forward and raised her dark brows in a suggestive fashion.

"Holy Mother," Doyle breathed. "It was *Acton* who logged-in as Williams?"

"I'm not allowed to say," the girl replied, as she gave Doyle another significant look.

Considering this unexpected news, Doyle leaned back in her chair, and blew a tendril of hair away from her face. Honestly, you had to admire the man; she'd wondered why he'd claimed that he needed a look at the database when he knew perfectly well who Lady Abby was, and here was her answer. He'd come in to the Garda, bold as brass, so as to muck up the evidence in the Father Gregory murder.

"Are you all right?"

Doyle did her best to look shaken by the news, and nodded solemnly. The poor girl might fear she'd facilitated an English peer's disgrace, but in fact Doyle had no such qualms; she knew her husband like the back of her hand, and it seemed very clear that there was some sort of misdirection play going forward. Acton was obviously trying to draw everyone off, and he knew that the best way to accomplish this aim was to draw attention to himself; no matter how much the locals might resent an arrogant English peer, they also knew upon which side their bread was buttered, and that said arrogant peer had connections who could no doubt make their lives very uncomfortable. He was uniquely able to absorb incoming fire without sustaining real injury, so the question remained; why would he do such a thing? Not exactly someone who'd sacrifice himself for the greater good, was our Acton.

The two girls were interrupted by Sergeant O'Shaughnessy, who approached from the front desk bearing a steaming cup of coffee. "D'you still love coffee, Officer Doyle?" He gave the intern a dismissive glance, and she promptly vacated her seat, and slipped out the hallway door.

Doyle smiled her gratitude and accepted the sergeant's cup, careful to hold it away from Edward. "I do, indeed, and thank you kindly, sir."

With a disclaiming motion, he sat down in the now-empty chair beside her. "You don't have to call me 'sir', lass; you're a sergeant now, too."

"Faith; it's an old habit, and I'd probably still be callin' you 'sir' even if they made me the queen."

They chuckled together, and she thought, interesting; he was a sergeant when I was here, and he hasn't been promoted in the years between. He was a drinker, Sister Luke had said, and Doyle drew the obvious conclusion.

O'Shaughnessy tilted his head toward the back hallway. "Sounds like they're goin' at it, hammer and tongs."

Irritated with her menfolk for having put her in this situation, Doyle tried to decide how she should play this, and concluded that she'd no choice but to fall in with Acton's unknown scheme, pending further information; hopefully, the Garda station wasn't about to meet with the same fate as Holy Trinity Church, but with Acton, one never knew. "Inspector Williams has always had a temper; I don't dare cross him."

He nodded in understanding. "London folk," he opined succinctly. "Are you happy, there?"

Doyle brightened. "I truly am, sir. Very happy—and I owe much of it to you."

He considered his own coffee cup for a moment. "And your mum? Was she happy there?"

Doyle could feel the sadness, emanating from him, and so she said gently, "She was happy to be with me, mainly. You've heard—you've heard that she was gathered up, a few years ago?"

He nodded, again. "I did. I'm sorry for your loss, lass, but heaven's the richer."

"Amen," she agreed.

He glanced up. "And your da? Did you say you never got a chance to look 'im up?"

"No—as it turned out, he died before I had the chance." Now, there was the understatement of the century.

With a small sigh, the sergeant shook his head. "That's a mournful shame, lass."

But Doyle found that she couldn't help but bristle. "He was a petty crook, sir. A no-account grifter."

"He was your da," the other insisted. "Blood is important."

"No," she said crossly. "It's not, and everyone needs to just get over it."

Startled by her reaction, he met her eyes. "I'm that sorry—I didn't mean anythin'—"

But whatever he was about to say was lost, as the entry door banged open and Acton stood on the threshold, looking very much like he wished he had some hounds to release. The sergeant hurriedly rose, and Acton fixed him with a cold gaze. "What is the meaning of this?"

"They're arrested Williams," Doyle offered helpfully.

The sergeant set down his cup and hurried back to his desk. "Oh, no, sir—no, not at all; the Inspector wanted to ask a few questions, is all—"

In clipped tones, Acton cut him off. "I would like to speak with the Inspector *immediately*. Are you all right, Kathleen?"

"Right as rain," she assured him. "They've yet to break out the thumbscrews."

The sergeant beat a hasty retreat toward the hallway, but there was no need to fetch the Inspector, because—having heard Acton's raised voice—he promptly appeared with a notably sullen Williams in tow. "Chief Inspector Acton, may I explain—"

But Acton wasn't having it. "Are you questioning my officer, Inspector?"

Doyle could only admire the Inspector's mettle, as he withstood a thousand-years blast of aristocratic condescension. In a calm voice, the man advised, "I am sorry, sir, but I have evidence that Inspector Williams is withholdin' important information about the Father Gregory Brown homicide. He refuses to cooperate, however—"

"I'd lock him up," Doyle suggested. "He's a rum 'un."

139

"And why is my wife here?" Acton demanded, his public-school voice tinged with incredulity. "Are you questioning her, also?"

"Not to worry," Doyle assured him. "I haven't said a blessed thing about your gun-smugglin' operation, or the bodies buried on your estate."

The Inspector stiffened, and replied in a stilted tone, "It is not a jokin' matter, perhaps."

"I should say not," said Acton, emphasizing each syllable. "This is an outrage, and I will speak to the Garda Commissioner at my first opportunity."

But Inspector Geary remained uncowed, and replied steadily, "A man is dead, sir, and I believe that you—and Officer Williams here—know more than you're sayin'."

There was a long pause, whilst the issue hung in the balance, and Doyle devotedly hoped that fisticuffs weren't about to break out amongst the four men. However, apparently Acton decided to defuse the situation, and so he bent his head, and offered in a constrained tone, "Very well, then. I will answer your questions, but I can only do so in strictest confidence."

The other man tilted his head with regret. "I'd have to hear it, first, before I make any promises, sir."

"Right, then." Acton nodded, and glanced in a considering way at the others who were present. "Shall we take a short walk? Perhaps we should leave our devices here."

Oh-ho, thought Doyle with interest; he doesn't want whatever he's goin' to say to wind up on surveillance tape, somewhere—which was just as well; the Pakistani intern shows alarming skills when it comes to that sort of thing.

"It should not take long," Acton assured the Inspector, and as the other man indicated his acquiescence, the two men walked out the entry door.

Chapter 23

It might be the last straw for the stupid twit, but the baby was still   a problem.

After the two ranking officers left out the door, Williams crossed over and bent to rest his hands on the arms of Doyle's chair. In a low voice he asked, "Could we wait out in front? I'm *persona non grata*, here."

"Whatever that means, but fine, Thomas; Edward's gettin' restless, anyways." Apparently, Williams wanted to speak away from eavesdroppers, and Doyle was perfectly willing to fall in with this plan on the off-chance that he would tell her the point of this little psychodrama.

As she gathered up Edward and rose, Sergeant O'Shaughnessy called out, "D'you need a lift anywhere, Officer Doyle?" He eyed Williams with latent hostility, obviously willing to step in to her rescue, if necessary, but Doyle assured him that she only wanted to take the baby out for a bit of air. In a stage whisper, she then leaned in to add, "And DI Williams needs to cool down his hot head—Acton's not at all happy with him."

With a knowing nod, the other man advised, "Give out a shout, if you need me," and then fixed Williams with a warning glare.

Once they were standing outside on the pavement, Doyle put the fussing baby to her shoulder, and began to bounce her knees gently. "Please, please, hold off a bit, Edward. We'll be home soon, I hope."

Williams leaned to look into Edward's little face, and took the opportunity to chide Doyle in a low voice. "Well, that was a near disaster. You shouldn't try to make me laugh when I'm doing my best to be an ass."

She quirked her mouth and glanced up at him. "You deserved it, my friend, for keepin' me in the dark about whatever plan has been hatched."

Williams glanced up the street, watching for the other two men. "I'm sorry Kath, but it's not my plan in the first place. And speaking of which, Acton's not going to be happy that I pulled you in; you're supposed to be back at the hotel, right and tight."

Doyle retorted, "Well, I wasn't about to abandon you, Thomas, and how was I to know that it was all a hum, anyways? What's the gambit—are you tryin' to infiltrate an Irish prison, or somethin'? Because from where I stand, it looks as if you and Acton are bound and determined to wind up in the nick."

He shrugged a regretful shoulder. "I can't tell you, Kath."

She eyed him with exasperation. "They're not nodcocks, you know—even though we're in the hinterlands, and not at the Met. They've twigged on to your muckin' about in the database, and I don't know how you're goin' to explain that one away."

He pressed his lips together. "I can't tell you—I'm sorry, but there it is."

Frowning, Doyle regarded him as she bounced, trying to soothe the baby. "I'm tryin' to imagine the type of crisis that would require you—and Acton, too—to be actin' like a couple o' jinkers in front of my home crowd, and I'm comin' up empty."

Williams glanced up the street again, and then bent his head to contemplate the pavement. "I have to defer to Acton, Kath. It's not my story to tell."

Doyle decided that she'd grilled Williams as much as she was able, and since he wasn't budging, she'd best offer an olive branch. "I'm that sorry I'm such an archwife, Thomas; but I'm not understandin' any of this, and it makes me very uneasy."

"He doesn't want you to know," Williams confessed. "And I have to respect his wishes."

With a small sigh, she shifted the baby. "All right, then; let's speak of other things so that we don't start shovin' at each other and give the desk sergeant an excuse to knock you down. How d'you like Ireland? Have you ever been?"

His hands on his hips, he surveyed the busy street and looked over the buildings that lined the quaint neighborhood. "No, I've never been before. It's nice enough, although everyone sounds like you, which is a little strange."

She laughed. "Now you know how I feel, Thomas, livin' deep in the land of the English-people. Will you have time to take a look 'round? Trinity College is pretty—that's where we went this mornin'. They've a huge library, and there's some famous book, there." Doyle furrowed her brow. "*The Book of Kelps*, or somethin' like that."

"Unfortunately, I won't be staying long," he reminded her. "Sightseeing will have to wait for the next time."

She made a sympathetic sound as she jostled the unhappy baby. "Well, you could always bring along Lady Abby and just give her a taste of the Taser, once in a while, so as to remind her what's what."

Smiling at the picture thus presented, he shook his head. "I don't dare; the Inspector would throw me in gaol in a heartbeat—he's looking for any excuse. I'd best go home straightaway."

Oh, thought Doyle in surprise; that's of interest—it wasn't at all true, and Williams was not, in fact, going home straightaway. Lightly, she teased, "Just don't let her cast her lures at you, Thomas; she's very wily, that way. Howard got himself fooled, after all."

"No; I've strict instructions, which is a shame, because it's always the crazy ones who are great in bed."

She made a moue of distaste. "Too much information, Thomas."

"Sorry. Speaking of which, when I went to drop off the packet, Acton's assistant gave me a bit of the green light, which was unexpected."

This was indeed unexpected, as Acton's assistant was notoriously anti-social, and wedded to her job. "Faith, it's a workplace-hazard, you are, Thomas. Watch yourself, or Tanya at the front desk will shiv the poor woman in a fit of jealousy, and then where will Acton be?"

He smiled. "I will do my best not to instigate a catfight."

"Our Munoz would probably join in, too," Doyle observed. "And if that were the case, Acton's assistant wouldn't stand a chance. So be careful—his assistant does a good job, and it can't be easy, workin' for Acton."

With a grin, he met her eyes. "You did."

"Case in point, my friend."

As he looked up the street again, Doyle tried to decide if she wanted to put poor Williams on the spot, yet again, and then concluded that yes, indeed she did. "So; what was in the packet, that had to be hand-delivered to his assistant? It must have been important."

But he only shrugged. "I don't know, actually—I picked it up from Layton. I had the feeling that it may have been money—cash."

Doyle raised her brows at this, as Layton was Acton's man of business. "A bribe for Lady Abby, mayhap?"

But he reminded her, "No—you've got it backwards; I wouldn't be handing it over to Acton's assistant, if that was the case; instead, she'd be handing it over to me."

"Oh—of course. Sorry; havin' a baby makes you lose a step, I'm afraid. Hopefully I can get back up to speed without feelin' that I should instead be mutterin' on a street corner, somewhere."

With an overly-casual air, Williams ventured, "Munoz is worried that you're not coming back."

He was worried too, of course, and so she hastened to reassure him. "Tell Munoz that of course, I'm comin' back—I've got to wave my commendations in her face at every opportunity."

They both chuckled, because Munoz was—by every measure—a better detective than Doyle, save for the unfortunate fact that Doyle had rescued the other girl out of the river, and so the CID brass were reluctant to promote her over Doyle.

She could feel his suppressed relief. "Good—we've a full slate of cases."

Thinking to explore yet another forbidden topic, Doyle probed, "I hear that there're some ugly spite-murders aboundin'."

"More than the usual," he admitted. "Nasty stuff."

In a dry tone, she noted, "As opposed to the tea-and-cake murders that we normally handle."

He met her eyes in all seriousness. "You know what I mean—these are vicious. *Cask of Amontillado*-grade stuff."

With some amusement, she glanced up from the restless baby. "Not a *clue* what that means, Thomas."

"You didn't read it in school? *The Cask of Amontillado* is a famous story about a spite-murder. The victim gets bricked up behind a wall and left for dead."

Amused, she ran a hand over Edward's unhappy head. "I don't think Irish nuns are goin' to be teachin' horror stories, Thomas."

He smiled in acknowledgement. "I suppose not."

"Here they come," she advised, as she spotted her husband's tall figure approaching from the distance. "What fish-tale has Acton told him, can you at least tell me that at least? I feel as though I'm a player in a play, but no one's given me my lines."

"What makes you think it's a fish-tale?"

She gave him a look, and he had the grace to look self-conscious. "I've no idea, actually; I don't know my lines, either."

"You know enough to be all secretive-like, and surly," Doyle retorted. "That's more than I know." With a knit brow, she watched the two figures approach. "Acton's drawin' him off," Doyle decided thoughtfully, "but I don't know how he's doin' it, and he doesn't want me to know, which is a bit alarmin'.'"

The two men halted in from of them, and the Irish Inspector shook Acton's hand. "Thank you for bein' so candid," he said. "I do appreciate it."

"Please contact me if you have any further questions," Acton offered. "We will be staying through the week."

They bid Williams farewell, and then Acton escorted Doyle and Edward toward the street. And although a cab promptly pulled up, it was not manned by their usual driver, and Doyle realized with some surprise that she'd known it wouldn't be him, but she didn't know why she knew that it wouldn't be him. She didn't have time to think about this, however, because Edward finally let loose with all the fury of a hungry baby, and the replacement cab driver could not get them home fast enough.

Chapter 24

It said something, that he didn't even trust Williams to do the delivery; he trusted her, instead. She'd not let him down.

Once back at their hotel, Doyle hurried the crying baby through the quiet lobby and into the lift, and then pulled up her blouse before Acton had even unlocked their suite's door, collapsing onto the settee with no further ado.

She winced as she adjusted the hungry baby—faith, he was acting as though he hadn't eaten in days, the wretched boyo—and blew out a long breath in relief. Into the blessed silence she rested her head on the cushions and asked, "What's the status of the retinue, husband?"

Acton loosened his tie and walked over to the cabinet to remove two bottles of water. "Mary should return at any moment, and she will see to Edward's nap. Reynolds took Gemma for lunch in Grafton Street, and they will stop to feed the ducks again on their way home."

"Returnin' to the scene of the crime," she observed. "Faith, she's probably sharpenin' up a stick as we speak."

"We can only hope that Reynolds acts as a check." He handed her a bottle of water and then sat down beside her.

After clicking her bottle against his in a mock-toast, she took a sip. "And where's Tim? Did the two of you manage to take a gander at the library-yates thing?"

Acton's chest rose and fell. "He is visiting St. Brigid's. I'd thought to give him a tour, but then I was unexpectedly called away."

There was a small, significant pause, and so she turned her head to face him, and touched his arm in apology. "Don't be angry at Williams, Michael; there was no way I was goin' to leave him without a back-up, and how was I to know it was only a holy-show, in the first place?"

After taking a long drink, he tilted his head toward her, clearly thinking carefully about what he wanted to say. "I would ask that you be a bit more cautious, Kathleen, now that you have Edward."

"You were countin' on my retreatin' into the hotel with the baby," she acknowledged. "Little did you know that the 'mother' instinct hasn't yet kicked in, and instead I was off to rescue Williams."

He leaned to kiss her temple. "You are a loyal friend, and I cannot fault you."

She glanced up at him, relieved that she'd got off so lightly. "Speakin' of which, Williams is that pleased to be back in your good graces, and so I'm happy that he's happy."

Although Williams normally acted as Acton's henchman in doing questionable deeds, in the recent past he'd tried to get himself out of a spot of trouble without Acton's knowledge, and with predictable results. Faith, the man should have known better—whenever you were in trouble, the best strategy was always to lay the whole before Acton, take your lumps, and let him fix it.

She paused in surprise, because her scalp was suddenly prickling. What? It went without saying that Acton would fix it—it was astonishing, sometimes, what the mighty Chief Inspector could accomplish, when all seemed lost. As long as he was motivated to help you, of course—and there were only a few people on earth who fit that category. Williams was one of them, if for no other reason than he was dear to Doyle, and in Acton's world, that was reason enough.

Acton's voice broke into her thoughts. "It was unfortunate, but Williams had to be taught a lesson. Hopefully, the lesson was learned."

She made a wry mouth. "It's lucky, I am, that you don't try to take the rod to me—you'd be doin' nothin' else."

In a tender gesture, he rested his head against hers. "I disagree; you are as close to perfection as it is possible to be."

"It's nicked, you are," she disclaimed fondly. "Although you're the lucky one, too; it could have been Lady Abby you saw out your window that day, and not just me."

"I am, indeed."

"So," she ventured; "Are you going to tell your almost-perfect support officer the workin' theory behind Father Gregory's death?"

"No," he replied, with a tinge of amusement. "I am not."

With a sigh, she turned her attention back to Edward. "Well, it was worth a try, and you can't fault me—you're bein' awfully mysterious, Michael."

After a moment's consideration, he offered, "I will say that I do not believe the investigation will go any further, and that the case will probably go cold. Although in the unlikely event that someone does ask, if you would put it about that Father Gregory was a beloved priest in our own parish, I would appreciate it."

This was untrue, of course, but it was plausible, since technically the now-defunct Holy Trinity was supposed to be their local parish instead of St. Michael's, the church that they actually attended. At the same time, however, it seemed a nonsensical cover-story, since a beloved priest's grisly death— or at least one would think—would incite a very determined quest for justice, and not the sweeping-under-the-rug treatment which was apparently to be dealt-out in this case. She raised her chin to eye him suspiciously. "Honestly, Michael; it would help to know what sort of rig you're runnin'."

"No," he said bluntly. "Believe me, it wouldn't."

This was true, but she felt at least she should warn him, "Well, just so you know, my friend; the Inspector's not buyin' whatever it is you're sellin'. He's pretendin' to be mollified, but he's on high alert, and as suspicious as a church-gaffer."

Thoughtfully, Acton raised his head. "Is that so?"

"'Tis."

Acton seemed distracted by this revelation, and was silent for a few moments, gazing thoughtfully out the window.

With some reluctance, Doyle felt she should add, "It may be because they know you're the one who hacked into the database, and not Williams."

As could be expected, this remark garnered his surprised attention. "And what would you know about that?"

Doyle shrugged. "The intern has mad IT skills, apparently."

He raised his brows. "And she told you what she'd discovered?"

"I did scold her about the protocols, but she wanted to warn me, nevertheless."

Again, he went silent, and seemed thoughtful.

With a sound of sympathy, Doyle shifted Edward to the other side. "Saints and angels, Michael—I almost feel sorry for you; you're used to doin' all your schemin' with the expectation that everyone will behave in a certain way, but we're talkin' about the Irish, here, who are an entirely different kettle o' fish."

Gently, he advised, "Nevertheless, please allow me to handle this particular investigation, Kathleen. I'll not have your visit ruined, and I'd request that you have no further contact with the Garda."

This seemed wholly unfair, and she protested, "But they're good people, Michael—"

To her immense surprise, her voice broke, and she paused, struggling to control her emotions. Immediately, Acton gathered her up into his arms, and ran a soothing hand down the back of her head as she buried her face in his shirtfront and fought an inclination to cry.

"Don't squash Edward," she warned in a muffled voice.

"No, I won't."

She took a long breath to steady herself. "They're good people," she repeated. "The Inspector's dedicated to doin' his job—no matter what—and the intern's as sharp as can stare. And the sergeant—well, it turns out that he wanted to marry my mum and raise me, so I suppose I feel a bit sorry for him because neither one of us would have wanted him to."

"I see," he murmured in a comforting tone against her head.

She lifted her face to his. "I'm not just defendin' them because they're Irish," she insisted. "I'm not, Michael."

"Of course not," he soothed. "All will be well, Kathleen; please don't worry."

She sniffed, and fiddled with one of his buttons. "And I don't know, Michael, as I'm very much interested in seein' my old house."

"Then we won't," he said. "Instead, perhaps a nap would be in order, and I'll see to it that you are not disturbed."

She closed her eyes and breathed in his scent, thinking that a nap sounded like heaven, just now, and trust him to know this. "I'm sorry I'm such a crackin' trial, Michael."

"Nonsense—of course you are tired. Let me take Edward to Mary; may I bring you anything?"

Smiling, she wiped her eyes with the palm of her hand. "An anti-hysteric. Or mayhap you can borrow Williams' Taser."

"To bed," he ordered. "I'll hear no more."

Chapter 25

The problem was she may not have another chance to get at the baby.

If Doyle was hoping to nap undisturbed, she was to be sorely disappointed, because yet again, she was confronted by the bishop, whose sense of outrage hadn't abated by one whit. With barely-controlled anger, he fixed her with a baleful glare. "You must tell them the truth! You must grant me justice!"

Bewildered, Doyle ventured, "Are you truly certain they're sayin' you're a Section Five, Your Excellency? Because I haven't heard a whisper about such a thing, and Acton's been as silent as the grave about it." She paused, stricken. "Sorry—not a good choice of words."

But her companion only drew himself up in outrage. "I am not a sodomite!"

"Of course not," Doyle hastily agreed. "And I'm not one to be correctin' anybody, but I think you're usin' the wrong word—weren't you a 'penderast', or somethin'?"

Seeing her confusion, the African man urged in unhappy frustration, "You will right the record! It is your duty!"

But at this repeated and insistent demand, Doyle suddenly knit her brows and regarded him with a puzzled expression. "I suppose I don't understand, Your Excellency; if the accusations against you aren't true in the first place, then why does the record have to be righted? You know the truth, and God knows the truth; I would think that's all that matters right now, in the grand scheme o' things."

But he was unmoved, and only stared at her in disbelief. "It is an outrage! You do not understand—it is not as simple as you say."

Frowning, Doyle thought this over. "I'll have to disagree, I think. When you get right down to it, indeed it is."

"Go!" the bishop ordered impatiently. "Grant me justice!"

"It's a bit tricky, just now," she ventured, and wondered if perhaps this particular ghost was unfamiliar with the facts on the ground—rather a surprise, since all ghosts she'd dealt with thus far had always seemed very much up-to-speed. "I'm in Dublin, on holiday."

But she was to receive no further answers from the ghostly bishop as instead, the hunched figure of Sister Luke rather abruptly took his place. As Doyle blinked at her, the elderly nun pursed her thin lips. "Fah—another baluba, like that Sister Roseline."

"You mustn't be so prejudiced," Doyle scolded. "We're all on the same team."

"No, we're not on the same team," the nun retorted. "And you'd do well to remember it, missy. It's the first rule of the Order of Operations."

As this comment seemed nonsensical, Doyle ignored it, and explained, "The bishop is angry because he hasn't been murdered for the reason that everyone thinks. He wants me to clear his name, so to speak."

The nun fixed her with the same expression that used to terrify the young Doyle. "Then he's a gobbin' fool, to be dwellin' on it, and you should pay him no mind."

After assimilating the extraordinary fact that a nun was willing to call a bishop a gobbin' fool, Doyle cautiously admitted, "That's rather what I thought, too—I don't understand why he cares so much."

The nun blew out a breath of impatience. "Of course, he cares—didn't you hear what I said? It's the first rule of the Order of Operations." Fixing her former student with an exasperated gaze, she scolded, "You never could remember it, no matter how many times I explained it to you."

Doyle considered this in abject confusion, since the mathematical term was something she hadn't thought about for many years. "The brackets?" she guessed. "Isn't that the first rule? In mathematics, the brackets take priority."

The nun made a derisive, mock-celebratory sound. "Holy St. Brigid's shoe, the girl remembers—quick, someone; give her a prize."

Frowning, Doyle bent her head—knowing that somehow, this was important, but at a loss as to why. "What has that got to do with anythin', though? Why are the brackets so important?"

The old woman lowered her chin, and intoned, "It's the way of humankind, missy, and it's the first rule. Mark me."

Doyle suddenly woke, her eyes flying open and her heart beating in her ears as she took in the dimly-lit room, with the curtains pulled against the sunlight. Not much of a nap, she thought crossly, rubbing her eyes, but then realized that she felt very much refreshed, despite having entertained two agitated ghosts in rapid succession.

Thoughtfully, she stretched her arms over her head and contemplated the ceiling. That they were both agitated seemed important, and that they'd visited in such a fashion—one right after the other—also seemed important, but she'd no idea why that was, or why it would be significant. Oddly enough, it almost seemed as though Sister Luke was there to operate as a check on the bishop—not that Doyle was going to run out the door and do his bidding anyway, since she couldn't very well solve his murder whilst here in Dublin. It was all a bit strange, actually; the bishop shouldn't be chastising the fair Doyle, Sister Luke shouldn't be chastising a bishop—for heaven's sake—and besides, the nun was not exactly someone who should be claiming higher ground in the first place as she was shockingly prejudiced.

In truth, it all seemed a bit bewildering, and Doyle still hadn't a clue as to what it was she was expected to do. That the bishop wanted her to restore his good name seemed clear—not to mention that he wanted the perp to be brought to justice—but there was little she could do at present, especially since Acton was maintaining radio silence so that she wouldn't find out that he'd been killed in the first place. She'd been barred from visiting the Garda, and even if she did get over there—by hook or by crook—the last thing the Inspector would allow, one would think, was to let the fair Doyle fiddle around in the database after her husband had already been mucking up the evidence like a shambler on the axe.

Shifting her head, Doyle contemplated the sliver of sunlight that came into the room where the curtains didn't quite meet. And besides, there was the other point that Sister Luke had mentioned, too; why would the bishop be calling for justice, and insisting that Doyle clear his worldly name? Of all people, he should forgive and forget, now that he was past worldly cares—he was a bishop, for the love o' Mike.

Makes no sense, she decided as she rubbed her eyes; so, I'll be a good detective, and marshal up what I know, and decide what needs to be discovered before I can come up with a plan of action. The facts on the ground are these: It seems clear that the poor man's been spite-murdered—if his wounds are any indication—and he's that unhappy that his murder is being lumped in with the other spite-murders that seem to be originating from the old corruption scandal. There were some nasty pedophiles involved—not to mention a bit of sex-slavery, on the side—and small blame to him, if he doesn't want to be painted with that particular brush; far be it for me—or Sister Luke—to be questioning his motives.

So—he's been spite-murdered, he keeps insisting that Doyle solve the case, but Acton doesn't want her to find out that he's been murdered in the first place and is taking enormous pains to see to it that she doesn't find out.

Frowning, she thought this over, and corrected herself; it could be that Acton didn't want her to investigate the murder, or it could simply be that he wanted to shield her from the bad news whilst they were on holiday—he did tend to shield her, bless him, not that it ever seemed to work out for the poor man, and she'd the bullet wounds to prove it.

With some reluctance, however, she was forced to acknowledge that the "shielding" theory seemed unlikely, mainly because there was a very unhappy ghost haunting her, and also because it seemed apparent that there was some sort of misdirection play going forward, with her wedded husband squarely in the midst of it.

So—if Acton didn't want her to delve into the bishop's murder, perhaps the murderer was someone she knew.

She held up her nails to examine them, and decided that this seemed very unlikely, as she could count no one amongst her acquaintances who'd be inclined to spite-murder a bishop—which was probably a good thing, all in all. Nonetheless, there was something here, and she'd best find out what it was; Acton knew something significant, just as he knew something significant about the Father Gregory murder—and it seemed to her that he was moving heaven and earth to draw everyone off, with Williams giving an able assist.

Once again, the unwelcome thought popped into her mind; could it be *possible* that Acton was covering for a pedophile? No, she thought immediately; both Acton and Williams were all about the bloody-vengeance when it came to pedophiles—it was how the two men had allied themselves to begin with, after all. And Acton wouldn't cover-up for a pedophile, if for no other reason than if his wedded wife ever discovered he'd done such a thing, the repercussions would be swift and terrible.

So, try as she might, she was unable to come up with a plan of action; the bishop-ghost wanted his killer brought to justice—and seemed insistent that it happen immediately—but she didn't see what she could do whilst she was here in Dublin.

Therefore, she'd concentrate on the second ghost in the rotation—Sister Luke, who was willing to criticize the bishop even though she was certainly not someone who should be spouting off advice, left and right. On the other hand, it couldn't be a coincidence, that the dead nun was hectoring her dim-bulb former student, and so the aforementioned former student had best find out why that was.

And so, after rolling out of bed, Doyle wandered into the main room to seek out Reynolds.

Chapter 26

She'd have to think of another plan to get rid of the stupid baby, but one thing at a time.

When Doyle entered the main room, Reynolds was seated at the table and studying a guidebook, but he immediately stood to sketch a quick, correct bow and pull out a chair for her. "Would you care for coffee, madam?"

"I would," she agreed, and sank into the chair as she tucked a casual leg beneath her. Acton was not on the premises, but this was not a surprise to Doyle, who'd known he wouldn't be, even though she wasn't certain why she'd been so certain—apparently, he and the African cab driver were off being mysterious, somewhere together.

"How were the ducks?" she asked Reynolds. "And more to the point, was anyone stabbed?"

"We had a very nice outing," the servant replied, as he poured out a cup of coffee. "And now Miss Gemma and Master Edward are napping. Lord Acton has gone for a walk, but wished to be informed when you awakened, madam."

Idly, Doyle sipped her coffee and duly noted that Reynolds' mobile seemed to be functioning just fine. "Well, let's wait a tick; he deserves a bit of free-range time, what with all the goin's-and-comin's. He's not used to havin' so many people underfoot."

"A very astute observation," Reynolds agreed. "Would you care for a refreshment? Perhaps I could ring for a tea tray."

"Best not," she decided. "If I start addin' an extra meal in the afternoons, I'll never get back to bein' my old skinny self."

"Something light?" he suggested. "Cucumber sandwiches, perhaps?"

She made a face. "I think whoever invented a sandwich made with cucumbers was just havin' a lark, and had no idea that anyone was goin' to take 'im seriously."

"Very good, madam." This was a lie, and Doyle suspicioned that the servant was a bit sharp-set, himself.

"Have you any plans for the afternoon, madam?"

That's the problem with traveling, she thought; everyone expects you to be loaded to the gills with plans. "Not as yet, but let me ask you, Reynolds; do you remember learnin' math—learnin' about the Order of Operations?"

If the servant privately thought this was an unlooked-for topic of conversation, he hid it well. "Certainly, madam. The sequence for problem-solving. BODMAS, I believe, is the pneumonic."

Doyle debated whether to ask him what 'pneumonic' meant, and decided she'd best stay on-topic. "Remind me what it means—the Order of Operations."

The servant paused to gather his thoughts. "When there is a lengthy mathematical problem, the various components must be resolved in the correct order, or you will not arrive at the correct solution."

"And you always start with the brackets," Doyle mused. "That's the first rule."

"Yes. All bracketed formulations take priority and must be resolved first. I believe the sequence is: brackets first, then orders, then multiplication-and-division, and lastly, addition-and-subtraction."

Doyle thought about this for a moment, and then shook her head. "If that's what she was referrin' to, I haven't a *clue* what she was talkin' about."

Carefully hiding his extreme incredulity, the servant ventured, "You were discussing mathematical theory with someone, madam?"

"No," said Doyle slowly. "And that's the rub—I don't think we were."

Reynold poured her a re-fill. "You've shown an extraordinary interest in the study of mathematics lately, if I may say so, madam."

Doyle held the cup between her hands for a moment, and idly watched out the window. "Not really, but I've an extraordinary interest in sortin' things out—and the sooner the better, before my poor husband bursts from tryin' to pretend that all is well."

The servant paused in surprise. "Is all not well, madam?"

With a small sigh, she took a sip. "No, it's not. But don't you dare say anythin', Reynolds, before I do sort it out—he's tryin' so hard, poor man. The way things are goin', he'll never go on holiday again, and small blame to him."

Clearly at sea, Reynolds lifted his brows. "Is this about the blonde woman at the desk?"

"That's only the tip of the iceberg, my friend." But to her surprise, her scalp started prickling like a live thing. What? She thought in surprise. The blonde woman at the desk was Lady Abby—who'd been disappointed in love, and was a bit crazed as a result. There was no mystery, there.

Again, her scalp prickled insistently, and she frowned, trying to decide why it would.

"Shall I phone Lord Acton now, madam?" Apparently, the servant was uneasy about his failure to comply with the head of the household's instructions.

"In a minute, Reynolds; first, tell me what a 'sodomine' is."

The servant considered this, frowning slightly. "I am not certain I am familiar with that particular word, madam. Perhaps you could give me the context."

I suppose I could, she thought with some amusement; I could tell him about the murdered ghost-bishop, but then I'd run the risk that Reynolds would hand over his notice—quick as a cat—and Acton has enough on his plate, already. Aloud, she offered, "Well, it sounded somethin' like that—sodomine, sodomite—"

"Sodomite, perhaps?" In a delicate manner, the servant explained, "A sodomite is Biblical term, and it refers to a man who prefers the company of men, as opposed to the company of women."

She stared at him in surprise. "Oh? Well, that's not the same as a Section Five, is it? I wonder why it changed?" She was certain the bishop was unhappy about being labeled a pederast—or whatever the other word was—the first time he'd appeared.

"I beg your pardon, madam?"

"Never you mind, Reynolds; I was just thinkin' aloud." Although she didn't even know what to think about in the first place; it seemed mighty strange that a bishop would be accused of these things—although the church had weathered a scandal or two in the past, and it was not unheard-of. He wanted to clear his reputation, apparently—grant me justice, he kept saying, like a flippin' broken record. She'd best watch herself, or she'd wind up being just as annoyed with him as Sister Luke was.

There was a soft tapping at the door, and the visitor was revealed to be Mary, bearing a fussy Edward in her arms, with Gemma in tow.

"Come on in, Mary," Doyle called out. "The boyo's hungry, I'll bet."

"That he is, Lady Acton—I'm glad we didn't have to wake you."

"I will ring for a tea tray," Reynolds decided.

"Make sure they'll have extra cucumbers, on the sandwiches," Doyle suggested, as she gathered up the baby. "How does our Mr. Howard, Mary?"

"We had a lovely morning, Lady Acton; thank you." Mary emanated the serene happiness of someone who's met her own true love, and as a consequence, was in love with the world. "And if it can be arranged, he'd like to spend some time with Gemma, this afternoon."

"We purchased a parcel of Mr. Howard's favorite candy this morning," Reynolds offered. "Didn't we, Miss Gemma?"

"Toffee," Gemma disclosed shyly. "Reynolds says the gentlemen are always fond of toffee."

"He will love it," Mary exclaimed, and gathered up the girl for a hug. "Thank you, Reynolds; what a kind thought."

Doyle bent her head over Edward, because suddenly she found—for the second time, this uneven day—that she was blinking back tears. Gemma had been a loose-end child—both parents dead—when Mary had stepped in, and—as though it were the most natural thing in the world—had taken in the girl as her own. And Reynolds surely must have mixed emotions about being supplanted by Mary's new beau, but he was also being selfless, and guided only by what would be best for the girl. Even Howard understood that in order to court Mary, he'd also be courting Gemma.

It quite restored one's faith in humankind, and Doyle could only wonder a bit guiltily if she would be as good, under similar circumstances—jumping off a bridge didn't count for much, in comparison to opening one's home to a stray child. Faith, she should be kinder to Sergeant O'Shaughnessy down at the Garda; he'd been willing to take in a loose-end child, himself, but hadn't been given the chance. Mayhap he would have curbed his bad habits, so as to be a good father to the fair Doyle, and a good husband to her mother—who's to say?

Gently, she stroked Edward's soft little cheek with a forefinger. And of course, the man who'd carried off the palm was Inspector Habib, her supervisor at the CID—his story was the topper to end all toppers, and if he were an RC, he'd be an easy candidate for sainthood. Detective Munoz's sister Elena had been caught up in the horrific sex-slavery rig, and Acton had recruited DI Habib to pose as a customer, so as to infiltrate the rig, and undertake a dramatic rescue of the girl. And not only had Habib rescued Elena, but—since it turned out she was pregnant—he'd married her immediately and claimed the child as his own. It was still a wonderment to her, that mild-mannered Habib had such hidden depths; especially when you considered the couple's divergent backgrounds—

With a sudden movement, Doyle's head snapped up as she stared out the window, and she had to make a mighty effort not to gasp aloud. *Holy Mother of God.* Holy, *holy* Mother of God—of course.

Chapter 27

He said she wasn't to tell anyone about the pay-off, which just went to show what an embarrassment his stupid wife was.

Doyle lifted Edward to her shoulder and began to distractedly pat his back as she tried to come to grips with her epiphany—it just went to show that motherhood made one's wits grow dim, and shame on her, for being as witless as they come.

Like a green recruit, Doyle had dismissed the Pakistani intern's theory out-of-hand, instead of taking the basic and most obvious good-detective step, which was to ask herself if she knew of any Pakistanis who would be willing to spite-murder one of the conspirators in the corruption rig.

The answer, of course, was yes—yes, in fact she did; and to make her lapse even more embarrassing, the murderer was definitely someone Acton would be willing to aid and abet. After all, Acton had recruited Inspector Habib to rescue Elena, and now Acton was not going to stand in the way of a bit of vengeance-taking, because there was nothing that Acton liked better that a bit of vengeance-taking, himself.

Father Gregory must have been Elena's rapist, or was one of them—mayhap he was even the true father of Elena's child. And so, Habib—who no doubt had fellow countrymen and the appropriate dagger at the ready—took an ancient and elemental vengeance on behalf of his new wife.

Doyle considered this revelation, shifting Edward to the other shoulder and watching the wait-staff as they came in with the tea tray. It was all a bit puzzling, because she knew—in the way that she knew things—that Acton hadn't expected the wretched priest's corpse to land on the Garda's doorstep; she was certain of it. Somehow, the priest must have got wind of his fate—or Habib had given him a hint of what was to come—and the panicked man had fled to find Acton, having already witnessed DI Drake's untimely death and guessing, perhaps, that these strange and unsettling events could be directly traced to the illustrious Chief Inspector.

Shyly, Gemma moved over to see Edward, and so Doyle willingly laid him out on her knees so that the little girl could have an unobstructed view.

"He's smiling," she exclaimed with delight, taking the baby's little hands in hers. "Oh—look!"

"Sort of," Doyle agreed, and then had to smile herself, as the little girl bent to make faces at the fascinated baby.

So—even though Acton had thought to be well-away from the Habib-vengeance fallout, instead, the whole mare's-nest had been deposited directly in his lap the moment they'd landed in Dublin, with the Irish Inspector correctly suspicioning that Acton knew more than he was saying. And—without turning a hair—Acton had immediately started behaving in a manner that could only add to the man's suspicions, so that any stray theories of Middle Eastern vengeance were drowned out by the psychodrama being laid out before him.

Faith, Acton had even called-in Williams to lend a badly-behaving hand, so as to add credence to the misdirection play—a misdirection play that would only result in frustration for the aforesaid Irish Inspector, since the poor man would find no evidence of opportunity or motive that could in any way connect Williams or Acton to the murder, despite their suspicious behavior in erasing evidence from the database.

A wily one, Acton was, Doyle thought in wonder for the thousandth time. Faith, even I was distracted, when I should have been asking myself the basic good-detective questions and paying no mind to Acton's attempts to stir up a dust shield.

But—dust shield notwithstanding—it all meant that Doyle was yet again squarely on the horns of the usual dilemma she'd faced many a time in the course of her short-lived marriage; a man had been murdered—no matter his sins—and vengeance was best left to God, not to angry Pakistanis or wily Chief Inspectors. What was the fair Doyle to do, now that she'd twigged on to the cover-up?

"Lord Acton will return shortly," Reynolds announced, as he put down his mobile.

"I believe I'll take the man for a walk-about," Doyle decided, as she gathered up the baby and rose to her feet. "If you wouldn't mind takin' Edward for a bit, Mary."

"With pleasure, Lady Acton."

"Lord Acton is just returning from a walk, madam," Reynolds reminded her. "Perhaps he'd like to partake in our tea, first."

"The poor man will have to go hungry," she replied easily, as she handed Edward to Mary. "Because a walk-about it is."

Reynold hurried to fetch her coat whilst Doyle moved toward the door and tried to decide how best to approach the subject that needed to be approached—no easy task, since her husband was a past master at turning the conversation if he didn't like where it was heading.

"Would you like an umbrella, madam?"

"No thanks, Reynolds; we'll take our chances." Absently, she wound the cashmere scarf 'round her neck, and tried to decide—in light of her new understanding—if it was possible that Habib's vengeance-killing was somehow connected to the dead bishop. Was it *possible* that the bishop was complicit in the sex slavery rig—like Father Gregory was— and that the gossip he was so worried about was true?

After a moment, she decided against it, as she reviewed her reflection in the entry-way mirror. No; the bishop was truly unhappy that he'd been lumped in with the evildoers—although for some reason he'd gone from being a pederast to a sodomite between her two dreams, and this was also important for some reason, although Doyle had not the faintest idea why. In any event, she didn't have the sense that there was a link between the two murders, even though they were very similar in many respects.

As she lifted her hair over her scarf, her fingers suddenly stilled. Come to think of it, that seemed a bit strange, all in itself; whatever-it-was that each of the two ghosts wanted, it seemed very clear that it had nothing to do with Father Gregory's murder. Neither of her ghostly visitors was remotely interested in the priest's grisly death, which—all-in-all—was a bit odd, since the ghosts were both consecrated members of the faith.

Slowly, she lowered her hands and knit her brow as she gazed at her own reflection. Instead, the bishop was stewing about getting the facts put straight—which seemed unseemly, for a holy man—and Sister Luke's motives were as yet unclear, except insofar as she'd demonstrated a shocking prejudice against African clergy and had disclosed Robbie's long-ago contretemps with Doyle's mother.

Which only meant that it was all centered on something else—something separate and apart from Habib's vengeance-killing of Father Gregory. Something was afoot, and that "something" was complicated—or leastways more complicated than a dead priest on a station-house doorstep—and that was an amazement in itself, that such an event could fall to second-in-line.

She didn't have a chance to dwell on the matter any further, because Acton was at the door and Doyle promptly informed him—with a firm hand on his chest—that she needed some air and he was to turn himself around and march his way outside again.

Chapter 28

The handoff was going to be in a public place. A bridge, somewhere.

Once in they were walking along the hotel corridor, Acton bent his head to Doyle's, emanating curiosity as to why he'd been turned him around at the door. "Everything all right?"

"Right as rain," she replied, and put her hands in her coat pockets.

"Are we escaping the retinue?" This said with a suggestive nuance.

Hopeful, he was, and she was almost sorry to dash those hopes. "I'm afraid there's no spontaneous sex in the offing, my friend."

"A shame," he teased, and she could sense that he was trying to gauge her mood. "Did you have a chance to sleep?"

"I did indeed—and thank you for it; I feel much better rested, and much less inclined to weep and wring my hands."

He pressed the button for the lift. "You may weep and wring your hands anytime you wish, Kathleen. I understand that this is a trying time for you."

"I may take you up on that, then. By the by; where's our Williams, this fine afternoon?"

She could sense her husband suddenly grow wary, although he gave no outward indication of it as they stepped into the lift. "Williams has agreed to spend the evening with

McGonigal. I think Tim requires company, just now, but he feels guilty about keeping me from you."

This was true, and so Doyle moved on. "Is Habib with them, or is he hidin' out somewhere else?"

There was a small silence, as they began the descent to the lobby. "DI Habib is at his desk at the Met," her husband replied evenly. "There is no indication that he has been anywhere else."

"Naturally," Doyle agreed, and then any further conversation was curtailed as they crossed the marbled lobby and headed out the entry doors. Once outside, she took a long breath, and lifted her face to contemplate the sky, which was strewn with gray-tinged clouds. It felt good to be outside, even though the breeze was a bit brisk, and even though she was engaged in yet another brick-bat discussion with her wayward husband—although Acton famously didn't care for discussions, brick-bat or otherwise, and avoided them whenever possible. Small blame to him; truly.

They walked along in silence for a few moments, until he ventured, "I don't suppose there is any hope that you will tell me how you guessed."

"None," she agreed. "Mainly because I'm holdin' out my own faint hope that you'll be unnerved enough to curb your ways."

He tilted his head in gentle correction. "Not my ways, this time."

With a sigh, she relented, and tucked her hand into his arm. "I know this, husband—spite-murders are definitely not your style; instead, you prefer it when people simply disappear, with no one the wiser. But the point is this, Michael; you can't allow people to go all bloody vengeance-mode, whether it's your bloody-vengeance or not. We're supposed to uphold the law."

Acton replied mildly, "I owed him a favor."

He was trying to remind her that Habib had been instrumental in saving Elena, and by invoking this reminder he hoped to thus muddy-up the fair Doyle's take on the whole matter, but she stoutly held her ground because she was wise to his wily ways. "It doesn't matter, Michael; we can't be lookin' the other way whilst spite-murders are bein' committed, otherwise where will it all end? Who's to say whether someone's fit o' spite is more worthy than someone else's? That's why we're supposed to be forgivin', and leave it up to God to come up with the who's-deservin'-and-who's-not."

He made no reply—mainly because he'd a different sort of philosophy altogether—and so she changed tack; if he couldn't be persuaded by the idea of heavenly justice, perhaps she should remind him of the tangle-patch that had been created in the here-and-now. "And now this whole unholy mess has landed on the poor Inspector's docket, even though it shouldn't be his concern to begin with. He's got to assign precious resources and do a lot of leg-work; in Ireland, a murdered priest is not somethin' that can be brushed aside or allowed to go cold, despite what you might think. Everyone will be up in arms, Michael—it's not like London."

"I will agree that matters have taken an unexpected and unwanted turn."

Exasperated, Doyle lifted her face to his, and tugged on his arm for emphasis. "Well, that's no surprise a'tall, because that's exactly what happens when everyone commits do-it-yourself vengeance, left and right—it's impossible to keep emotions in check, and then it all spins out of control and turns into a crackin' bloodbath. Faith, Michael, we've seen the results more than most."

"I cannot disagree."

She blew out a frustrated breath at his unwillingness to budge a fraction of an inch on the subject. "This is one of those 'debt of honor' things, and don't think I don't know it."

"I did owe him a favor," Acton repeated.

She retorted with emphasis, "But your debts of honor shouldn't trump the law, Michael. There's no such thing as a 'just' murder."

There was a small pause, and so she made a wry mouth, and was forced to backtrack. "All right—I know 'just cause' can be a defense, but it's fallen out of favor, and with good reason; there's truly no such thing."

That this remark was heresy to him went without saying, and so he made no response.

They walked along for a short space, and—after having cooled down a bit—she offered, "I know this one's a sticky wicket, Michael—and a wicket that you weren't expectin', to boot—but it just goes to prove my point about how things tend to spin out of control, in the vengeance-takin' business."

"Yes," he agreed. "It is not at all what I wished for your first visit home. I am sincerely sorry, Kathleen."

Abruptly, she closed her eyes and confessed, "It was never goin' to be smooth sailin' to begin with, because you were right; bein' here makes me miss my mum—or miss her more than usual, anyways. I'm constantly fightin' an urge to hide in the room, and not go out anywhere a'tall."

He bent his head to hers in silent sympathy for a few moments, and then suggested, "Perhaps it would be helpful to immerse yourself in the memories—it may work to lessen the sadness."

But she flinched at the very thought and shook her head. "I can't imagine any good would come of probin' that wound, Michael—best to let it lie." Curious, she raised her face to his. "Did it help you, to bring your own memories to mind?"

He lifted his gaze to contemplate the street ahead for a moment as he tried to come up with a truthful answer. "Somewhat."

She smiled slightly at this equivocal response. "Well, yours were not the same sort of memories, I suppose. Mine are bittersweet, whilst yours are just bitter, with an extra helpin' of mayhem on the side. I'd trade yours for mine, any day o' the week, and shame on me, for bein' such a baby about it."

He squeezed the hand in his elbow against his side. "You are not being a baby at all; it is only to be expected, coming back for the first time without your mother."

Reminded, she asked, "Speakin' of which, can you tell me what it is that you're hidin' about my father?"

She'd surprised him, and she could sense him suddenly become wary, yet again. "In what respect? You have seen your father's criminal record."

She shook her head, slightly. "Not the worst of it, I think. I heard someone describe him as an 'evil' man, and petty griftin' doesn't qualify as evil, I think."

Acton lifted his head to contemplate the tree tops, then reluctantly revealed, "He was never charged with a Section Five, but he had a taste for young prostitutes, and it might have been headed in that direction."

So; this was what Sister Luke had been hinting at, and now Doyle knew that Acton was indeed willing to cover for a budding pedophile, so long as it would spare his bride. "I'd a feelin' that it was somethin' like that."

Again, he bent his head in sympathy. "I think it was just as well that he wasn't involved in your life, Kathleen."

"A good riddance," she agreed. "And thank you for tryin' to spare me, even though you shouldn't have been muckin' about in those records, either."

Being as he wasn't remorseful in the least, he made no reply, and she leaned her head against his arm. "I want to smooth your way, too, you know—this marriage business is a two-way street, my friend. Can you tell me about whatever-it-is that's botherin' you? I think it has somethin' to do with the fact you've become a person who travels by public cab, and the devil take the hindmost."

He didn't speak for a moment, and then said only, "I would rather not say, Kathleen. But I promise that all will be well, and very shortly. Forgive me, if I have been distracted."

"I think," she ventured, "that you are very unhappy about somethin', and it's not just the fact that Habib's spite-murder has caused such an Irish ruckus."

But he lifted a shoulder in disagreement. "On the contrary, I am very unhappy that Habib has caused such an Irish ruckus. You deserve a better homecoming."

Doyle duly noted that he'd neatly sidestepped her question, and so she responded with no little irritation, "Well, let this be a lesson about this bloody-vengeance business, Michael. No one is goin' to sit quietly by and just allow you to spite-murder them—which is how we get to the crackin' bloodbath part of the equation."

"That is often the case," he agreed.

With a mighty effort, Doyle decided to let it go; they could go 'round and 'round for hours but there was no point to it—if Acton didn't want her to know whatever-it-was, she'd not find out, or at least, not find out from him. In the meantime, she was over-troubled, he was over-troubled, and fortunately there was simple cure for this sad state of affairs. "All right; I can see I'm makin' no headway, and anyways, I don't want to be pullin' caps with you, just now. Instead, let's table this discussion until we've figured out a good plan for a hearty bout of spontaneous sex."

Surprised, he lifted his head to regard the street before them. "I think that is never not the right answer."

"So—put that brain of yours to a better use, for a change; how do we duck out on the retinue?"

Acton paused so as to contemplate the small, rather seedy hotel that fronted the pavement where they'd happened to stop. "Shall we see if we can reserve a room for an hour?"

"Michael," she laughed. "They'll be scandalized—they'll think I'm a two-penny brasser."

He couldn't resist a half-smile. "I can't imagine that anyone would mistake you for a two-penny brasser."

She teased, "I do have the bosom for it."

"Point taken."

Giggling, she pulled him toward the hotel's door. "So to speak."

Chapter 29

She took the train, careful not to let the packet out of her sight.

In much better spirits after their afternoon tryst, Doyle had gone out to dinner with her husband at the corner pub—so as not to be too far from Edward, if needful—and there she very much enjoyed listening to a fiddle-band play Irish music as she feasted on bangers and mash. She'd suggested that they ask McGonigal to join them, thinking to cheer him up, but Acton had reminded her that Tim was spending the evening with Williams.

And that's another thing that's a bit strange in what seems like an unending list, she thought, as she tapped her heels and watched the patrons folk-dance to the exuberant music. If Acton had pulled Williams away from the Met so as to beef-up their security, one would think the man's duties wouldn't include baby-sitting a lovelorn surgeon. But she made no inquiries, having decided that she wasn't going to berate her husband any more about whatever-it-was that he was worried about. In Acton's world, anything that caused her to be upset was a serious matter, and so rather than double his troubles, she'd resolved to be more upbeat, and not so moped.

They walked home in the cool evening breeze, Doyle well-content as she strolled beside her husband. "Have you spoken to Lady Abby as yet?"

"Howard has."

Thoroughly alarmed, she looked up at him. "Oh—I don't know, Michael; was that wise?"

He lifted a shoulder. "Sometimes it is therapeutic, for the victim to confront the Section Seven."

"And sometimes it's dangerous," she added, treading a bit carefully because—after all—Acton was a bit of a Section Seven, himself.

"True. I have no real fears, though; recall that she did not bring a weapon to the lake."

"No; it seemed clear that she was anglin' for a screechfest, instead," Doyle agreed. "And since she knows that's not the way to win him back, she was just hopin' to take a revenge on him—and mayhap frighten his new sweetheart away, too. It was all strictly selfish acting-out, so as to make herself feel better—but the only thing she's accomplished is to thoroughly prove that he was wise to step away from her."

"I doubt she sees that, though."

"*Love does not rejoice in wrongdoing,*" Doyle quoted. "Or at least it's not supposed to, but sometimes it does, anyway."

"But then it is not love," said Acton. "I think that was the point."

She smiled. "You sound like Sister Roseline, over at St. Brigid's. She said the exact same thing—no shades of grey, for the two of you."

She paused in surprise, because she'd caught a flare of emotion from her husband—something rather grave, that was quickly suppressed. What? Sister Roseline had the right of it, of course; it was Doyle who kept thinking that love could still be love, even if it turned corrosive—probably because she was married to Exhibit A, here.

"Speaking of which, I may be called away for an hour or two tomorrow morning. I'm afraid it can't be helped."

Remembering her new resolution, Doyle replied easily, "No worries, husband; and whilst you are about it, why don't you go back to the Garda and throw some chairs about—I'm sure they miss you."

He smiled in acknowledgement. "I'll ring you up, if I need bail money."

"No, you won't; I don't have mobile service," she retorted. "You'll have to look to yourself."

That night, Doyle had barely fallen back to sleep, after giving Edward his midnight feeding, when Sister Luke appeared, thoughtfully chewing on her gums whilst her rheumy gaze rested on Doyle.

Since the ghost-nun made no effort to speak, Doyle decided she may as well get the ball rolling. "Who's the harmonic divisor? I don't think it's Acton—he's not very harmonic, and there's no mistakin' that sad fact."

"Fah," the elderly woman said in disgust. "You never did pay attention."

"I'm tryin'," Doyle protested. "I figured out that Habib was the murderer." As there was no discernable reaction to this disclosure, Doyle remembered that it didn't seem that the nun cared much, either way. "It's hard to believe, that he'd do such a thing."

"Best believe it, missy; it's what I've been tellin' you."

"About the brackets?" Doyle asked with some skepticism. "I don't know as people can be pushed into mathematical formulas in the same way that numbers can."

Affronted, the nun scowled at her. "A' course they can; after all, it's the first rule." She paused. "And there's the Rule of Three, too."

"Three what?" Doyle asked.

But the nun had moved on. "That little girl—the one you've got with you. The butler thinks she's God's gift."

Exasperated, Doyle replied, "Gemma. Her name is Gemma, and you mustn't be such a spy."

"Well, the poor thing should go play at the school—it would do her good to run about."

Whilst Doyle's first impulse was to disagree with anything the nun suggested, she had to admit that this seemed like a good idea. "I suppose that's true—she has no one to play with, here. And it would give her a taste, since she's to enroll in St. Margaret's, soon."

The nun nodded smugly. "I know my girls, I do. It would do her a world of good."

Lifting her chin, Doyle warmed to this idea. "I'll take her myself, tomorrow; that way Mary could spend another mornin' moonin' about with Howard, and Acton can go off and wrangle with stupid Lady Abby."

"Take your guard-dog," the old nun warned, and then she was gone.

Crusty old thing, Doyle thought uncharitably; you'd think she'd make a push to be a bit kinder, all things considered.

And—speaking of the unkind—she was hoping against hope that the outraged bishop would not follow his usual pattern, and turn up after the other ghost's departure, but in this she was to be disappointed since the murdered ecclesiastical suddenly stood before her, once again the picture of frustration. "I did not pay an exaction—I was not being bled! It is not true—it is a foul calumny, and I call upon you to right this wrong."

Doyle stared at him for a moment, and then ventured, "If you want my help, Your Excellency, you've got to use words that I understand—Reynolds is going to think that I've lost my mind, after the last two I threw at him."

"You are the police! There must be justice!"

He regarded her, unhappy and unyielding, and so Doyle offered tentatively, "You'll have justice, Your Excellency, but you may not recognize it—it's beyond our ken, after all. Instead, our job is to forgive, and to try not to get overly-frustrated about how it all works out."

With an abrupt, frustrated gesture, he conveyed his extreme disagreement with this assessment and then disappeared, leaving Doyle rather thoughtful, as she lay in the bed and listened to see if Edward was still asleep.

I wasn't paying attention—she admitted to herself—because he's a respected member of my tribe, but now I can see that he's so angry he's forgotten what's what. Hopefully, he'll cool down and remember the basics—the last needful thing was for the fair Doyle to have to lecture a bishop about grace and forgiveness.

And so, as Acton readied to leave the next morning, she informed him about the planned visit to St. Brigid's. "We'll just go over to the schoolyard, so that Gemma can play with the children for a bit—I'd rather not go inside for another ceremonial visit; it makes me very uneasy to have the Mother Superior bein' all nice and respectful-like."

He considered this, and she sensed that he was not best pleased with the plan.

"I'll take Trenton," she assured him. "I'm not sure Gemma truly needs him, but he can act as her back-up, if anyone tries to push her off the swing."

"All right," he agreed. "Shall we meet back here for lunch?"

"Right-o," she said cheerfully, and tried not to notice his aura of wariness—he wasn't happy about the pending meeting with Lady Abby, and small blame to him; who knows what sort of scene the woman might pull off, if she thought it would garner more attention.

But she couldn't dwell on it for long, because Mary was readying Edward for their trip to the school whilst Trenton was heading down to the lobby to arrange for transportation, and so time was short. "Reynolds," she asked. "I've yet another one for you; what's it mean, an 'exaction'?"

The servant raised his brows. "An exaction? Could you give me the context, madam?"

Frowning, Doyle explained, "It wasn't at all a nice thing—it was a 'fowl culinary' or somethin' like that."

"A foul calumny, perhaps." He paused, thinking about it, and then offered, "It may refer to blackmail, madam."

"Blackmail." She turned this idea over in her mind for a moment, and then slowly shook her head. "That doesn't make much sense, though. If it wasn't true in the first place, unlikely that he'd be willin' to pay blackmail."

With an air of stoic resolution, Reynolds suggested, "Perhaps a bit more context, then, madam."

Making a mighty effort, Doyle closed her eyes and tried to remember. "He said somethin' about 'bein' bled'."

"Ah. Then it *is* blackmail." The servant then ventured with some delicacy, "If I may ask, who is 'he'?"

"Never you mind, my friend." And then, sensing his flare of alarm, she hastened to assure him, "It's not Acton—or anyone else you'd know, for that matter. It's just a case—a puzzlin' one."

Much relieved, Reynolds offered, "I see. I always stand ready to assist you, madam—you have only to ask."

"You're a trump, Reynolds." But the words were said absently, because there was something here—something important, that she didn't understand. If the dead bishop was not a practitioner of those things he'd been accused of, why would he pay blackmail—or at least, be accused of paying blackmail? And why was he ordering the fair Doyle to get it straightened out?

The answer presented itself almost immediately, and she made a face at herself in the entry-way mirror for being so dim-witted, as she threw on her scarf. Of *course*; someone must be framing him—faith, that would explain *everything*, and she'd been a crackin' knocker not to think of it sooner. He was being framed for someone else's crimes in the corruption rig, and he wanted to see justice done so that the true villain got his comeuppance.

It was a huge relief, actually—she'd entertained the uneasy feeling that he was seeking some type of unbishop-like personal vengeance, and now it seemed clear he only wanted to place the blame squarely where it actually belonged. It would also explain the manner of his death—someone was framing-up the bishop, and so it had to appear as though his killer was an angry victim—or the parent of a victim—in order to lump his death together with all the other spite-murders that were suddenly springing up.

His was a shadow-murder, then—one committed in the hopes it would be framed on another murderer—and Acton must already suspicion that this was the case, which was why he was trying to keep the fair Doyle from finding out about it; he was afraid that she'd cut their holiday short and race back to London so as to clear a prestigious member of her tribe.

It can keep, she decided, relieved to have unraveled at least one ghostly problem. Once we're back in London I'll get to work on it—after all, the killer doesn't know we've twigged him, so that should help matters.

"Here's Edward," Mary said, and then helped her fasten-on the chest carrier. "And thank you so much, Lady Acton—Gemma will love it."

"As will Howard," Doyle added with a smile.

The woman beamed with happiness. "Yes—as will Nigel. Thank you again."

A couple of saps, being all sappy, thought Doyle with indulgence, and then she headed out the door.

Chapter 30

She'd do the deed and then return straightaway; her desk was a disaster.

Once at the St. Brigid's schoolyard, Doyle signaled to the aide who was supervising the children and explained her request.

"Of course, Lady Acton—and hello, Gemma." The older woman smiled kindly upon the little girl, who was clinging shyly to Doyle's legs. "Please come in, and I'll fetch Sister—"

"No need," Doyle hurriedly interjected. "I truly don't want anyone to make a fuss. I'll just sit on the bench with my baby, and keep a low-profile."

"I understand completely," the aide replied with a sympathetic smile. "It must be a bit strange, to be you."

"It is very strange to be me," Doyle agreed, and then took a seat to watch as the aide led a timid Gemma over to the slides in order to introduce the girl to the other children. In a short time, she was climbing and sliding with the best of them, and Doyle congratulated herself on a job well done—although it was technically Sister Luke's idea in the first place and all credit should be given, no matter how reluctantly.

The older-grade children were still in class, so that the laughing little faces arrayed before her belonged to the youngsters, who'd only be in school for a half-day. And over in the sand-box was another aide, playing with a little boy who was even younger—in fact, he didn't seem old enough even for pre-school, so perhaps it was a day-care situation.

How extraordinary, Doyle thought, as her idle gaze rested on the small boy who was playing in the sand. Why—why, he looks exactly like Aiki's little boy. Almost without conscious volition, she called out softly, "Jean Luc," and the child immediately looked up, and tried to trace where her voice was coming from. It was him.

Her mouth suddenly dry, Doyle slowly rose, and debated what was best to do. Jean Luc was Aiki's child—and Nanda's too, of course; Nanda who'd been dating Tim McGonigal. How—how could he have come to be here, of all places? Holy Mother of God, the boy must have been kidnapped, and they taught you if you had any suspicion that you'd come across an exploited child, you had to take him into custody immediately, and ask questions later.

It would create an unholy scene—here, where she'd hoped to stay under the radar—but she'd no choice. Perhaps—as unlikely as it seemed—Nanda had up and moved to Ireland without anyone's mentioning it to the fair Doyle. She'd investigate, but in the meantime, her course was clear, and she'd have to take the boy.

Doyle advanced toward the sand box and bent to take the child's hand without asking the aide—the aide may not be trustworthy, after all. "I don't think this child belongs here," she said firmly. "I'm a police officer, and he's comin' with me."

The young woman stared at her in abject surprise as she scrambled to her feet. "Oh—oh, no—" Clasping her hands in dismay, she called to the older aide. "Marian—oh, Marian; this lady says she's the police—"

As could be predicted, Trenton materialized at Doyle's side even before the older aide did. In an undertone Doyle said to him, "Best call Acton," and then was rather surprised when the man made no move to do so.

"Lady Acton," the first aide said in alarm, as she walked up to Doyle, who was still firmly holding Jean Luc's hand. "Whatever has happened?"

Now that she'd reinforcements in the form of Trenton, Doyle decided that it might be a wiser course to ask a few questions before she removed the boy. After all, McGonigal was here in Dublin, and it was hard to believe it was a coincidence; hopefully Tim hadn't kidnapped Nanda's child. "I recognize this child, and I don't think he belongs here."

"Oh." Both aides stared in surprise at Jean Luc, and the older one offered, "His mother is a guest of Sister Roseline; Nanda, I think is her name."

Now it was Doyle's turn to stare in surprise. "*Nanda* is a guest of Sister Roseline?"

"Yes—although I understand she'll be leaving us today." The woman checked her watch. "I've strict instructions to bring him out to the curb, exactly at the top of the hour."

Completely flummoxed, Doyle looked from one to the other, but didn't have the sense that they were anything more than they appeared—bewildered school aides who meant well. "Let's go inside, then, and have a talk with his mother."

"I'm afraid," Trenton spoke up, "that you are not to go inside, ma'am. I have my orders."

Thoroughly astonished at being thus countermanded, Doyle retorted crossly, "Everyone seems to have orders save me. You will tell me what's afoot immediately, Trenton, or I'll give Gemma a stick and let her have at it."

But whatever response Trenton thought to give remained unspoken, because they could suddenly hear a keening cry, and Doyle whirled around to see that Nanda herself had appeared in the gateway that opened into the side street, wild-eyed and pointing an accusatory finger at Doyle, as she swayed slightly on her feet. "You—you are liars! You will take my son away from me!"

"Nanda," Doyle responded, trying to stay calm and unconsciously tightening her grip on the little boy's hand. "There's been a misunderstandin', is all—" Either that, or Doyle was hallucinating, because Nanda was dressed as a nun—not only dressed as a nun, but a strange caricature of her former self, as she was now almost painfully thin, her cheekbones showing prominently in a face contorted by rage.

"Let him go!"

"Nanda," Doyle tried again. "It's only me—Kathleen, remember? Jean Luc is safe, and everythin's all right—"

After taking a tentative step forward, Doyle then leapt back and gasped in dismay, as Nanda pulled a kitchen knife from her habit pocket and brandished it before her a bit wildly; turning in a nervous circle as though she feared attack from behind. "Liars! You will not take my son!"

Trenton had moved his hand to the inside of his coat, where presumably his shoulder holster lay, but Doyle murmured in an undertone, "Let's wait, and give her the twelve. Any closer and all bets are off." For self-defense, they taught you that if an attacker with a knife came within twelve feet, your use of deadly force was justified, because knives were very hard to defend against. Nevertheless, Doyle was very much hoping that Nanda would stay where she was and be calmed if no one else moved—and also that she wouldn't want to resort to violence in front of her small son. It was touch-and-go, though, because it seemed very clear that the woman was not in her right senses.

"Back inside, children," the older aide said briskly, and quickly herded the confused students toward the opposite side of the yard, and into the school.

"Nanda!" Breathlessly, Sister Roseline appeared at the gate, taking in the tableau before her with a horrified gaze. She then addressed the distraught woman in a language that was unfamiliar to Doyle, and appeared to be pleading with her.

Nanda flinched, and the whites of her eyes showed as she rolled them toward the nun. "*Oya,*" the distraught woman responded, shaking her head from side to side like a wounded animal. "*Oya.*" Her gaze rested on Jean Luc, and as she took a tentative step toward him, Doyle held up a desperate palm. "I can't let you come closer, Nanda—please drop your weapon, first, and then we'll sort this all out. I can't let you hurt Jean Luc, or Edward—Edward is my baby, remember? Drop the knife, Nanda—please. And then we will talk it over."

But it didn't appear as though the other woman was listening, as she licked her lips and clenched the knife, and Doyle could feel Trenton tense for action.

"*Kobwa.*" A deep voice could be heard from the gateway, and Doyle glanced over to behold their African cab driver, his booming voice suddenly solemn as he spoke to the frantic woman in her own language; quietly, and with palpable sympathy. "*Reka.*"

Nanda turned to him and gesticulated wildly as she strung together a faltering cascade of unintelligible words. In response, he stood placidly in the gateway, his deep tones soothing as he stood very still, and continued to address her.

To Doyle's surprise, upon hearing his words Sister Roseline suddenly broke down and began weeping into her hands, her shoulders shaking uncontrollably as she fell to her knees.

As Nanda stared at the distraught nun, her own mouth began to tremble and with an anguished cry, she too collapsed to the asphalt, the blade falling from her nerveless hand as she lay on the ground, wailing in abject misery.

His lumbering form moving forward, Mr. Mensah knelt down beside her, and continued to speak in quiet tones whilst he stroked her back, as though he were soothing a small child.

The woman sobbed and moaned but appeared stable, so Doyle started forward to secure the weapon, but Trenton immediately held her back with an outstretched hand. "Stay here, please."

And so, it was with little surprise that Doyle beheld Acton and Williams, bursting through the gateway on a run, and then rushing to converge on the distraught woman.

"She'll need to be sedated," Acton called out to Trenton. "Ring up McGonigal."

Chapter 31

A miserable place, Ireland. So damp and dirty.

Doyle and McGonigal were seated side-by-side in the convent's chapel because, Doyle acknowledged to herself, that was where their tribe tended to retreat after they'd suffered an upset. The place was empty because it was between services, and they were listening to Acton as he leaned a hand on the pew-back in front of them, giving them an update in quiet tones. "I believe it would be best to maintain the original plan, Tim. We will book her on a later flight, is all."

"Williams is goin' with her?" Doyle asked. She'd realized that the Williams-escorting-Lady-Abby-home ruse was actually a cover story for Williams' whisking Nanda away. And why the Rwandan woman needed whisking became very apparent when she began waving the business end of a knife around like someone who was well-familiar; Nanda had murdered the bishop, and Acton was moving heaven and earth to cover for her—or to cover for McGonigal, more accurately. After all, Acton owed Timothy a favor, too.

Acton nodded. "Yes. Williams will take her and the boy to Paris, where they will be met by an agency representative, who will escort them back to relatives in her old country."

As McGonigal indicated his sad acquiescence, Acton met Doyle's eyes in a question. She nodded, to reassure him that she was all right, and then he pressed the other man's shoulder, briefly, before moving away.

Doyle sat with McGonigal for a few moments in silence, trying not to wince at the exhausted mix of miserable emotions that emanated from the man.

"I'm so very sorry, Kathleen."

"Whist," she said. "It's me who's sorry for you—who'd have guessed?"

"Acton warned me," he confessed. "The bishop was—he was from a different tribe, and—apparently—his tribe had slaughtered her tribe, years ago. I couldn't understand it—it wasn't as though the bishop himself had done anything wrong. But she became—she became almost unhinged about it, and—and obviously, with hindsight—I should have believed her. I thought—I suppose I thought it was nonsense, and that she wouldn't risk our life together—wouldn't run the risk of Jean Luc being left with no one at all. But Acton warned me that I should take it seriously."

Doyle took a long breath. "Acton knows how this all works, Tim. He's seen it too many times."

"I'm so ashamed, but I can't go away with her—I can't leave my life. And I don't think I could be with someone capable of doing such a thing."

"There's no one to blame to you, Tim. I certainly don't."

He drew a breath. "I should go—go say goodbye, even though she's been sedated. Poor Jean Luc."

But Doyle assured him, "He'll be all right—if an agency is involved, they'll make sure of it. And you must know that Acton will see to him, Tim."

With an air of determination, her companion rose. "Yes; I need to find out how much this is all costing Acton—so as to pay him back for every penny."

"My advice," Doyle warned, "is to never mention such a thing. If you were in your right mind, you'd never have brought it up."

With a small, sad smile, he nodded. "Right then."

Doyle noted that Sister Roseline had come down the center aisle, to slide into the front pew. Rising, Doyle sidled out after McGonigal, and then went over to sit next to the still, silent nun. Another one, she thought with resignation, as she steeled herself against the waves of sadness, shame and misery that emanated from the quietly-sitting woman. Faith, it's been a ragged, ragged day, and it's not yet noon.

If the nun was in prayer, Doyle didn't want to interrupt, but apparently this was not the case, as Sister Roseline asked quietly, "How is your baby? Is he all right?"

"Slept right through," Doyle said, peeking down into her chest carrier. "Which only goes to show you that he's the male of the species." After they'd all retreated inside the school building, the older aide had offered to take Edward until everything had been sorted out, but Doyle found—almost to her own surprise—that she wasn't about to let anyone touch this baby; not yet. I must have grown a maternal instinct somewhere in the cross-fire, she thought; fancy that.

"You must think me a terrible nun, Lady Acton."

"Whist," Doyle demurred, yet again. "I'll not be judgin' you; obviously it's somethin' I couldn't understand unless I'd lived your life—yours, or Nanda's."

"I should know better," the other insisted heavily. "Of all people, I am called to forgive; I am called to have more faith."

Frowning, Doyle thought it over for a moment. "Forgiveness is a hard, hard thing—the hardest thing of all, I think. It's why practicin' the faith is not for the faint-of-heart. I keep tellin' my husband this, but I'm not sure he's buyin' it."

With a world-weary sigh, the nun bent her head. "Yes. I couldn't forgive, no matter how hard I prayed, and no matter how many years had passed by. *If I give away everything I own, and if I hand my body over so that I may boast, but do not have love, I gain nothing.*"

"I'll not believe that," Doyle protested softly. "You've love in spades, Sister."

But the nun only shook her head. "And now I've dragged my Order into this—this terrible scandal." Raising her face, she gazed upon the altar. "I've asked them for permission to take a leave of absence, and the Council is having an emergency meeting about it. I'd like to go back to my old country, so as to help care for Nanda and Jean Luc." She paused, and then added quietly, "I don't know as Nanda will live much longer; I've seen it before—it eats at you until you'd rather give up, than live with the memories."

In sad acknowledgment, Doyle quoted something the African cab driver had said, that first day when they'd arrived. "You try to get away from the troubles, but the troubles find you anyway."

"Yes—exactly." Glancing at her, the other woman added, "I was always so concerned with being the perfect nun, so that no one would know that I couldn't forgive. And I came here, to the end of the earth, and tried to hide."

Doyle protested again, "It's not as though your life has been wasted, here; far from it."

Again, the nun sighed sadly. "Perhaps. But I've always felt out-of-place—as though I was pretending to be something I was not. Sister Luke knew it, and she always felt a bit sorry for me. She urged me to go back to my country—she told me I should do social work, there, and that I'd be happier."

Doyle raised her brows in surprise. "Now, that's hard to imagine, as Sister Luke's is the picture they use in the dictionary next to 'old battle-axe'."

The other woman smiled, and her mood lightened slightly. "No—not really. It was only that everything was cut-and-dried, for her, so that she had no patience with foolishness." She nun paused. "She had a lot of insight, I think."

This couldn't go by without protest, since Doyle herself was a font of insight, and the ghost-nun was about a million times more annoying than insightful. "But people don't fit into equations, Sister—with Nanda servin' as an excellent case-in-point."

Thoughtfully, the nun tilted her head as she contemplated the altar before them. "In a way, they do, though. I was hiding from who I am—from my memories, and it is time to stop hiding. I'm not a very good nun; when your husband told me of the bishop's murder I leapt to help him hide Nanda. But I shouldn't have; love shouldn't rejoice in wrongdoing—or brood over injury—and I was such a hypocrite, to lecture you about what the Apostle meant when I wasn't able to see it, myself."

"It's the way of humankind," Doyle said, quoting a certain old battle-axe. "The brackets take priority, and Nanda was a member of your tribe."

But the nun only shook her head. "No—I was wrong; so wrong. The Order is my tribe, and I hope they will forgive me." Again, her dark mood lightened a bit, and she lifted her chin, as though struck with a sudden thought. "You know, our Order has no House in my home country, as yet. Perhaps I will start one, if they give me permission."

Doyle found this an excellent idea. "We'll help, you know—if you need any fundin', or if Jean Luc needs anythin' at all; his father was a friend of mine. Or I suppose I should say that Acton will help, more correctly—since he's the one with the money— but he'll do it if I ask him to."

The nun turned her head to Doyle and smiled a more genuine smile than she ever had previously. "You are lucky, in your husband."

"It's a mixed bag," Doyle admitted, "but we're in our own little bracket, together, and I wouldn't change it for the world."

Chapter 32

He'd asked that she not try to contact him once she'd arrived, and she could see why; his stupid wife could ruin everything.

Rather than retreat back to their hotel, Doyle decided to allow Gemma to keep playing at the school whilst Acton accompanied Williams and Nanda to the airport. "I think it would be best to go on as though nothing out-of-the-ordinary has happened," she explained to Acton. "And so long as Gemma doesn't start tellin' tales about the-lady-with-the-knife to her mother, hopefully no one will be the wiser."

He'd agreed—mainly because Trenton would remain behind with them—and so Nanda was discreetly bundled into Mr. Mensah's cab out the side entrance, and then they were gone.

Doyle resumed her post on the schoolyard bench and fed Edward, watching as the children ran about—it was the older group, now, but Gemma seemed to have found her sea legs, and managed to keep up.

I should be more relieved than I am, she realized, as she shifted the baby to the other side; all mysteries have been solved—albeit a bit messily—and now I know why my better half was shoveling money over to a tam-o'-shanter-sporting cab driver, and why he was taking extreme measures to keep me well-away from a certain spite-murder.

Her scalp prickled, and she frowned because her trusty instinct was acting up, and she wasn't certain why this was. Of course, it might be because she could sense a black mood coming on—she knew the signs.

On occasion—most notably when something had penetrated his substantial defenses and upset him, somehow—Acton would retreat into a black mood that was a bit fearsome in its intensity. She'd weathered more than a few, and had come to the conclusion that the best aid his helpmeet could offer was to ride it out with him—that, and provide a hearty helping of sex, usually the rougher the better. So—on the one hand, it was a shame that he'd been hit with multiple emergencies that had required him to exert himself to no small extent; but on the other hand, she'd no objection to another round of carnal goings-on once they were back at the hotel, and so it was a clear case of all's well that ends well.

And that it had ended as well as it could have seemed to be as clear as could be. Despite the fact that Doyle could not approve of these two spite-murders, she was reluctantly aligned with Acton's interest in keeping it all quiet. If Habib were indicted for Father Gregory's murder, his selfless acts in support of Elena and her child would have been for naught. Not to mention, of course, that Acton himself may have ended up being exposed for his role in the affair.

And the same thing applied to Nanda's spite-murder; Acton had worked his trail-covering magic so as to spare McGonigal—and the fair Doyle's church—from the horrific scandal that would have ensued, and—try as she might—she could find no fault with it. Perhaps—even though there was no such thing as a "just cause" murder—sometimes there may be just cause in containing the fallout, although that seemed to be a weaselly attempt to thread a fine needle, and she should repent fasting for harboring such weaselly thoughts.

And—to further excuse her general weaselly-ness—there was yet another element to these spite-murders that couldn't be discounted, because she'd seen the results firsthand. Law enforcement had to step carefully when it came to tribal allegiances, because the respective tribes would leap to the defense of the accuser or the accused, depending on which side they were on at the time. Old hurts would be remembered, and old scores would be dredged up—often in a shockingly violent manner. It was the first rule of humankind, Sister Luke had said, and it was hard to argue with her—the brackets indeed took priority.

Still and all, Doyle was left with a residual uneasiness; justice was supposed to be blind, and not caught up in the tangle-patch of trying to decide which was the greater good—especially when it came to spite-murders, which were nasty, vicious affairs. But—that being said—thank all the blessed saints and holy angels that Acton had saved the day, even though she was roundly a hypocrite for feeling so.

Idly, she pulled out her mobile, thinking to ask Acton for his ETA—best be home when he arrived back from the airport, so as to get started on the cure for the black mood—but yet again, her mobile phone was not working.

Almost immediately Trenton appeared beside her bench. "Do you need anything, ma'am?"

"No, Trenton; I'm just waitin' for the boyo to finish up."

Interesting, she thought, as she turned her attention back to Edward; my mobile's still not working and Trenton is still clinging like a barnacle, even though all the flash-fires have supposedly been put out. That it was happening on her husband's orders went without saying, of course, and so Doyle wondered if there was yet another, unknown crisis looming on the horizon—hard to believe, for the love o' Mike; there was no one left standing to spite-murder anyone else.

Firmly, she made an attempt to rein in her rather alarming sense of unease; Acton was simply being over-cautious, which was not a surprise a'tall, since he tended to be over-cautious when it came to his tends-to-take-the-bit-in-her-teeth bride. But still and all, it seemed a little strange, and thinking to explore this sudden and unwelcome train of thought, Doyle offered, "Thank you for not shootin' Nanda dead on the spot, Trenton. You've nerves of steel."

"Not at all, ma'am."   Not a chit-chatter, was our Trenton.

Watching the children for a minute, Doyle turned over possibilities in her mind, and then remembered a blonde loose-end in the form of Lady Abby—how could she have forgotten? The woman's general deranged-ness was the cover-story for Williams' trip, but since she'd been swapped-out for Nanda, presumably she was still at large, and still deranged. Although it almost strained credibility to think that Acton would allow the woman free rein to stalk and harass them— surely, he'd have clipped her wings by now.

May as give it a try, she thought. "So, Trenton; have we heard from Mary and Howard?"

"No, ma'am," her companion replied.

In a teasing tone, she offered, "Well, mayhap they've eloped, and there's no one to blame them, what with Lady Abby runnin' amok." Casually, she glanced over at him. "D'you know what's happened to Lady Abby?"

"No, ma'am," said Trenton, and it was a lie.

So, she thought; it sounds as though Acton has indeed curbed Lady Abby's wicked ways, but Trenton's not going to give me any insights, so I'll have to go to the source and winkle it out of him.   I'll catch him at a weak moment—which reminds me that we should go back soon, and I wish I could stop at a lingerie shop along the way.

To Trenton, she instructed, "May as well head back to the hotel, I think—if you're wantin' to call the service."

In an overly-casual manner, Trenton began to move over toward the gateway. "If it's all the same to you, ma'am, I'll just call a cab."

Oh-oh, she thought with a jolt of dismay; more trouble to be had.

Chapter 33

As directed, she checked into her room, and stayed off the phone.

Once back at their hotel, Doyle delivered Gemma over to Mary and then was not at all surprised to find that Reynolds was hovering in the hallway outside her suite, waiting to waylay her. "Acton's come back?" she asked.

"Indeed, madam." The servant was emanating a low-level anxiety behind his wooden expression. "And just so that you are aware, Lord Acton has expressed a desire to rest."

"We'll need a bottle o' scotch," Doyle advised. "Pronto."

"Already provided, madam."

"Good one, Reynolds." With no further ado, she handed the baby over to the servant. "Make yourself scarce, and don't show your colors until I've given the all-clear. If Edward gives you any trouble, tell him he's been pushed down in the peckin' order, and see if he'll accept a shot of baby formula, or somethin'."

The servant tucked the baby into the crook of his arm and bowed with some relief. "As you wish, madam."

Doyle pushed open the door to the suite, and then had to adjust to the dim light for a moment; Acton had pulled the curtains nearly all the way, but he was illuminated by a slant of sunlight at the table, where he sat gazing out the gap in the curtains to the street below which—she was unsurprised to note—gave him a view of her arrival. On the table was a bottle of scotch, and in his hand was a tumbler, already nearly empty.

"No time wasted, I see," she observed, and unwound her scarf.

He didn't say anything for a moment, and then lifted the glass to finish it. "I feel badly; I should have offered to stay with Tim."

With a smile, she threw her coat down over the settee. "It's me, Michael, remember? You don't feel badly at all."

"No," he agreed, with the ghost of a smile. "But I should."

She settled into the chair beside him and crossed her arms on the table, gazing alongside him out the window. "No, you shouldn't. He's got to work it out on his own, poor man, and there's not a blessed thing anyone can do."

There was another long pause, whilst they both contemplated the outdoor scene. He asked, "Where is Edward?"

"He'll have to fend for himself, for a change. It will be good for him."

Acton bent his head to contemplate the tabletop, and his dark hair fell across his brow. "I am not good company just now, Kathleen. Perhaps you should stay with him, instead."

She made an impatient sound. "Whist, man; enough of that—of course you're drinkin' like an alderman. It's truly amazin' that you've managed all this on the fly, and away from your natural habitat; my hat's off to you—have another, on me." Taking the bottle, she poured him another glass. "I'm hopin' to get you bosky enough to tell me how it all went down, since I'm roundly flummoxed, and can't quite piece it together."

He glanced up at her as he lifted the glass in his long fingers. "I would be very surprised to hear it. I have underestimated you far too often."

She quirked her mouth. "Well then; I'm goin' to disappoint you because I'm thick as a plank, apparently. I can't understand how you knew that Nanda had up and murdered the bishop, since we were off the grid on account of Habib's murderin' Father Gregory—and that's assumin' I'm keepin' all my spite-murders straight."

"Mr. Mensah," he replied, and took a healthy swallow. "Mr. Mensah—by an extraordinary coincidence."

Astonished, she raised her brows at him. "Unsnabble, and immediately, Michael; whatever do you mean?"

"That first ride; he found out we were from London, he knew we were RC, and almost immediately he asked if we'd heard about the holy man's murder."

She frowned, trying to bring that first conversation to mind. "But—but wasn't he speakin' of Father Gregory?"

"No. Father Gregory wasn't wearing a Roman collar, and he was a John Doe until we ID'd him, just a few minutes before our cab ride."

"Oh," she breathed, as the light dawned. "Oh—you are *somethin'*, Michael."

He took another drink. "It helped that I was already worried about such a possibility."

Gazing out the window in wonder, she thought this over. "So; you scrambled Williams—along with Timothy—and hoped against hope that no one would connect Nanda to the murder before the two of them could spirit her away so as to hide her up here."

He bent his head and swirled the amber liquid in his glass. "Time was of the essence; there would be fingerprints at the scene, and her prints were already in the database because she worked in health care."

With a knowing look, she glanced over at him. "But her prints aren't in the system anymore—I'll bet my teeth."

He took another drink, and made no comment.

Sinking back in her chair, she blew a stray tendril of hair off her forehead. "Holy Mother, Michael, it was one disaster after the next—what with Father Gregory bringin' his spite-murder straight to your doorstep, and Nanda decidin' it was the time to right all past wrongs."

"Indeed. Not the holiday I had envisioned."

She hid a smile; when Acton drank, his tones became clipped, and very House-of-Lords—which only went to show how much he reined it in whilst speaking to his hardscrabble bride. "But aren't you afraid that they'll twig on to Nanda, even though her prints aren't in the system? The man was a bishop, after all, so it's hard to believe they won't be turnin' over every possible stone—we're in Ireland, remember." Thinking about it, she reminded him a bit uneasily, "Mayhap somebody will remember how Nanda was givin' him the side-eye at your confirmation, and start to connect some dots."

Acton tilted his head slightly as he gazed out the window, and she could sense that he was debating whether or not to tell her something.

"If you've concocted some sort of alibi, it's only fair that I hear it," she prompted. "And I would guess that it has somethin' to do with bein' all lord-and-conqueror with local law enforcement personnel, although I haven't the ghost of an idea why that was at all necessary."

He fingered his glass. "The bishop's case will not be solved, but there is circumstantial evidence that would show it was Father Gregory who killed him, then fled here."

She blinked in surprise. "Now, that's convenient—and again, my hat's off to you, Michael, for cobblin' that theory together at a moment's notice."

"Indeed." He lifted the glass to take another drink.

Covertly gauging the amount left in his glass, she decided that two glasses-full was more than enough, and after that she's pull out the heavy artillery—in the form of her impressive bosom—if he showed any inclination to pour himself a third. Sometimes sacrifices were needful and necessary, but first, she'd try a bit more winkling. "So—if

Father Gregory killed the bishop, then who's killed Father Gregory?"

But Acton—being Acton—had a ready answer. "His murder will be pinned on a blackmailer. The evidence will show that Father Gregory—along with the bishop—were being blackmailed over their role in the sex slavery rig."

"Oh," breathed Doyle in wonder. "That's truly an impressive fake-workin'-theory, Michael."

His gaze a bit unfocused, her husband continued to gaze out the window. "Yes. It allows for the evident reason Father Gregory was seeking me out, and it also allows for the reason he was ultimately killed on the Garda steps; he was desperate to expose the blackmailer to law enforcement, and so the blackmailer had to stop him." He paused. "It would also explain the reason for the gruesome murder, as the blackmailer wished to send a message to all other potential grassers."

Doyle regarded him in all admiration. "Mother a' mercy—there's a round tale for you. And any potential clues would only double-back into dead ends."

He contemplated his almost-empty glass. "Yes. It does hang together."

Suddenly, the penny dropped, and Doyle straightened up in her seat. "You told Inspector Geary that they were lovers—the bishop and Father Gregory—and that's why you took him on the walk, so as to be all discreet-like. You told him they were bein' blackmailed because they were lovers." Not to mention it would explain why the poor, outraged ghost-bishop went from being a pederast to a sodomite, depending upon which cover story Acton was pitching at the time—it all made sense, now.

Acton surveyed the street below, and made no response.

"Holy Mother, but you're a crackin' magician, Michael," she proclaimed. "The Inspector's goin' to be very reluctant to pursue the bishop's case—as it would make his own RC tribe look bad. And that's also why you told him that Father Gregory was our beloved parish priest, so that he'd be even more reluctant to pursue it, because it might look as though he was bein' petty, and tryin' to stick it to you."

Her companion did not confirm or deny, but only finished off his scotch.

As she contemplated all the efforts he'd taken to thoroughly extinguish all pending flash-fires, she could only shake her head. "Saints, husband; you're like one of those birds that draw people away from their nest by pretendin' they've a broken wing."

A smile tugged at his mouth as he set the empty glass on the table with a click. "I confess I never would have hit upon that particular metaphor."

"Then you need to read more," she advised. "And there's some story about a cask of wine behind a wall that's also apt, apparently."

He was very much amused as he glanced up at her. "You astonish me, Lady Acton."

"Well, that's not all I'll do, husband. Despite all your impressive broken-wing-pretendin', I've half a mind to brain you with the nearest fire-jack."

Watching her, he shook his head slightly. "I cannot apologize for trying to help McGonigal."

"Another tedious debt of honor," she observed. "Hopefully, there's the end to them."

"Indeed."

Fairly, she couldn't help but admit, "And I've no real cause to complain; you did the same for me, once—swung into action, to cover up a murder."

He bent his head. "I was not going to mention it."

She sighed. "I suppose these are just the latest in what seems like a long list of 'just cause' murders. But it makes me very uneasy, Michael, when you act as judge and jury."

"I know this, Kathleen; believe me."

She made a wry mouth, and placed a hand on his forearm, where it rested on the table. "Which is why you never want me to find anythin' out. So, if you want to avoid havin' these sorts of dreaded discussions, husband, mayhap you shouldn't go about killin' people to begin with."

He glanced up at her. "Here is where I point out that I was not the one who went about killing people, this time."

She blinked. "Oh—oh, you're right. I'm sorry, it's just an automatic reflex." Frowning, she wondered why her scalp was prickling.

He fingered his empty glass. "I so did not want you to be troubled, on your first visit home."

With a smile, she leaned to look up into his face. "Home's in London, because home's with you, my friend. And I haven't been troubled—not truly; instead, I've learned a lot, and I suppose it's all to the good." After pausing for a moment, she offered, "I sat with Sister Roseline in the chapel for a bit, today. She was wearin' a white wool scarf—the kind you buy for a pound from the street vendors—and I caught that scent, the scent of cheap wool. All of a sudden, I was reminded of how my mother smelt when she used to carry me over her shoulder—she'd a scarf just like it. It was such a happy memory, and completely unexpected, in the midst of all the misery and despair."

He raised his head to meet her eyes, and then lifted her hand to kiss the knuckles. "I love you. I don't tell you near enough."

"Don't be a sappy-drunk, husband; and is there any chance you're sober enough to combine your well-deserved tipple with a round of hearty sex?"

He contemplated the empty glass in his hand for a moment. "I suppose I could make the attempt."

"There's my man—never one to shirk a challenge. Come, up on your feet—if we can't make it to the bed, the floor will have to do."

As they rose, he put an arm around her waist and kissed her neck. "I have very fond memories of the floor."

Laughing, she allowed him to pull her down. "For old time's sake, then."

Chapter 34

A shame, that she couldn't check in with him, but she understood the need for discretion.

That night, Doyle addressed Sister Luke from her windy perch. "It's you, who's the divisor. You warned my mum away from my da. And you told Sister Roseline that she should stop hidin' at St. Brigid's, and go back to Africa."

"It took her long enough," the elderly woman observed in a sour tone. "Paid me no mind, she did."

But Doyle disagreed. "No—she knew you were right, I think, but she didn't want to face her memories." She paused. "Rather like Acton."

"Rather like you," the nun retorted with a baleful eye.

There was a moment's silence. "Aye," Doyle admitted. "I didn't realize how painful it would be—she should be here, but she's not. Everythin' seems wrong, and out-of-place."

"*Love bears all things, believes all things, hopes all things, endures all things,*" the nun quoted. "It won't seem wrong for long."

"I'm not that brave," Doyle protested. "Everyone thinks I am, but I'm not."

"Tell the boyo," the nun directed sternly. "Sing him the songs."

Slowly, Doyle nodded. "Aye; I'm not the child, anymore—he is. I have to put aside childish things."

"Do so," the nun commanded. "And Robbie needs a bit of a push."

"Oh," said Doyle. "Right, then."

Suddenly, the figure of the bishop could be seen, stern-faced and hovering behind the old nun. "It is unfair! You will not do as I ask!"

"That angry lady—the one with the knife—she killed the wrong baluba," Sister Luke explained. "This fellow was a priest during the civil war, and he dug a secret escape tunnel under his church. Saved a lot of her people."

"A foul calumny," the man repeated, crossing his arms. "Bah!"

"Oh," said Doyle. "I see; but it truly doesn't change anything—not really. No one deserves to be murdered for the sins of their tribe in the first place. I'm truly sorry that you were murdered, and I'm truly sorry there won't be earthly justice for you, but that's the case for a lot of people, I think." She frowned, thinking about it. "I suppose—I suppose it all goes back to forgiveness bein' the hardest thing of all."

"Did you hear that?" the nun advised the bishop. "Now, leave her alone, you; she's got enough on her plate without worryin' about your hurt feelin's."

As the nun adjusted the long sleeves on her lap, the bishop disappeared and Doyle asked a bit warily, "What else is left on my plate? Everythin's been resolved—Acton's seen to it that it's all dead-ends and cold trails."

With a great deal of impatience, the nun fixed her sunken gaze on Doyle. "It's the Rule of Three, like I told you, child. D'ye *never* listen?"

Reluctantly, Doyle admitted, "There's somethin' Acton doesn't want me to find out, but whatever-it-is, it's well-hidden."

The nun snorted indelicately. "Well-hidden! Ha—good luck to him, then. I always knew you were fey, even if your mum didn't see it."

Doyle admitted, "I didn't like to see it, myself—I was that fearful."

"*There are many gifts,*" the nun reminded her. "Bein' fearful isn't one of 'em."

Doyle ventured, "That's easier said than done, though."

"Nonsense," the old woman retorted. "You need only have a reason to be brave."

Thinking it over, Doyle had to admit the truth of this, and confessed, "I wish I'd been kinder to you."

But the nun only regarded her with impatient derision. "Fah—such nonsense, child. I couldn't have asked for a life more suited to me." She paused, and then added, "When I was a postulate, the Order sent me to take some courses at Trinity College—took the bus, every day. I had to fight the sin of pride, to be amongst so many clever people, in such a grand place." There was a moment's silence, whilst her dim, old eyes considered a far-off memory. "I never told anyone, but the Chair took me aside, and told me I had a gift—that I should join the staff, there. It was a pint full o' ridiculous, of course—I had to get back to my girls."

"*Love is not pompous; it does not seek its own interests,*" Doyle quoted softly.

"No need to go mawkish," the woman advised with some distaste. "I never had any truck with such."

Teasing, Doyle agreed, "I don't think anyone would argue with you about that."

Lifting her chin, her companion chided, "I'll have none o' your sauce, missy. I always told the truth, with no bark on it."

But Doyle couldn't let this pass without reminding her, "Except you told me that my poor husband killed you."

The old nun drew her thin brows together in disbelief. "Fah—it's true as true can be. It was my time to go, but they told me you were comin' to visit, and so I hung on for just a wee bit longer." The aged eyes scrutinized Doyle narrowly. "This strange business—what with marryin' a *sassanach* lord— I wanted to make sure your mother's daughter hadn't done anythin' foolish." She nodded in satisfaction. "All's well with you, though, so I went on my way."

With a small smile, Doyle remembered, "You always sent a bag of rice home in my rucksack, every week. You told me it was to help my mum and me practice my countin'."

"You were a such a skinny little thing," the nun sniffed. "And there was no need for me to confess it—it wasn't stealin', technically, since I didn't keep it for myself."

"Thank you," said Doyle gently. "Thank you for everythin'."

The nun turned her head and looked into the distance for a moment. "Hard to know, sometimes, what's right, and what's not."

"That's why there's the Rules that out-rank even the Rules of Operation," Doyle teased. "Only there's ten of those rules."

"Think you're so clever," scoffed the nun. "Doesn't fool me; I know better."

And with that, she disappeared.

Chapter 35

He said not to speak to anyone; just hand the packet over, and leave.

The next morning, Doyle tried to decide how she could go about having a private conversation with Sergeant O'Shaughnessy without her husband or Inspector Geary—or both—descending on them like a couple of bristling terriers. And then there was the added problem that Acton had requested she make no more visits over to the Garda, which meant she'd have to hit upon an excuse to bring the mountain over to Mohammad, so to speak—no easy task when one was dealing with a desk sergeant who's supposed to be manning the front desk.

I'm as bad as Acton, she thought a bit crossly; I spend half my holiday cooking up schemes so as to hoodwink my better half.

As it turned out, though, Acton said that he needed an hour or two at the Garda in the morning so as to work on his caseload, and so the fair Doyle was afforded a bit of maneuvering room, which she promptly put to use by announcing to Reynolds that she was going down to the lobby to fetch a newspaper.

Since Doyle was not one to read newspapers, the servant was understandably surprised. "I will be happy to fetch a paper, madam. Do you have a preference?"

"It's an excuse to have a walk-about," she explained patiently. "Faith, Reynolds; you'd think you'd know me by now."

He bowed his head. "Very good, madam."

Doyle fastened on the baby carrier. "Havin' a baby makes you stir-crazy, so I'll pass the time by takin' Edward for a lap around the lobby. I'm sick to death of starin' at the four walls."

"Very understandable, madam. And I believe when Lord Acton returns, you are scheduled to take a tour of the cathedral, so that should make for an interesting outing."

Doyle stared at him. "The cathedral? Is that what Acton said?" This was alarming, in that it would seem to indicate that the poor man had had his fill of spontaneous sex.

The servant had the grace to look abashed. "Perhaps I shouldn't have said, madam; it may have been a surprise. He specifically mentioned it would be a chance for the two of you to have some time together."

Ah, thought Doyle—good one, Acton; it must be a cover-story for round two at the hotel seedy. Although she should have guessed as much immediately; if Acton truly stepped into a cathedral he'd probably bring down a plague of locusts, or something.

The servant helped Doyle strap Edward into his chest carrier and then, with a casual air, she wandered out the door and down the hallway. As soon as she emerged from the lift into the lobby, however, she sized up the personnel at the front desk and then approached a likely-looking young man.

"Hallo there; I'm Lady Acton, and I was wonderin' if you'd mind lendin' me your mobile for a moment? Mine's out, and I was wantin' to check in with a friend."

With a smile, the fellow pulled his mobile. "Certainly, Lady Acton."

In a joking manner, Doyle offered, "It's not Acton's blonde girlfriend that I'm callin', I promise you."

Chuckling at this, he handed the mobile over to Doyle. "If I may be askin', ma'am, what's happened to that young woman?"

"I'm not sure," Doyle admitted. "But here's hopin' that neither one of us will ever be seein' her again."

The young man lowered his voice and leaned in a bit. "It must be difficult, ma'am—I mean to have to deal with daft women who are tryin' to get your husband's attention."

"It is difficult," she agreed; and decided not to mention that they'd a few dead bodies, here and there, to show for it. "She was a crackin' pest."

The man nodded knowingly. "And it wasn't even the lady he thought it might be—he advised that we were to be careful not to allow the other one access, either."

Here was a wrinkle, and Doyle kept her reaction matter-of-fact as she turned over a list of possibilities in her mind. "Tasza?" she guessed. "Was she tall?"

The desk clerk shrugged in apology. "I don't know—he only showed us a snap on his mobile." With a smile, he joked, "I wish I had scads of pretty blondes chasin' me, but there you go."

But Doyle could only give him a courtesy-laugh, because her scalp was prickling and her instinct was warning her that this was important—this has happened before, she realized in surprise. Acton showing a photo, but hiding who it actually was—

Watching her, the clerk suggested, "Would you like me to dial the number for you, ma'am?"

"If you would." Doyle smiled and handed over Nazy's card, all the while trying to decide what it was that she was alarmed about. There was another blonde in the picture, apparently, and Acton didn't want that one coming into the hotel, either. *Could* it be Tasza? But Tasza was a Commander at MI 5, and it seemed very unlikely that someone of her stature would be actively stalking Acton or trying to storm their hotel—not to mention she wasn't the crazy-type, she was more the admire-from-afar type, although Doyle wasn't the best assessor of such things, as experience had sadly shown.

But if it wasn't Tasza, then who could it be? She was running out of blondes.

Still frowning a bit, she watched as the young man rang up Nazy, and then thanked him as he handed Doyle the phone and discreetly walked away. "Hallo, Nazy? It's Officer Doyle."

"Officer Doyle." Doyle could hear the suppressed excitement in the intern's voice. "How good it is to hear from you."

"Well, I'm that sorry to be botherin' you, but I was wonderin' if there was a chance that Sergeant O'Shaughnessy could escape for a quick visit to my hotel. I don't have his number, and I have a gift I'd like to give him."

"Oh—I could ask, Officer Doyle, but I'm sure he can't leave any time this morning. There's no one left to cover the desk, since everyone else is setting up an operational command for the trap-and-seizure."

This was related in the important tones of an intern who'd recently learned the jargon, and Doyle tried not to sound too jaded. "Are they? Well then, I suppose he'll have to stop by after the perp's been nicked, then."

The intern lowered her voice. "Will DI Williams be involved? Are you allowed to tell me?"

Doyle paused, confused. "Involved in the trap-and-seizure?"

"Oh—sorry, I thought you'd know. Since it is related to DI Williams' case, I wondered if he was involved."

"I'm not sure," Doyle replied carefully. "Perhaps." Mother a' mercy; *what* trap-and-seizure? If the intern thought Williams was involved, then the trap-and-seizure must have somethin' to do with Father Gregory's murder, which the Irish contingent had been led to believe was related to the corruption rig. But that was all a fish-tale, surely? Acton had arranged for the trail to go cold—with his doubling-back story about forbidden lovers and blackmail—so that all inconvenient loose ends were tied up in a cold-case bow, never to be investigated again.

The more Doyle puzzled over it, the stranger it seemed—faith, the whole point of Acton's tale was to make certain there would be no further investigation but for some reason, the Irish police thought they had themselves a perp. It all made no sense—the intern must have got it wrong—and Doyle decided to ignore the inconvenient fact that her scalp was prickling and that she had a heart full of disquiet.

"It's rather exciting," the intern continued. "The Inspector thinks we'll have the suspect, dead to rights."

"That is excellent," Doyle replied, frowning into the mobile. "Who is the suspect?"

"I don't know," Nazy confessed. "They're keeping it very quiet." She lowered her voice. "I think they are keeping it quiet because it involves corrupt law enforcement."

Stranger and stranger—it did indeed sound like a Williams case. "Oh. Then I suppose I haven't heard about it because Acton tends to be very tight-lipped about such things."

Of course, he was tight-lipped, the wretched man, mainly because he didn't want his better half to twig him out, which meant—apparently—that he was up to something that could not withstand the light of day, and his aforementioned better half had best find out all there was to find out.

"Hang on for a moment," said Doyle. "You're breakin' up."

She moved away from the desk and bent her head to think. Acton had said he'd need a couple of hours this morning, but her trusty instinct was telling her—unfortunately—that there was yet another Acton-scheme afoot; a scheme that she'd only unearthed thanks to a happenstance call to the intern.

Nazy thought it might be a Williams operation, but Williams was out of the country—that much was certain—so what was the gambit? Was it possible that Acton was having them run an operation to catch a suspect who didn't really exist, just to add credibility to his blackmail-and-corruption story? This seemed very unlikely; after all, the last needful thing—or at least one would think—would be for Acton to allow the suspicious Irish Inspector to try to take a pretend-suspect into custody and in the process find out there was really no such person.

Unless—unless Acton was running some sort of misdirection play, of course; a possibility which should never be overlooked, as she'd learned many a time to her sorrow.

"Mother a' mercy," Doyle said crossly. "My head hurts, just tryin' to sort it out."

"I beg your pardon, ma'am?"

Doyle took a long breath and was reminded that there was supposedly something left on the fair Doyle's plate—according to Sister Luke—and that it had to do with the Rule of Three. Three what? Was there was a third spite-murder, on the come—could that be it? But whose? And why would it be here in Dublin, of all places, if it was connected to the corruption rig back home?

Coming to a decision, Doyle asked, "Where's the trap-and-seizure, Nazy, d'you know?"

"Ha'penny Bridge," the intern disclosed in the tones of one who is aware she is not supposed to be giving out such information. "I heard them talking about it."

Doyle nodded, as the bridge was not far—only minutes away. "I'll tell you what, Nazy—if you will drive me over there, we'll watch the operation unfold and I'll explain all the protocols to you from the perimeter. It will be a good learnin' experience for you."

The intern could barely contain her excitement. "Oh—oh, that would be wonderful, Officer Doyle. Should we report in? Perhaps if we ask, Inspector Geary would allow us to join operational command."

"No," Doyle replied firmly, "We're not reportin' in, and we won't go anywhere near operational command. I'm goin' to stay well-out of it, because every time I try to go chargin' in like the cavalry I wind up with a commendation for bravery, and I'm pig-sick of it."

"I see," said Nazy, although she didn't see at all.

Thinking rapidly, Doyle said, "It sounds like we haven't much time, so if you'll drive by the hotel curb, I'll dash out, quick-like." This tactic was necessary because Doyle needed to slip her leash with no one the wiser, but there was no need to mention this unfortunate fact to the intern, as it would only confuse the issue.

Nazy thought this an excellent plan. "I'll be there straightaway, Officer Doyle."

Doyle rang off, absently rubbing Edward's back through his carrier and trying to make sense of it. That something was afoot seemed inarguable—Acton was unavailable for the next couple of hours, he'd been showing the people at the front desk a photo of a blonde who wasn't Lady Abby, and there was a trap-and-seizure going down that Nazy seemed to think was related to Habib's death, even though Acton had carefully buried that homicide into a cold-case vault.

So—what was it? Nanda had murdered the bishop, Habib had murdered Father Gregory, and now—unless she very much missed her guess—there was a third spite-murder to be addressed, and for some reason it had been placed firmly on the fair Doyle's plate.

With a pretend-negligent air, she returned the young man's mobile, and then sidled over to the door nearest the curb so as to keep a weather eye out for Nazy.

Chapter 36

It was not the first time his stupid wife had caused a massive problem—she'd got herself trapped at Wexton Prison, like an idiot. He'd been half-panicked—not his steady self at all—and that's when she'd realized that something had to be done.

They were approaching the north shore of Ha'penny Bridge, and as she watched out the windscreen, Doyle asked Nazy, "Where is operational command set-up, d'you know?" She wanted to reconnoiter a bit since there was always the off-chance that the trap-and-seizure was not some sort of Acton-scheme, and if that were the case she didn't want to throw the cat amongst the pigeons and interfere with a legitimate arrest.

"I'm not sure," the girl replied. "I think they've set it up in a business building along the embankment, but I'm not certain where."

Doyle leaned forward to glance up at the buildings on the far side and thought this sounded likely; a second story was always useful so as to keep a clear view of the trap-site. "Do y'know which end of the bridge the suspect's comin' from?"

"No," Nazy confessed. "But I wish I did—it would be so exciting to participate in the take-down, Officer Doyle."

But Doyle shook her head slightly, as she sized up the scattered pedestrians who were walking in the area. "You'll have to wait until you've been trained, Nazy—otherwise you'd be more trouble than help. And anyways, it's not a'tall like the police shows on the telly; most of the time it's all a bit anticlimactic, and there're reams of paperwork, afterwards."

The girl nodded. "Oh—oh yes, I suppose that is true."

Doyle glanced around. "Let's park here, since it gives us a fairly clear view from this end. We'll stay in the car—so that we're well-away from everythin'—but we should still be able to see whatever happens. And it gives me a chance to feed Edward, since he's due."

Doyle could feel Nazy's discreet embarrassment as she wriggled out of the carrier's straps to put Edward to the breast, but Doyle had learned almost straightaway that having a baby meant that one threw one's dignity to the winds, and the strait-laced intern would just have to get over it.

With a watchful air, Doyle surveyed the area, and reflected that it had been a long time since she'd been across Ha'penny Bridge, which was an old-fashioned, cast-iron pedestrian bridge more than a hundred years old. A favorite with tourists, it spanned the river and served as a convenient short-cut between the river banks—and a prime place to feed the ducks, if you didn't want to walk all the way to Stephen's Green.

"It's very quiet," Nazy noted, as she watched out the window. "There are not a lot of people around, at this hour."

Doyle explained, "That's why—if they're doin' an operation in a public place—they like to do it durin' off-hours; they don't want lot of people about."

With a knit brow, Nazy ventured, "You'd think they'd rather keep it quiet, and go to the suspect's home, instead."

"There's no arrest warrant, yet," Doyle reminded her. "They need to catch the suspect in the act, or with incriminatin' evidence—which is why this is a trap-and-seizure instead of an arrest. And having it in a public place tends to cut down on any idea of resistin' arrest—the suspect is out of his element, and doesn't want to cause a ruckus." She paused, so as to shift Edward to the other side. "Usually, there's a lure—a person who's undercover—who tries to get the suspect to incriminate himself."

Nazy nodded, her gaze taking in the scene with intense interest. "There is a woman who is standing on the bridge. Do you think she is the lure?"

Doyle had already noted that a woman was leaning on the bridge's iron railings at the mid-point, watching the water. She looked like she was a professional on her way to work, since she was dressed smartly and carried a small valise. It did seem a bit odd that she was lingering, though; one would think she should be getting to work, rather than dawdling on the bridge.

Suddenly struck, Doyle narrowed her eyes and stared intently at the distant figure. "D'you have a field kit, Nazy? I wish I had a pair of binoculars."

"I do not," Nazy said in apology. "Why—do you recognize her?"

"I think—holy Mother, I think she's Acton's assistant from the Yard, but I can't be sure."

Nazy turned to address Doyle with suppressed excitement. "Then she must be the lure, and DI Williams must indeed be involved."

"Mayhap," Doyle replied, thoroughly confused— although it did seem that Williams had slain yet another heart. One thing that she knew for certain, however, was that Acton's assistant was a blonde, and *surely* she shouldn't be here of all places, leaning on a bridge in Dublin and leaving Acton's desk unattended whilst he was away on holiday. Therefore, Acton must be involved in this operation—it was impossible to believe he didn't know his assistant was here, big as life. That, and she definitely looked as though she was here on business, and not larking about—it *couldn't* be a coincidence, she must be part of this trap-and-seizure, but what part?

Very uneasy with this latest unlooked-for turn of events, Doyle tried to come up with a working theory. Was it his assistant's photo, that Acton had shown to the desk clerk at the hotel? If it was, that led—one would think—to one of two completely divergent working theories; either Acton's assistant was the suspect, or Acton was laying the groundwork to nab someone at the hotel's front desk by using his assistant as the lure.

Doyle considered these options, and couldn't help but think they were both very far-fetched. It was true that Acton's assistant wasn't a fan of the fair Doyle, but she'd loyally served him for years—it seemed very unlikely that she'd be all the way up here without his say-so. Besides, if she were a suspect for some reason, it also seemed unlikely that she'd be standing on a bridge in the midst of a sanctioned Irish operation; if she'd been committing misdeeds, she'd have been nabbed at home with no further ado.

On the other hand, why on earth would he use his assistant as a lure in an Irish-sanctioned operation? There were plenty of Irish policewomen who were available for undercover work—unless—unless, he was trying to pull a fast one on the Inspector, for some reason, and was having his assistant pose as a villain.

That's it, she realized, her scalp prickling as she made the intuitive leap; Acton had arranged for his assistant to pose as a villain for the Irish Inspector. There was no longer any need to dupe the Inspector, though—all trails were slated to go cold—so this little holy show must mean that Acton truly wanted the Inspector to arrest his assistant.

Doyle suddenly caught her breath. According to Sister Luke, there was a third spite-murder brewing, and the old nun seemed to think it was something that the fair Doyle was destined to deal with. If the assistant was in Acton's black book for some reason, then it didn't take a genius to figure out who would be willing to arrange for her arrest and subsequent spite-murder, so as to resolve this particular blonde-headed problem. And if the Irish Inspector happened to twig on to that same conclusion, the illustrious Chief Inspector from Scotland Yard could be in for a world of hurt. Therefore, it would probably be best if the fair Doyle erred on the side of keeping said Chief Inspector out of prison, and thwarting a third spite-murder as an added bonus.

Having come to her decision, Doyle said to Nazy, "If you would hold the baby, I'd best wander over to check it out."

"Oh—oh, of course." Nazy seemed surprised by Doyle's sudden change in attitude as she accepted Edward. "But won't she recognize you?"

"Indeed, she will," said Doyle, and closed the car door on the confused intern with no further explanation.

Be careful, Doyle warned herself as she pulled the empty carrier's straps back up over her shoulders; you're being the cavalry, again, and that never seems to work out very well for you. Best do a bit of cautious probing, so as to get a glimpse of which scenario it truly was—hard to believe, that Acton was willing to set-up his assistant to be murdered, but there was definitely something afoot, between Sister Luke's warnings, and the strange matter of the other blonde in the photograph.

Doyle began walking in a leisurely fashion toward the bridge, her hands in her pockets and the baby-carrier giving the appearance that she was a new mother, out for a stroll. I hope I'm not being foolish, she thought, but I'm trained—and armed too, after Acton's reminder—so surely, I can handle this one; after all, the assistant's a bit of a preener, and doesn't know that I'm suspicious. On the other hand, I'm headed to yet another rendezvous on a bridge, and not a fond memory, that one is.

Affecting an air of causal disinterest, she entered the pedestrian bridge, and approached Acton's assistant.

Chapter 37

It seemed clear he'd unload his stupid wife after this fiasco, which would leave only the baby to be dealt with.

Doyle noted that the assistant had a conscious air about her—keeping her head down and not showing even an idle interest in the people who passed her by, which rather went to the theory that she was indeed a lure, and waiting to be approached. Still and all, best not get too close, and so with a cheerful air she hailed the girl from a small distance.

"I thought it was you," Doyle called out brightly. "Are you on holiday also?"

Startled, the assistant looked up with profound irritation. "*You*? What are *you* doing here?"

Doyle stopped out of arm's reach but noted that the girl had made no attempt to take her hands off the railing, which was a good sign. "I suppose I could be askin' the same thing."

With a dismissive air, the other girl turned back to contemplate the water below. "I'm not surprised he didn't tell you. Go away, before you ruin everything."

This opening seemed to indicate there was indeed a trap-and-seizure underway that didn't involve Acton-style vengeance, but Doyle's instinct was telling her to be wary, nonetheless. "Oh—are you here on an assignment, then?"

Her companion tossed her head. "Of course, I am; you don't think I'd come all the way up here for fun?" The girl made a face at the muddy water that streamed by below. "But you've got to leave immediately, so that I can do my job."

With some puzzlement, Doyle took a glance around. "Who's the perp?"

With a snide little laugh, the girl gave Doyle a sidelong look. "You're the perp."

Strangely enough, this was true, and Doyle could only stare at her in abject confusion. "I don't understand."

In a tone laden with contempt, the girl retorted, "I think he's finally sick of your nonsense, and not a moment too soon. What did you do, this time?"

A bit shocked, Doyle hastily reconsidered her options because the assistant's barely-concealed hostility—which she'd only show if she was certain there'd be no retribution from the boss—seemed to swing things back into the Acton-is-setting-up-his-assistant-to-be-murdered territory, and Katy bar the door if that was true; he'd show no mercy to a turncoat—not that he tended to show mercy to anyone, turncoat or otherwise.

Slowly, Doyle replied, "I think the proper question is what did *you* do?"

Jerking up her head, the girl regarded Doyle in scornful disbelief. "What do you mean? I'm making the Chief Inspector's life easier, like I always do. It's something that you'd never understand."

Doyle decided she'd best cut to the nub, since her red head was certainly visible from where ever operational command was located, and therefore time was short with respect to saving Acton's stupid assistant from her stupid fate. "I'm worried that he's angry with you about somethin'."

The girl's face grew flushed with fury, as she whirled on Doyle. "What *on earth* are you talking about? It's not *me* he's angry with, it's *you*."

Again, this rang true, but if Doyle knew anything at all, she knew that Acton was incapable of being angry with his unlikely bride, and so this meant that he was feeding his assistant some sort of fish-story, which did not bode well for the girl's continued health and well-being. She also noted that her companion had become far too angry far too quickly, and so Doyle immediately changed tactics, and instead of confronting her, attempted to soothe her by affecting an air of wounded sensibility. "Oh? Never say so—why's he angry with me?"

"You've embarrassed him, as usual," her companion retorted, and struggled to regain her equilibrium as she scowled at the river below. "And now he's got to cover it up, somehow. Go—go on your way and leave it to the two of us to handle the problem."

"Officer Doyle?"

Doyle turned to see that Nazy had approached, awkwardly holding baby Edward in her arms. "Is everything all right?"

The intern had no doubt been alarmed as she watched the other woman's angry reactions, but Doyle couldn't be best-pleased that she'd brought Edward into this volatile situation, and so lifted her fingers slightly in a surreptitious signal to stay back.

"And now who's this?" The assistant looked from Doyle to Nazy, her eyes narrowing with suspicion.

"The nanny," Doyle explained, and then she smiled at the intern. "Go on back to the car, Mary, and I'll be there shortly."

"You're 'Mary'?" The other woman eyed Nazy's hijab with palpable disbelief.

"Yes," Nazy replied. "I am Mary."

It seemed clear that the intern was loathe to leave Doyle without support—which was commendable—but as Doyle didn't want Edward anywhere in the vicinity, it created quite the dilemma. It was a shame the intern didn't speak Gaelic, but on the other hand, she did speak police-code, and probably better than Doyle did.

Still lifting her fingers in a quiet warning, Doyle pretended to look at a non-existent watch. "I'll need to take that t-call at code two, Mary." The code referenced an emergency situation, and a request for back-up. "Would you mind goin' back to the car, and ringin' them up?"

"Yes, ma'am," said Nazy, and she turned to go, her calm demeanor hiding her extreme alarm. It went without saying that the call was probably unnecessary, as operational command was no doubt watching events unfold with a great deal of chagrin, but at least she'd warned Nazy to leave—and to take Edward away—with all speed.

"Oh—wait; is that Edward?" Quickly, the assistant took a step around Nazy, effectively blocking the girl's exit from the narrow bridge. "Let me see him—I only saw the snap on the birth announcement." She reached to take the baby from the intern.

With an abrupt movement, Doyle stepped between the other two girls and lifted Edward from Nazy's arms. "He'll be needin' a nappy change, I'm afraid." With one hand she held the baby firmly against her chest, and with the other began to wriggle the carrier up around him. "Go make the call, Nazy."

"Mary," said Nazy.

"Mary," corrected Doyle.

But with a calculating expression, the assistant again reached for the baby. "Come—let me hold him; just for a moment."

Suddenly, the assistant began to forcibly pull at the infant, and the next thing Doyle knew, she was engaged in an all-out tug-of-war over Edward, handicapped by the fact she was desperately trying to zip up the carrier so as to secure him against her chest.

"Stop it," Nazy demanded in acute dismay, and pulled at the assistant's shoulders. "Stop it—you'll hurt him."

But Doyle had seen the fanatical determination in her opponent's eyes, and her heart froze with horror—if Edward went into the river, they'd never find him in time. "GAT,

Nazy!" she shouted, as she hung on to the baby with both arms wrapped around the half-zipped carrier. "My ankle!"

After a second's pause, Nazy knelt to frantically feel around Doyle's legs whilst she resisted the assistant's determined efforts to seize the baby. Vaguely, Doyle was aware of shouts coming from the near distance, but she dared not relinquish her concentration for a moment as she clung to Edward with all her strength, throwing her weight backwards.

"Give—him—over," the assistant ground out, and then abruptly stopped pulling to instead shove Doyle, so that she fell backwards over the kneeling Nazy.

Whilst Doyle desperately tried to scramble away with one hand on the ground, a carrier strap fell from her shoulder and the assailant grasped it with a jerk, yanking so hard that Doyle was hurled forward as she attempted to regain her feet. The abrupt movement caused her to crash sideways against the railings of the bridge, unable to defend herself because her arms were locked before her, shielding the baby.

With a mighty effort, Doyle threw her weight backwards, bracing her feet against the assistant's greater strength and hanging on to the baby's carrier like grim death. "Nazy!" she shouted with some urgency, "Hurry—get the gun!"

As Nazy again crawled to feel around Doyle's legs, the assistant made repeated, yanking attempts to pull Doyle toward her by means of the loose shoulder strap, but the strap on Doyle's own shoulder had caught 'round one of the decorative spikes that lined the rails, so that the carrier—and Doyle—wouldn't budge.

Furious, the assistant changed her focus to the baby himself, trying to pull him out of the carrier with Doyle trying to counter-pull, handicapped because she was stuck against the railing, and she dared not cease pulling backwards for a single moment, lest the carrier come off completely.

More shouting could be heard—closer, this time—and then Doyle heard the blessed sound of Velcro being released as the intern freed her weapon. "Quick, quick—" she gasped, as the assistant furiously renewed her efforts to pull the baby directly out of the carrier. Heaving with all her strength, Doyle threw all her weight the opposite way so as to give the intern sufficient clearance to shoot, and prayed the strap that was stuck on the rail-spike would not break.

"Now, now," she panted, and glanced over to see that the intern stood in uncertainty, holding the weapon in the manner of someone who was unused to handling such, her eyes wide with fear.

"Shoot her," Doyle ordered, shielding the baby tightly with her arms. "Now!"

But Nazy could be seen to hesitate, and instead turned the gun butt-out, and stepped forward as though to use it to hit the other woman.

"No—no! Don't get close or she'll take it—"

But the warning was too late, and as her attacker grabbed the gun, Doyle frantically released a hand so as to gouge her nails into the other's face, aiming for her eyes.

With a cry of pain, her attacker turned her face away, and although Doyle could hear the sound of running feet on the deck behind her, she dared not shift her focus for a moment, lest the tension on the shoulder strap lessen, or the assistant make use of the gun that was now in her hand.

And then rescue came in the form of the young DC, who flew in to grasp the other girl's wrist and forcibly wrench it up and away. With a cry of pain, the girl dropped the weapon as he used his other hand to punch upward beneath her jaw with a sharp, hard blow. Instantly, the girl collapsed limply to the ground, her eyes rolling back in her head.

A textbook take-down, Doyle thought, bending over to catch her breath and nearly dizzy with relief; I hope Nazy's paying attention.

In a flurry of activity, Inspector Geary and two PCs converged on the unconscious woman as Acton bent next to

Doyle, an arm around her as he assessed the damage. "All right? How's Edward?"

"All's well—Mother a' mercy, cuff her quick, before she gets a second wind." With one arm holding Edward a bit too tightly, Doyle straightened up whilst her son made the annoyed little sounds that a baby makes when someone has awakened him too soon.

As the DC and the two patrol officers none-to-gently trussed-up the assistant, Doyle looked over so as to reassure poor Nazy, but saw that the intern was retching miserably over the side of the bridge, and decided to leave her alone.

"Let's take her in," said the Inspector. He signaled for the two officers to lift the suspect, and bent to carefully tag the valise, so as to take it into custody. Glancing over to where Doyle stood beside Acton, he then said, "When you are able, Officer Doyle, we'll need a statement."

"I'm willin'," Doyle agreed, but before she turned to leave, she gave a last, fond squeeze to the old cast-iron spikes, where she and her mother used to stand and watch the waters of the River Liffey.

Chapter 38

She refused to give a statement and waited for word. It must be part of his plan—he was an amazing planner.

They'd been back at the Garda for several hours, with Doyle reciting her statement to the recording officer and carefully avoiding any explanations that involved crazed jealousy.

"She was that unhappy that I'd interrupted whatever-it-was she was doin'," Doyle explained, which was the truth, more or less. "And then she started fightin' with me, and tried to throw my baby in the river."

The young officer leaned back to whistle softly. "Bad luck—she was makin' a drop, and you were in the wrong place at the wrong time. And now you've got the bruises to show for it."

"I bruise easily," Doyle said, as she examined the black marks on her arms. "Nothin' to signify." Casually, she asked the officer, "So, what was the trap-and-seizure about? Hard to believe Acton's own assistant was up to no good."

"She was blackmailin' some players from the old corruption scandal," he confided. "I suppose she got the information when she worked on your husband's cases, and then decided to run a rig on the side. My chief says they've got her dead to rights, because the money she was carryin' can be traced right back to the corruption rig."

"Oh—is that so?" Doyle replied, and thought, you don't know the half of it, my friend. "Will they do a psych evaluation?"

The young man raised his brows in surprise. "I don't think so—or at least, no one's said as much. She had a pretty well-thought out scheme goin', so I think that rules out a psych defense."

At this point, Inspector Geary entered. "About done, here? Chief Inspector Acton would like us to wrap it up."

"Yes, sir." The officer recognized a dismissal when he heard it, and with a final nod to Doyle, gathered up his things and left.

There was a moment's silence whilst Doyle and the Inspector regarded each other warily. She decided to go on offense, and said, "If you're lookin' to browbeat another confession out of me, best watch yourself; I fight like the dickens when I'm cornered."

The Irishman tilted his head. "No—you're not an easy mark, Officer. That much had been made clear."

"I'm not as dumb as I look," she agreed.

"Me neither," he returned with a level gaze. "Can't say I enjoy havin' the wool pulled over my eyes."

With a reluctant smile, she offered, "Join the club."

To her surprise, he chuckled, and bent his head for a moment. "Aye—I suppose there's the nub of it. Well, whatever's the real story here, there's no question that the perp deserves to be put away, so I'll have to be content with that."

Since Doyle had the sense he was fishing for insights, she didn't give him any—mainly because she had little to give. Hopefully, Acton was going to fill her in, but as the wretched man was a wool-puller of the first order, those hopes were not very high.

"I understand that the weapon found on the scene was yours."

Nonplussed, Doyle didn't respond, mainly because it would be illegal for the fair Doyle to be carrying such a weapon in the Inspector's fair city.

With a small smile, the Irishman pulled her pistol from his pocket, and placed it on the table with a click. "I can't fault your husband; if I had a wife, she'd be carryin', too. Just make sure it doesn't make another appearance, Officer."

"Yes, sir," said Doyle, and slid the weapon into her carry-all. She'd forgotten, in the this-tribe-against-that-tribe metric, that the law enforcement tribe tended to close ranks to protect its own.

Hard on this thought, Acton gave a cursory knock at the door and entered with no further ado. "Are we finished, here? My wife should rest, after her ordeal."

"I wouldn't mind an ice cream," Doyle agreed.

"Then you shall have it." Acton addressed the Inspector. "If you need to do any forensics on my assistant's office electronics, you have only to let me know."

The other man nodded. "We will need your testimony, of course. Once we're at that point, I'll contact you for convenient dates."

"Willingly," said Acton. "I am at your disposal."

"If you wouldn't mind," Doyle ventured, "I'd like to speak with Sergeant O'Shaughnessy, for a moment. I have a small somethin' for him."

"Of course," the Inspector stepped out into the hallway to go fetch him.

Acton took the opportunity to run a worried hand over Doyle's head. "Tell me the truth. Kathleen; are you all right?"

"I am," she said steadily, "my hand on my heart." Poor man; he wasn't all right—not at all. Best not mention the bruises; he'd see them soon enough. "Just let me talk to the sergeant—five minutes, Michael. Then we'll be off."

He nodded. "I'll be in the waiting room, then. Do you want me to take Edward?"

"I do," she said, thinking that the baby might provide some distraction for her unhappy husband. "He's a trouble-causer, though; keep a sharp eye out."

With the shadow of a smile, he lifted the baby and moved toward the door just as Sergeant O'Shaughnessy came in. "There's the boyo," the sergeant said in a jovial manner. "Lucky he didn't have to learn to swim on this fine day."

"Indeed," said Acton, and shut the door a bit harder than he needed to.

The sergeant pulled up a chair to sit across from Doyle. "How are you, lass? They say you fought like a Viking."

"I didn't have much choice," she disclaimed. "There was nothin' for it."

"Good one," he said approvingly. "I always knew you had mettle."

This was not exactly true, but it provided a good opening for Doyle to say what she needed to say. "I have somethin' I wanted to give you—it's my Garda badge." She pulled the small item—wrapped in a cloth—from her carry-all, and pushed it across the table. "I owe you a lot, and I'll be ever grateful."

Touched, the other man ran his fingers over it. "Your mum would be that proud, lass."

"She was," Doyle said, and knew that it was true—her mother had been a bit bewildered by her daughter's out-sized interest in law enforcement, but nevertheless, she'd indeed been proud.

He bent his head for a moment. "I hope—I hope she didn't suffer much, at the end."

"No—no, she didn't." This was not exactly true, but Doyle didn't want to think about it, herself. "She always spoke very fondly of you." This was also a lie, but Doyle felt she'd already headed down this road, and so she may as well be hung for a sheep as a lamb.

Her companion was unable to conceal a smile beneath his gruff manner. "Well—well, I thought often of her, too." He lifted the badge, and said, "Thank you, lass; it means a lot. Don't be a stranger."

Doyle took a breath. "I wanted to mention—I wanted to mention that they've need of a new mathematics teacher at St. Brigid's, what with Sister Luke dead."

The sergeant lifted his brows in surprise. "I'm a copper, lass."

Gently, she replied, "Not a happy one."

He made a gesture so as to disclaim, but then met her eyes and after a moment's hesitation, shrugged. "No one's a happy copper."

She reached to clasp the hand that held her badge. "I am, thanks to you. But now there's a new crop of little girls who need help with the Order of Operations. Get yourself to a support group, and straighten yourself out."

Surprised, he lowered his gaze to the tabletop, and struggled with his emotions. "I already tried, a couple o' times."

"This time it's goin' to work. My promise on it."

There was a small silence, whilst he turned the idea over in this mind. "I could volunteer, mayhap," he mused cautiously. "And see if I'm suited for it."

"Please do," said Doyle, and squeezed his hand. "And let me know how it goes."

"Aye, then." He pushed out the chair, and she rose with him so as to walk down the hallway toward the Garda's entry. Someone had to be the harmonic divisor, now that Sister Luke was dead; the old nun had spent a lifetime planting younger feet on a better path—Doyle's mother, Sister Roseline, and countless unknown others. Although—apparently—Doyle didn't require any divising from Acton, which seemed like a good sign, all in all. Of course, it may have been only that the nun's head had been turned by his handsome face; she wouldn't be the first.

With a smile, Doyle met her husband in the waiting room. "Let's go, Michael. I'm ready."

Chapter 39

They were all a bit rough and unkind, here, and she'd lodge a complaint, just as soon as she had the chance.

Doyle had decided that her post-baby diet had been preempted by all the dire events, and so she was busily plowing through an enormous chocolate sundae which she was supposedly sharing with Acton even though she wasn't giving him much of a chance.

They were back in the suite at the hotel, and Edward was napping whilst Reynolds was trying to control his extreme agitation with only limited success. "I can scarce believe it, madam."

"It turns out she was a blackleg, through-and-through," Doyle informed him through a mouthful. "A nasty piece of work—had to try and scratch her eyes out." She paused, thinking about it. "She tried to throw Edward in the river, but the river wasn't havin' it."

"So distressing," the servant tut-tutted. "To think that you harbored such a serpent."

"Very distressin'," Doyle agreed, as she shoveled in another spoonful.

Acton ventured in with his own spoon, hoping for a bite, and she paused so as to allow him one. As he was thus distracted, she lifted her gaze to Reynolds' in a signal that he should make himself scarce, and the servant very obligingly made his excuses, and left. Very quick on the uptake, was our Reynolds, and between him and the resilient baby carrier, she'd be hard-pressed to choose which was the more valuable member of the retinue.

As soon as the door closed, Doyle laid her hand over her husband's. "I'm that sorry I gave you such a scare, Michael."

He paused to take a long breath, as he contemplated the sundae. "The fault is mine; I should have warned you, but I'd thought to keep it quiet. We were handling enough trouble as it was."

"How did you know that she was the one behind the train attack?" That the assistant had been somehow behind it now seemed clear, and it was equally clear that he'd known it almost immediately, because from that moment onward he'd changed up their travel arrangements and had avoided all pre-booked services.

"It was not a difficult conclusion to make. Literally, no one else knew the particulars of our travel schedule, and it seemed clear the attack on the train was planned."

"Not a very good plan," Doyle noted, and decided to take just one more bite—one needed to keep up one's strength, after all.

He ducked his chin in acknowledgement. "No—it wasn't a very good plan, which was actually another clue. She is not a planner; she is someone who implements other people's plans. I knew she'd be stymied, if the first attempt didn't work and if we used unpredictable transportation going forward."

Doyle cast him a sidelong glance, and then decided she may as well do a bit of probing—there was always the off-chance he'd tell her something remotely useful. "So now she's on the dock for blackmail, with a side helpin' of conspiracy-to-murder Father Gregory and the bishop."

Lifting his spoon, he made another foray into the ice cream. "Not to mention she publicly tried to murder an infant. They'll not go easy on her."

Doyle shrugged, slightly. "No, they won't; but it will be easier than what she faced from you, Michael. Confess; you were goin' to see to it that she didn't survive the take-down—in the best Kevin Maguire fashion—and now I've gone and sounded the knell to all your wicked spite-murderin' plans."

"No," he replied evenly, and met her eyes. "I didn't plan to kill her in the take-down."

To Doyle's great surprise, this was true, and as a reward, she rose up so as to lean across the table and kiss him soundly. "Well then, I'm that proud of you, Michael. Faith, I was wantin' to shoot her dead myself, because—as it turns out—the 'mother' tribe is the most ferocious one of all."

"I'm glad you didn't shoot her," he said with all sincerity, and—again, to her great surprise—this was also true.

"Well, they're not goin' to do a psych-eval," Doyle informed him as she addressed the melting remnants of the sundae. "But sooner or later, someone's bound to see that she needs one."

"I will monitor her case, and see to it that she gets the proper treatment."

Doyle nipped one last tiny bite, equal parts impressed and relieved by her better half's unexpected show of restraint. She was also content in the knowledge that Acton—even though he was trying to turn over a less bloodthirsty leaf— wasn't about to let his assistant get a second bite at the Edward-apple; Acton may no longer be a cask-behind-the-wall person, but he wasn't one to let bygones be bygones, either, and he'd keep a close watch on his erstwhile assistant.

And to the good, there'd be no third spite-murder, so Doyle felt that she could pat her own back for a job well-done; Sister Luke would be that proud.

"I am so sorry, Kathleen. You've had a very forgettable homecoming."

The black mood hovered—as it had since the bridge incident—and so Doyle teased, "Whist; never had a nicer time, I assure you."

"You deserved better," he insisted.

She reached to take his hand, across the table. "It truly hasn't been all bad, Michael, my hand on my heart. Instead, a lot of good's been done, believe it or not. You're the one who's had a terrible time, having to scramble-drill for three separate disasters. And on top of that, you're minus an assistant, which will be quite the handicap when you take up your miserable caseload again."

Acton tilted his head. "I have asked Ms. Chaudhry if she would be interested in the position."

"Nazy?" Doyle blinked in surprise. "Truly? I thought she wanted to be a detective."

"Apparently, she has changed her mind."

Thinking on this, Doyle could only concede, "Aye; she wasn't happy about the bridge-brawl. Which just goes to show you that not everyone's cut out for this kind of work."

"I rather wish you weren't."

There was a small silence, and when he wouldn't meet her gaze, she reached to take his other hand, so that she held both of his in her own. "My work is important, Michael. Look at where I came from—saints in heaven, who would have imagined someone like me would wind up at the CID, fightin' the good fight and clobberin' the villains, left and right? When you think about it, I'm a bit like Gideon, who couldn't quite believe he was slated to do the things he was supposed to do, and thought that maybe God had got it mixed up, somehow. But here I am, and best not argue about it."

"Yes," he agreed—although with some reluctance. "You are extraordinary."

"Extraordinary at givin' you grey hair," she teased. "But I'm handy at givin' you the other kind of heir too, which is a mark in my favor."

"Yes. I suppose I must accept the good with the bad." He was trying to make light of this latest disaster, but she could see that his heart wasn't in it; shame on her, for wanting to chit-chat when she should be getting on with the cure for the black mood, and with no further ado.

"Choose your poison, then; scotch or ice cream." With a provocative gesture, she took a spoonful of the melted ice cream and dribbled it down her blouse and into her impressive cleavage.

He offered a half-smile, as the black mood retreated. "Ice cream it is."

A short, blissful time later, the bedclothes were in disarray on the floor and Doyle was lying in his arms, watching the curtains flutter, since they'd opened a window to combat the steaminess of the sex.

They hadn't spoken for a time, until Doyle ventured, "I do have a request, Michael, if you wouldn't mind throwin' open the vault."

"Certainly." He was a bit drowsy, and had to struggle to pay attention.

"Could we establish a mathematics scholarship at Trinity College? In memory of Sister Luke." She thought about it for a moment. "For a local girl, who wouldn't be able to afford it, else."

She could feel his abject surprise. "Certainly," he said again. And then, because he couldn't quite believe it, "A scholarship in mathematics?"

She smiled. "Aye, that—Sister Luke was my mathematics teacher, Michael."

She could sense that he debated whether to say something derogatory, and then merely said, "You are very generous."

With a small smile, Doyle watched the curtains move in the breeze. "It's not me, that's generous."

"Consider it done, then."

"The Garda could use some new equipment."

His chest rose and fell. "I see."

Smiling, she turned her face to him, and teased, "Layton must be wonderin' what on earth has come over you, throwin' your money to the winds."

He responded by rolling so that he lay atop her, and leisurely began kissing her throat. "Actually, I don't think he wonders much at all."

Giggling, she happily settled in for round two.

Chapter 40

She couldn't wait any longer, and would phone him at her first opportunity. These people were intolerable; it was nothing like London.

It was their last day in Dublin, and Doyle and Acton were walking down a rather cramped back-street—just a stone's throw from St. Brigid's. The church bells were ringing in the background as they stepped across an intersection, Doyle carrying Edward in his chest carrier, and Acton walking along beside her. Neither one of them had spoken for a small space of time.

Doyle paused. "This is it," she announced, although she knew it was unnecessary; Acton would certainly know her old address. That very morning, he'd presented her with a cheap wool scarf—the same kind Sister Roseline had worn—and Doyle had promptly embarrassed herself by crying into its folds like a big baby, and not like someone who was a mother, herself.

Resolute—and with the scarf wrapped around her neck—she'd decided that they would take Edward over to see her old house, and shame on her, for being so afraid of her memories. After all, her memories were good ones, and—thank God fasting—nowhere near as painful as the memories shared by Nanda and Sister Roseline; horrific memories that had left them wounded for life.

I can do this, she thought; *love bears all things*, after all. And so, with Acton standing in sympathy beside her, she regarded the window where her mother used to watch for the young Doyle to come home from school.

Self-consciously, Doyle propped up the baby so that his face was turned toward the building. "D'you see, Edward? That's where your gran lived. She was very special." Her voice broke, and Acton pressed her to his side as she took a long breath, to steady herself. "I lived there, too, alongside her."

Whilst she struggled with her emotions, Acton asked gently, "Shall we go in? I am certain if we explained, they'd let us have a look 'round."

"No—I can't do it, Michael. And besides, there's no point; that chapter's closed."

He looked over the little place for a moment. "I wish I'd known her."

"She'd love the way you love me," Doyle said diplomatically. Her mother would have goggled at the idea of meeting a real English lord, let alone bringing one into their tiny little house. Or having an English lord for a grandchild—she'd have laughed at the very idea.

She wiped away tears with the palm of her hand. "Just so as to give you fair warnin', I'm goin' to start singin' some songs to him—the same as my mum used to sing to me."

"We shall sing them together, then."

Touched, she looked up with a wobbly smile. "Where no one can hear us."

"Nonsense; you have a very clear soprano. I will provide harmony."

"Watch yourself," she teased. "Next thing you know, you'll be buyin' yourself a piano."

There was a small pause, whilst her husband kept his gaze on the old building. "We shall see."

She had to chuckle—so happy that they could joke about everything that had happened to them. "Faith, but we're a couple of saps, Michael."

"Don't tell anyone," he cautioned, and leaned to kiss her over Edward's head.

Epilogue

Ridiculous, that she'd been held without bail, and way up here in Maghaberry, when she shouldn't be in a Class A prison to begin with—it was positively claustrophobic. And the cold climate must be affecting her; she felt a bit odd, a bit woozy. It was very hard to focus, this morning, and she needed to focus; needed to discover why her solicitor wasn't returning her calls.

CPSIA information can be obtained
at www.ICGtesting.com
Printed in the USA
LVHW04s1248191018
594144LV00002B/19/P